SUBJECT X

EMMA G. HUNTER

OMNIFIC PUBLISHING

LOS ANGELES

Omnific Publishing
1901 Avenue of the Stars, 2nd floor
Los Angeles, CA 90067
www.omnificpublishing.com

First Omnific eBook edition, January 2016
First Omnific trade paperback edition, January 2016

Library of Congress Cataloguing-in-Publication Data

Hunter, Emma G.
    Subject X / Emma G. Hunter – 1st ed.
    ISBN: 978-1-623420-90-1
    1. Science Fiction — Romance. 2. Superhero — Romance.
    3. Biotechnology — Fiction. 4. Philadelphia — Fiction. I. Title

10 9 8 7 6 5 4 3 2 1

Cover Design by Micha Stone and Amy Brokaw
Interior Book Design by Coreen Montagna

Printed in the United States of America

To my lovely husband

July 5th

I've never been so aware of the sound of my own steps as I make my way to the front desk, my new heels clacking on the hard white marble. I flatten my skirt and fiddle with my suit jacket in an attempt to look like a serious career woman and not the sweaty mess of a girl I feel like.

It's 8:00 a.m., and it's already over eighty degrees outside and humid as a rainforest. I've just walked about a half hour to the business district in Philadelphia from my apartment in South Philly, and as my dress shirt starts to stick to my lower back, I'm thinking I should have coughed up the ten dollars for a cab. I'm momentarily relieved that I'm in a suit — in general, being in a suit makes me feel like I'm in a grown-up costume, but at least today the jacket hides the sweat stain I'm sure is appearing above my butt. I didn't expect to be nervous — I know I'm a good candidate for this job — but something about the stifling heat and a looming sense that today is the first day of real life has me a little off.

"Charlotte Kane. I'm here for the research assistant program at Genesis Life Systems," I manage to get out without stuttering when I reach the large and imposing security desk. In smart charcoal suits with crisp white shirts and earpieces, the two men at the desk look more Secret Service than receptionist.

Genesis Life Systems is the biotech research arm of the multinational conglomerate Garrison Holdings, headquartered in Center City, Philadelphia. The lobby of the Garrison Holdings building is beautifully sterile—all white marble and stainless steel. Since the interviews I had for the job all occurred in the career center at school, this is my first time actually inside the building, and it's even cleaner and colder than I expected. I now understand why it's simply referred to as "the Garrison."

"ID, please," says the older of the two men as he starts typing my name into the computer.

I dig my driver's license out of my purse. He shines one of those purple pen lights on it and tilts the card back and forth, scanning it carefully.

"Welcome to Garrison, Miss Kane," he says, handing my ID back. "Please look into this camera so I can take a picture for your temporary badge."

I'm not sure if I should smile or not and settle on what must be an awkward-looking half-smile.

"You're the first to arrive from your program. You'll be taking the east bank elevators up to the forty-sixth floor—behind us and to the left." He points in the general direction as the printer below the desk spits out a card. He clips the card onto a lanyard—an orange one with the blue Garrison Holdings logo every few inches—and hands me the badge over the desk. "Make sure you keep this with you at all times. Don't even go to the bathroom without it. You'd be surprised how many locked doors there are in this place."

I thank him and try the barcode on the gate to the left of the desk. The waist-height glass panels retreat soundlessly into the stainless steel dividers.

As I make my way toward the far left elevator bank, I inspect the temporary badge. My half-smile looks more like a lame smirk, and I hope these pictures aren't used for anything else. Below my name, it reads "CLEARANCE LEVEL: 1" in bold red letters, and there is a red border around the entire badge. I have to assume that means there are a lot of places in this building I'm not supposed to be.

The ride up to the forty-sixth floor is surprisingly fast and quite silent. Alone in the elevator, I can almost see my reflection in the glossy marble of the wall, and I try to smooth my hair and blot the little beads of sweat from my forehead with the back of my hand. I'm glad I'm early—I'll have plenty of time to find a bathroom and make myself a touch more presentable before I meet the other new recruits.

There's a sign where the elevator bank meets the hallway that reads:

GENESIS LIFE SYSTEMS
RESEARCH ASSISTANT ORIENTATION:
ROOM 46D

It's printed on glossy orange poster board with the Garrison logo printed lightly in navy blue every six inches or so like a watermark. I follow the arrow pointing left down the hallway, and I'm happy to find a ladies room just a few doors down. Looking at my reflection, I wonder how my hair can possibly look both flat and frizzy at the same time. After help from my very girlie college roommate, I'm actually surprisingly capable of blow-drying my hair to look halfway decent, but apparently I missed the lesson on managing humidity. I fish an elastic out of my purse and pull it into a loose bun.

I'm not wearing much makeup—I almost never do—just my regular mascara and a little brown eye shadow, so there's not much to touch up, but I do pull an almost-never-used nude lip gloss out of my bag and swipe a layer on. The added bit of shine makes me feel a lot more made-up and a little out of my element, but this is my first day, so I should try to make a good impression. I still have some time before orientation starts at 8:30, so I get out my phone and check my email. There's a brief note wishing me good luck on my first day from my mom. This does give me just a tiny bit more confidence, so I take one last look in the mirror and head out into the hall.

Room 46D has a podium at the front and four rows of tables, each with eight chairs. In front of each chair is a stack of folders and books—all orange and blue, lest we forget which company we work for already—and a folded name card including university and major. I find mine in the third row.

CHARLOTTE KANE
HARVARD UNIVERSITY
BIOMEDICAL ENGINEERING

I'm the only one in the room, so I hang my purse on the back of my chair and start rifling through the orientation material. It's pretty dry stuff—a big packet of HR material about benefits and such, a single sheet of information about my lab placement, and two spiral bound books: the *Garrison Holdings Code of Conduct* and the *Genesis Life Systems Manual of Policies and Procedures*. They're each close to an inch thick.

I'm hoping the rulebooks are just for reference when I hear the door open at the back of the room. Two guys walk in, both in suits with badges around their necks like mine. One of them is pretty cute. They both smile and walk toward me. When we shake hands, the cute one holds my hand just a moment longer than seems natural.

"Kyle Harris," he says, glancing at my ID. "Nice to meet you, Charlotte." He holds my gaze a little longer than is comfortable. Is he flirting with me?

While I'm still an absolute tomboy and nerd at heart, over the course of college I made somewhat of a transition to at least look like a girl. More or less appalled with my baggy jeans, sweatshirts, and constant ponytail, my roommate insisted I start to buy clothes that fit and learn to apply make-up. She wore me down, and by the end of college, I actually enjoyed looking a little feminine. I'm still not used to being noticed, though, and my first assumption tends to be that guys are just being awkward or friendly. My best friend, Maddie, says my flirt-dar is all screwed up.

I don't have much time to wonder if Kyle is flirting with me before the door opens again and several more new recruits come in. Before long, the room is full, and a thin woman in her mid-thirties heads to the podium and asks us to take our seats. I hadn't noticed that the name card next to mine is Kyle's; he gives me a quick smile as he slides into his chair. His eyes are bright, and I notice his shoulders are broad and square when he shimmies out of his suit jacket. I debate doing the same, but the thought that I might still have a sweat stain on the back of my button-up stops me.

The human resources woman introduces the first speaker, a gray-haired guy named Jack Green. When he takes the podium, I realize where I've seen him before. He's the president of Genesis, and he's on the news from time to time whenever there's a significant new product or drug from the company, or any kind of controversy. Most recently I've seen him talking about a highly anticipated obesity drug scheduled to hit the market next year. I think he was interviewed by Anderson Cooper.

I'm oddly star-struck for a brief moment—Jack Green is no celebrity, but he's huge in the world of biological sciences, and I certainly wasn't expecting to be in the same room with him in the first ten minutes of my career. He starts out by telling us about his first day at Genesis, in the research assistant program forty-two years ago when there were just two recruits each year. His spiel is a little cheesy, and I'm sure he gives the same talk every year, but I can't help being a little excited to become part of an organization that has made so many important advancements.

After several more speakers and just before noon, the HR woman steps back up to the podium and informs us that we'll be served lunch on the top floor of the building — the Garrison Holdings executive floor. The Garrison is the tallest building in Philly, and I look forward to seeing the view as we pile into the elevators.

Kyle walks with me the whole way, asking what I thought of the speakers and what I know about the lab I'll be joining.

"Not much, just that it's Pod F and the name of my manager. Isn't that what your orientation material had?"

He pauses. "Well, yes, I'm Pod D, but my manager also called me two weeks ago to introduce himself and tell me about the work going on in his lab. He sent me some papers to read to prepare." Kyle must be able to read on my face that this is worrisome to me. "Maybe my boss is just an overachiever or a micromanager," he adds quickly. "I'm sure yours will go over everything with you when we get into the labs on Monday."

I don't have much time to think about this because we're just getting to lunch and I'm distracted by the sign outside the meeting room. Printed, of course, in blue on Garrison orange, with the Garrison logo watermarked all over it.

Genesis Research Assistants
Welcome To The Annual Meet-Your-Manager Lunch

I guess I'll find out more about my potentially neglectful manager earlier than I thought. I follow the other research assistants into the room, and we find nametags on a table by the door. There are maybe twenty older Genesis employees milling around the room, and within a few minutes, the other RAs have all found their bosses and stand chatting in small groups. I do a second lap, reading every nametag, and then circle back toward the door. There's one lonely remaining badge.

Todd Strickland
Pod F

Great. Not only did he fail to reach out to me ahead of time, but he hasn't even bothered to show up at our welcome lunch.

The HR woman notices after a few minutes that I'm standing around awkwardly.

"I'm so sorry, Charlotte. We're not sure where your manager is at this moment. I've sent my assistant down to your lab to try to find him."

I nod, unsure of what to do with myself, then walk over to a table with soft drinks and take my time opening and pouring myself a Diet Coke. I hear the HR woman ask everyone to seat themselves, and I'm glad the round tables are large — at least I won't be sitting alone.

"Charlotte, come sit with us," Kyle says, laying his hand on my shoulder from behind. I nod, grateful for the distraction, and follow him over to a table.

He introduces me to his manager and makes a real effort to involve me in the conversation as we work on our appetizer salads. It's sweet of him to try to make me comfortable, and it's definitely nice to have an ally so early on. A cute ally.

As I take my last bite of some fancy baby green, I notice there's a tiny blue Garrison logo in the center of my plate. Even the china in the executive meeting room is Garrison branded. Kyle still has a few bites left, and I point it out to him as he finishes up. He rolls his eyes and giggles quietly.

"Tomorrow's orientation activity," he whispers, mimicking the buttoned-up effect of our HR leader, "includes the mandatory Garrison tattoo. Please select a butt cheek this evening, and I advise you to bring along a topical anesthetic if you so choose."

I've just taken a sip of my soda, and I almost snort it out my nose. I'm still laughing when I notice Kyle look over my head toward the door.

A bedraggled middle-aged man is pinning a nametag to his shirt. He's still wearing a lab coat — a wrinkled and stained lab coat — and thin, mousy hair sticks up all over his head. It looks like he's been in the same clothes for days. All of the other managers have worn suits for the occasion.

He stands looking confused for a moment before the HR woman escorts him over to my table. The seat next to me is empty, and I stand uncomfortably to introduce myself. For a moment, I have a glimmer of hope that he's one of those oblivious geniuses so immersed in his work that he doesn't have room in his brain for understanding social norms or operating on a regular schedule. I could learn a lot — I had a professor like that in college, and he was tough, but I got a ton out of his fluid dynamics course.

"I'm Charlotte Kane," I say, holding out my hand. "Your new research assistant. Nice to meet you."

"Todd Strickland," he says with a brief, clammy handshake. "I know who you are."

He sits abruptly in the seat next to me. I'd have expected an apology at least, but the servers have just set our entrées down, and Strickland picks up his fork and digs in immediately.

The conversation is awkward. I ask a few questions about the lab, but Strickland gives curt answers, like he really doesn't have any interest in whether I even know what the lab does. After a halting five minutes or so, he takes the napkin from his lap and drops it on the Garrison-stamped plate. I'm maybe half done.

"Charlotte, I have to get back to the lab. Come in Monday morning ready to work." With that, Strickland stands up and walks out of the room.

July 9th

I have nervous jitters Monday morning when I make my way to my lab station on the forty-seventh floor for the first time. Five minutes after I arrive, Strickland walks in carrying a vat of Starbucks and looking even more disheveled and cranky than he did at the manager lunch. I hope this isn't how he is every morning.

"How much experience do you have running tests on blood samples?" he asks me. "Oh, welcome to the lab." His greeting sounds like a forced afterthought.

My heart sinks a little.

"Um, not a ton," I say. "We did a few blood tests in my cell biology course, but most of the electives I took were in medical robotics."

Literally the first question my boss asks me, and my answer is disappointing. Strickland looks a little irritated, and I already want to crawl under my lab bench.

"You'll have to learn fast. We have a lot of samples to get through today." He turns and walks away, gesturing for me to follow. He then removes a rack of test tubes from the bank of glass-doored refrigerators behind his station. The tubes of blood look almost black under the lab's fluorescent lights.

"Watch me first, then ask questions," he says and then explains what we'll be testing for.

What Strickland shows me seems pretty straightforward. After five minutes or so, when he's done dipping test strips and making slides to send to the micro lab, among other things, he looks up at me.

I don't really have any questions about the procedure. It's maybe fifteen steps or so, but none of them seem particularly complicated, and I've written each one down in my notebook. I'm fairly certain I could replicate it already.

"What's this study about?" I ask. "What are we looking for in the results?"

Strickland again looks a bit irritated, like I'm wasting his time with silly questions. I'm self-conscious for a moment, but he can't possibly fault me for being interested in the work.

"It's a drug study," he says, "a drug Genesis is hoping will improve liver function. We're looking to see if it does, in fact, improve liver function." There's a condescending edge to his voice, which really doesn't sit well with me.

I take a deep breath. I am definitely not going to get into it with my boss on my very first day in the lab.

"Why don't you try this one." He hands me a tube of blood, effectively dismissing my interest in the actual study. "I need to know you'll be able to handle the rest of these today. I have to do some work on another study—a confidential one." Again, there's that edge, like he wants it very clear that he has far more important things to do than help me learn on my first day.

I breeze through the procedure, recording the results on the station laptop precisely as he showed me, and I know I've done well. Strickland nods.

"I'll be in my office. If you need me, knock loud." He walks away without another word.

A "good job" would have been nice.

I finish the rack of blood around lunchtime. For the first few samples, I still had to pay attention, but since the fourth or fifth one, I was basically on autopilot. Getting through the remaining sixty or so tubes was one of the most excruciatingly boring things I've done, even with my headphones blaring Lady Gaga.

Just as I'm starting to panic a bit that I've made a big mistake in taking this job, someone taps me on the shoulder.

"Hi," says a redheaded girl who looks a few years older than me. "Charlotte, right? I'm Hannah." She reaches out to shake my hand. Her hair is pulled back, and she has no makeup on, but she's unobtrusively pretty in a way that makes me think she must be a real knockout done up. She has kind eyes and is smiling at me.

"Looks like you've had a pretty exciting morning," she says. "Strickland isn't exactly the most welcoming boss in the world, is he? Come on, I'll take you to lunch."

I nod. I could use a break before going back to Strickland for my next task, and my stomach is grumbling. Wouldn't hurt to have a friendly face or two in the lab either.

On our walk to Potbelly Sandwich Shop, Hannah tells me she's been at Genesis for five years. She started out in the research assistant program like me and was promoted after two years to researcher, which from what I've gathered is pretty fast. Kyle told me last week that only about a quarter of the research assistants get promoted after two years, about half after three, and then the rest either get fired or moved to another division within Garrison. So, we're basically in direct competition with each other. I don't find this surprising, but it is a little nerve-racking, especially given that my incoming recruit class seems pretty academically competitive.

"How do they decide who gets promoted after two years?" I ask Hannah once we're seated with our sandwiches. My turkey and cheddar on a whole grain roll hits the spot, and I take a long drink from my bathtub of Diet Coke, which I hope will be enough to keep me awake through the afternoon.

"They say they look at your progress in the lab, but since it's not like research assistants are getting their names on any papers or anything, I think it's really more about the review you get from your manager."

So Strickland, who already dislikes me, will decide my fate after two years. If I even make it that long.

Worry must show on my face, because Hannah holds up her hand and continues. "I know, he seems like a real hard-ass, but he's actually pretty fair to his researchers. I thought he hated me for at least a year, but everybody thinks that with him. I'm pretty sure every RA he's had has been promoted after two years."

That's a bit of a relief to hear, but now I have to worry about being the first to break the streak.

Most of the rest of our lunch is spent getting to know each other. Hannah has been married for about a year to her college sweetheart, an architect who works at a nearby firm. They live in the Art Museum district and have a rescue shepherd mix named Lola. My enthusiastic jealousy over their having a dog seems to win her over. She's down-to-earth and sweet, and I hope she'll be a friend to me at work.

I'm feeling a little more optimistic about my job by the time I get back to my lab station. Strickland's door is still closed, so I head over and knock. I wait a few seconds, and he doesn't answer. I assume he's at lunch and am about to head back to my station when I hear a faint banging from inside his office, like he's moving chairs around. It sounds like a door slams, and a moment later, the office door swings open in front of me. Strickland looks irritated again, like he was in the middle of something. I'm momentarily thrown off.

"Hi, Todd. Uh, sorry to bother you, but I finished the blood tests from this morning and wanted to know what to work on next."

A surprised look crosses his face. "You finished already?" His eyes dart to my lab station and then back at me. "Ah," he says. "You finished the *first rack*." He glances at the clock. "Still not bad. The rest are in there."

He points at the glass refrigerator behind his station. My heart sinks. There must be at least ten more racks.

"Try not to bother me until you've finished the rest," Strickland says matter-of-factly and closes the door in my face.

July 16th

"Starting Wednesday," Strickland says as soon as he sees me the following Monday morning, "we're going to have a lot of subjects coming through here, and I'll need your help taking and organizing all the samples. We'll analyze them starting next week."

He doesn't waste any time with the typical pleasantries, but my being involved with actual subjects is good news, I think. At least I will have a break from running tests.

"Which study are the subjects from?" I ask. I might as well read up on it so I don't sound like an idiot if any of them ask me questions.

"I find it most efficient to have designated sample-taking days, so they are from several different studies. This week, we'll be busier than usual. We have all our monthly subjects coming in as well as our bi-annuals. I guess you got lucky, lots of practice." Strickland turns. "Follow me."

It dawns on me that tons of subjects this week means days and days of busywork running all of the tests next week. I'm not sure I'd call it luck, but I am sure I'll be an expert by the end of it.

The subject reception area looks like the waiting room of a doctor's office. There are a bunch of chairs gathered in twos and threes and little side tables in between, each with a neat pile of magazines.

Strickland sits down at one of the computer stations on the reception desk and motions for me to pull up a chair. Behind us is the door to the sample-taking rooms, four little exam rooms off a short corridor. At the end of the corridor is the door back to our lab.

Strickland shows me how to pull up the subject calendar on the computer.

"When a subject comes in and tells you his name, first ask to see an ID, and then find him on the calendar. Click the 'checked in' box here, and then double-click on his name." He clicks on a subject scheduled for Wednesday and pulls up his file. "We'll print all these out too, so we don't have to do it day of. Actually, you can do that. Make sure it's done Tuesday night before you go home."

Great. A printing job. Aren't there assistants for that? I nod and jot myself a reminder in my notebook.

"Why do we have to check IDs?" I ask. "Who would fake being a subject?"

Strickland nods. "I know, for most of the studies it seems pretty unnecessary, but we do have a couple of more…sensitive studies, so it's become company policy. It can get awkward when you're asking someone you've seen every month for two years to see ID, but company policy is company policy."

I nod, wondering what all these confidential studies are. Maybe running hundreds of the same test could be slightly more engaging if the study itself were at least interesting.

Strickland goes on to show me where in the files to find the pertinent information about each subject and which samples need to be taken. It takes the rest of the morning for him to show me all the supplies, how to take each type of sample, and how to do all the office tests. The blood tests are the hardest, but Strickland tells me that his colleague in another lab is doing the same thing and will send over Kyle, his RA, this afternoon so we can practice on each other.

Awesome. Not only will I have to stick the one cute guy from training over and over with a needle, but unless Kyle happens to be a phlebotomy prodigy, I'm likely to look like a heroin addict by the end of it. I guess it's better than somehow having to practice on myself, though, and it was actually fairly thoughtful of Strickland to set up. It's nice to have my boss actually take the time to teach me, but something still seems a little off about him, a little hurried and frazzled.

"I'll start out here with you on Wednesday morning, but by mid-morning, hopefully you will be fine on your own. Friday we have some subjects coming in for studies you are not cleared to work on, and some from our longer running studies, so I'll be in and out."

"I actually wanted to ask you about that. What do I need to do to get a higher clearance level and how long does that usually take? I'd be interested in working on more of the studies."

Strickland snorts. "I think you'll have your hands full as is. If I start seeing exceptional work from you, I'll recommend you be considered for clearance level two. But you should know, some of the studies we run in this lab are much more classified—some you'll never be able to work on."

He sounds a little haughty, like he wants me to think I could never be as important at Genesis as he is. I'm irritated, but I resolve to do a good job this week with the subjects and ask him again in a month or two.

July 19th

It's been a nice change to be chatting and poking and prodding rather than sitting at my lab station all day, buried in samples of blood and urine.

By the time Thursday afternoon rolls around, I've gotten a little bored with all the small talk, but also quite fast at taking samples. I've made it a little game with myself, to see how quickly I can get people in and out. The majority of the subjects on Thursday just need to give two vials of blood and pee in a cup, and my best time so far is seven minutes. Looking at it as a game seems to make the day go a little faster, and I'm really looking forward to getting home. Thursday is reality TV night with Maddie, and we have *The Bachelorette* and *The Real Housewives of Orange County* on the DVR. Half the time we just talk over the TV and don't really watch anyway, but it's always fun. Way more fun than labeling cups with pee in them and poking subjects with needles.

It's 2:57 p.m., and I have eight subjects left—one every fifteen minutes until five o'clock, at which point I'll need to spend an hour or so picking up and filing. Three more hours; I can handle that. I look at the calendar—Jennifer Champlain should be here in the next few minutes. If I can get her out by 3:06, I tell myself, I'm going to use the extra nine minutes to run downstairs and treat myself to a latte.

I hear the door to the reception room open and look up from the computer. That is *not* Jennifer Champlain.

Walking toward me is pure, distilled masculinity.

My breath hitches in my throat as my eyes drift over the figure in front of me. A crisp navy suit, cut close and impeccably tailored, drapes elegantly over broad shoulders and hangs from slim hips. The unbuttoned neck of a white dress shirt exposes just a bit of collarbone, two strong slashes across what I can tell is an exquisitely muscled chest. My eyes snag on that little divot between them at the base of his neck, and something small and frantic flutters inside me as a fleeting image of my own tongue dipping into that dent flickers through my mind. I'm near shocked at the direction of my thoughts—all of this and I haven't even made my way to his face, so mesmerized am I by his all-but-tangible virility.

I almost wince as I allow my eyes up to his face.

He is absolutely devastating.

I'm a sucker for bone structure, and his is like none I've ever seen. High cheekbones are just a touch wider than his heavy jaw, both so strong I wouldn't be surprised if they were reinforced with steel. He doesn't quite have dimples, just a bit of hollowness to his cheeks that only serves to emphasize the flawless wide line of his mouth. His nose is ruler straight but not too narrow or sharp; just a trace of cleft mars the tip.

Everything about his face is strong and purposeful—he's been drawn with a Sharpie and everyone else with a pencil. My heart beats in my ears.

But it's when his ice-blue gaze fixes on mine that the rest of my field of vision darkens and blurs, like I've dialed the brightness on my laptop all the way down in full sunlight. For a second there's something distant, maybe even sad in his deep-set, almost aqua eyes. Then he blinks, and when his eyes reopen, something is different. They're somehow softer, the glimpse of melancholy suddenly evaporated. And though he hasn't moved, I swear the space between us is shrinking. With my feet planted firmly on the ground, I'm still floating toward him, unable to keep a comfortable distance between us.

I'm not usually one to get tongue-tied around good-looking men; I think an entire childhood playing ball and riding bikes with the boys has left me pretty unintimidated by the opposite sex. But as this man stares me down across the desk, the thought does cross my mind that I may not be able to speak at all. I use every ounce of willpower in my being to tear my eyes from his and look down at the computer in a vain attempt to distract myself. I check the next slot in the calendar, thinking maybe he's just early, but it's another woman due at 3:15. I look back up.

"Warm one out there today, huh?" he says to me, his voice low and resonant with just a hint of roughness. It's the kind of voice that could make a mediocre-looking man hot, and on this specimen, it's nearly ridiculous and hits me like a fist to the gut.

He begins to remove his suit jacket. This man undressing in my presence is not going to make it any easier to speak, and an unexpected image of him removing a lot more than his jacket pops into my head.

"Yeah, the humidity is a killer," I manage and immediately wish I'd come up with something better. Short, light brown hair — or maybe it's a dark blondish red — frames his perfectly proportioned face. It's just long enough to be a little mussed up, and I can't tell whether the bit of messiness is purposeful or not. Whatever it is, it's disastrously hot. Despite his striking appearance and the paralyzing effect he seems to have on my brain, he doesn't have the air of a guy who spends a lot of time in front of the mirror. Before I can think of something else to say, he extends his hand to me over the reception desk.

"Owen Becker," he says. "You must be new. I'm sure I'd have remembered seeing you here before."

His eyes lock on mine again, and a slight smile crosses his lips. Is he flirting with me? No. Sexy and friendly are not mutually exclusive; he's just being nice. Plus he's a subject. I don't remember too much of the Genesis policy manual in great detail, but one rule definitely stuck out in my mind.

Genesis Life Systems Policy #38: A Genesis researcher may not date a subject of a study from his or her lab pod. Should a researcher begin a relationship with a subject, he or she will be immediately removed from that study. Any inappropriate behavior by a researcher toward a subject could qualify as grounds for termination with cause.

I thought it seemed unnecessarily strict, given that the extent of researcher/subject contact seems to consist entirely of brief, periodic appointments, maybe a needle stick or two, and a little bit of small talk. But this is my first real job, and I have no excuse not to follow the rules.

I realize after a moment that I've gone way too far down this path anyway. A good-looking subject walking into the lab and introducing himself is no reason for me to start worrying about company dating policy—"good-looking" being the understatement of the year. I suppose I don't have a great sense of what league I'm in, but I'm pretty sure he's out of it.

"Charlotte Kane," I say, taking his outstretched hand. A tiny but searing current of electricity buzzes through me when my skin touches his. His lips part almost imperceptibly, and some hopeful part of me wonders if he felt the same thing. His hands are big, his handshake warm and firm. "You're right. I'm the new research assistant. I've been here about two weeks."

I realize I'm not sure how long I've been shaking his hand and quickly release my grip. But he holds on just a fraction of a second longer and then lets his fingertips trail lightly over my palm as he pulls his hand away. An unfamiliar wave of something like heat flows downward through my abdomen at the unexpected touch. Did he mean to do that? He hasn't looked away, his stare unnervingly intense.

My brain lurches into first gear. I'd better find out why he is here. He's not in the calendar for today, so either there is a mistake or he's not a subject. Maybe he's selling something—that would explain the hot suit and the flirty line. And I don't recall any Genesis policies on salesmen.

"Do you have an appointment?" I ask, focusing on the screen to avoid being pulled right over the desk by the odd magnetic power in his gaze. "I don't see you here in the calendar."

"I should be in there for three. Usually Strickland meets me out here."

Strange. It seems like Strickland has been more than happy to pass off as much of his work as possible on me, and I can only assume he's done the same with his other RAs ahead of me.

"Have you been a subject for a long time?"

"A while." He wrinkles his nose, which makes the corners of his eyes crinkle. "I think this year makes twenty-seven."

My eyes widen. He looks to be in his mid-thirties. That would mean he's been coming to Genesis since he was a small child.

"Twenty-seven years. I didn't know we even had any studies going on that long."

"Lucky me," Owen says with a hint of a smile, turning up only one corner of his mouth.

It dawns on me that Strickland said some of the longer-running subjects are due Friday, so I scroll through the calendar to tomorrow. There he is: Owen Becker, 3:00 p.m., July 20. Tomorrow.

"Ahh, okay," I say. "Here you are, three o'clock tomorrow."

"So strange. I could have sworn the scheduling woman said the nineteenth, but I must have gotten mixed up. I'll have to rearrange a case meeting tomorrow, but that's okay. I know you guys are always booked back to back."

My stomach tumbles as I realize I don't want him to leave. He's off limits as a subject, not that I'd have a chance anyway, but Genesis policy can't keep me from enjoying his hypnotic presence for a few minutes.

"Well," I start, "my three o'clock subject isn't here yet, and I've been running ahead of schedule. I'll squeeze you in if you like." Before the words are all the way out of my mouth, I'm wondering if I'm even going to be able to keep my hands steady enough to draw his blood.

"Could you? That would really be great. And I'd much rather get stuck by you than that old hack." He smiles. That seems like a line, but for some reason, it sounds almost earnest coming from him.

"I'm sure you'll be more fun to stick than my three o'clock anyway." I'm surprised to hear that come out of my mouth. For me, at least, that's a little bold.

His smile broadens slightly, and I notice that his mouth is a touch asymmetrical; he has a strong cupid's bow, and it's a little higher on his right side than on his left. I know lots of studies have shown that humans find symmetry to be beautiful, but this small asymmetry somehow makes his face even more masculine.

"Let me just grab your file, and we can get going."

Owen starts to come around the reception desk. He clearly knows where the exam rooms are, but then I realize I've been too distracted to follow protocol and ask for his ID.

"Oh, before we go, can I take a quick look at your ID? I know it's—"

"Silly, I know, but company policy," he says in an uncanny impression of Strickland. "Don't worry, Strickland has been carding me for fifteen years. At least you have the excuse of having only just met me."

He hands me his ID. I take a moment to note that he's thirty-four, and he lives on Rittenhouse Square, which is one of the nicest places in Philly. The bit of boldness sweeps through me again. "You must be very photogenic. You even look good on your driver's license."

Owen bites his lip, and there's that softness in his eyes again when I look back up at him. As I hand him back the card, the afternoon sun streaming in from the windows catches something on his hand, and I see a glint of gold. A ring. My stomach sinks, and I want to kick myself immediately for the reaction. There does seem to be a spark—I wonder briefly if this is what people mean when they talk about chemistry—but he's a subject, so it really doesn't matter if he's married or not. He's off-limits either way. Maybe I'm reading into it and he's not even really flirting with me in the first place; I'm certainly not known for reading these things well. But I don't really want to give up the fantasy that this perfect man could be interested in me. And if he's married, either he's interested and not perfect, or he's not interested.

I watch his hands as he puts the card in his wallet. My heart basically leaps into my throat when I realize I was too distracted by this Owen Becker's charm to notice which hand it was on. On further inspection, it's some sort of class ring, and it's on his right hand. His left hand is clean.

He catches me staring.

"Is…is that your class ring?" I'm not sure if that's a weird question, but I felt like I had to say something about his hands that wasn't *Thank God you're not married.*

"My dad's, actually. I've been wearing this ring since my hands got big enough to keep it from falling off." He spreads his fingers and looks thoughtfully at the ring. It certainly means something to him.

"Can I see?"

He holds out his hand to me, and rather than just lean forward to look, I take it and hold it closer to my face. The electricity tingles through my forearm again as my skin touches his. My heart pounds against my ribcage, and his eyes burn into me as I inspect the ring, noticing his long fingers and cleanly clipped nails.

Just then, I hear the door to the reception area open, and a woman in her forties walks in. I'm still holding his hand and give him an embarrassed smile as I release it. But he doesn't pull his hand back right away, and he looks at me steadily. Like he doesn't care if someone sees him holding my hand.

"Hi, Jennifer?" I call to the woman. She nods. "We're running a little late, but I should be able to get to you in ten or fifteen minutes. I'm sorry, I hope that's not too much of an inconvenience."

"No problem," she says, settling into a chair by the windows and pulling a Kindle out of her purse.

The short distraction of greeting my real three o'clock is enough to briefly stop the runaway train of sexy-older-man fantasy barreling through my head. He's still a subject. Given that he's about a thousand miles out of my league, it's probably not going to be company rules that keep us apart, but my stomach still sinks a little when I remind myself of the very explicit Policy #38. I resolve to enjoy the ten minutes or so I'll have in his presence and move on.

I look back at Owen, and he leans toward me like he's going to say something. I instinctively lean in as well, and when our faces are just a few inches apart, he whispers, "I'm definitely more fun than your three o'clock." He doesn't smile. His look is serious — sexy — and I'm struck again by that floating sensation that threatens to pull me right into him. Then his eyes wander down my face and stop for a few seconds on my mouth. Is he thinking about kissing me? That can't happen. Yet I indulge in a split second of thinking about what his mouth would feel like on mine before I straighten.

"Let's find that file and get started," I say quietly, turning toward the file cabinets against the wall and steeling myself with a deep breath. I've left all the printed summaries for Friday's subjects at my lab station, but the information should be in his paper file too. I find it quickly and pull it out of the cabinet. It's light. Opening the manila folder, I flip through the few papers inside. There's a list of samples needed and tests to run, like would be on a typical subject summary, but none of the information about the study. Very odd. The other few pages are Owen's results from last month. Wow, they really test him for *everything*.

"Shall we?" I say to him, and he picks his suit jacket up off the counter and comes around to the other side of the desk. Physical proximity seems to amplify his magnetic draw, and the hair on my arms stands on end as he gets closer to me. My nerves hum.

"After you," he says, then follows me through the door.

I have the file open as I walk back toward the exam rooms, and it's astounding how many samples they take from this guy. Ten vials of blood, urine, hair, fingernails, a skin scrape, and a cheek swab, to name a few. I'm about to take him into the first exam room when the door at the end of the corridor opens and Strickland strides in from the lab. He looks from me to Owen and back to me, and he does *not* look pleased.

"Owen—hi—what are you doing here? And Charlotte, what are you doing with him?" His eyes burn into me, and he snatches Owen's file out of my hand like I'm a child caught stealing candy.

"Owen's appointment time got mixed up, so I'm squeezing him in between the other subjects," I say. "I didn't want him to have to make another trip." Somehow it feels like I'm being caught red-handed, when, really, from Strickland's perspective at least, I'm just trying to do the right thing for the subject. I don't think he'd be pleased about the flirting, but unless he has a security camera in the reception room, all he has seen is me bringing Owen to one of the exam rooms to take his samples.

Strickland turns to Owen. "Owen, I'm sorry, but I'm going to have to ask you to come back tomorrow. Charlotte is not cleared to work on your study. I'm the only one that can take your samples, and unfortunately I have to run to a meeting right now. Sorry for the mix-up." He sounds like it's taking a lot of effort to keep his voice at a normal volume.

Owen looks at me and then back at Strickland. "Todd, it's just taking blood and yanking out a hair or two. I'm sure Charlotte is cleared for that." The heat of his quick glance flashes across my skin.

Strickland looks annoyed, and his face flushes slightly. "Owen, I know it's a pain to come back, but I really can't let her. It's—"

"Company policy," Owen says, "I know. Okay, I'll see you tomorrow." He turns to me, and once again I'm snared by those deep-set eyes. "Charlotte, it was lovely meeting you." He holds my gaze for a few moments—long enough that I'm sure Strickland notices—and then blinks away the magnetic pull, nods, and heads for the door.

"You too."

Strickland is pissed. After the door closes behind Owen, he turns to me, and his face is red with anger.

"Charlotte, what the hell do you think you're doing? I *told* you that you couldn't work on the higher-clearance studies. You could get fired for this. Hell, *I* could get fired for this." Is he serious? How could this possibly be that big a deal?

"Todd, I'm sorry, I didn't know it was restricted. I didn't see anything; there's almost nothing in his file," I say, doing my best to keep my voice even and calm despite the nerves trying to close my throat.

"Did you not notice when you clicked on his name in the calendar that it was security protected? You saw that it was restricted, and then you still went digging for the paper file?" He might even be getting angrier.

"No, no, no." I hold up a hand in protest. "I never clicked on his file. I didn't have the printouts for Friday with me at the desk, so I thought it would be faster to just pull the paper file than wait for the summary to print out. Since I was trying to be accommodating and squeeze him in, I wanted to be efficient." I suppose that last part is not entirely true, since I would have stood there flirting with him at the desk indefinitely, I think, had the next subject not shown up.

"It sure looked like you were trying to be *accommodating*," Strickland says, and there's a mean focus in his eyes for a moment before he takes a breath and seems to calm himself.

But now I'm angry. That sounded accusatory and gross. The last thing I need is my boss accusing me of violating company policy in my first two weeks. I might have thought things that were wildly indecent, but what actually happened was harmless flirting, and I know I didn't actually do anything wrong.

"What is that supposed to mean?" I demand. Reminding myself that a screaming match with my boss is probably not a great idea, however, I resolve to choose my words carefully from here on out.

But he backs down. "Sorry," he says. "I didn't mean anything." He's lying, but at least he apologized. "Just…If any subject comes in at the wrong time, you call me before you go changing anything around. And Owen Becker is off limits. I've been working on his case for fifteen years, and I will not have it compromised by your carelessness." He doesn't even look at me, and before I can say anything else, he turns and stomps back to the lab.

The rest of my subjects run pretty smoothly on Thursday, though by the end of the day, I do worry that I've been rudely quiet. I've played through my entire interaction with Owen in my head at least ten times, picking apart each flirty moment over and over. Does he have that same arresting effect on every woman he meets? I determine that either he's a very well-practiced flirt or he really was intrigued by me in some way and didn't feel the need to hide it at all. I just didn't get the sense he was playing with me.

I am dying to know about him, but I'm not sure how to find out more. I certainly can't look in his file. If Strickland caught me anywhere near it, I'm sure I'd be out on my ass in minutes. How quickly Strickland snapped about the whole thing does make me wonder, though, if there's something significant about Owen's study. His reaction didn't seem like one that was entirely based on "company policy" — he was *really* mad, like how I'd expect him to be if he thought I had almost caught *him* doing something shady. Strickland does seem like a bit of a loose cannon, though. Maybe I'm just being paranoid.

By the time I pack my stuff up at the end of the day, I've determined that, if nothing else, I'll at least try to run into Owen tomorrow when he's back for his appointment. I'll have to avoid Strickland, but maybe I can catch Owen on the way in or out. I don't know what I'll gain by seeing him again since it would be against the rules to ask him for his number, even if I were the kind of girl who had the balls to do that sort of thing. Which historically I haven't been. But I'm just so drawn to him, like I'd be powerless to pass up even a few more moments in his presence.

A few of the other RAs in my program have planned to have drinks after work, and I'm glad they've invited me. I could really use the distraction. The gorgeous and unattainable stranger plus my little run-in with Strickland have me a little shaken. I walk the two blocks to the bar after hanging up my lab coat for the night and find my colleagues with nearly empty glasses.

Kyle sees me coming and opens his arms wide for a hug. I'm not one of those people who claim to be "not a hugger" or anything, but I'm also not sure that I should be on hugging terms with Kyle at this point. Maybe he's not on his first drink, or maybe he thinks repeatedly sticking me with a needle has brought us closer. It does occur to me that if I wasn't so completely taken with the subject from the afternoon, I might even be excited about the attention from the cute guy in my program. Regardless, I don't want it to be awkward, so I give him a quick hug and then say hi to the other RAs. Those three—two guys and an otherwise very shy girl—are already talking loudly and laughing. Maybe they've all been here for a while.

"When did you guys get here?" I ask. "Maybe I need to find a new lab, seems like you're having more fun."

"I think you need to catch up." Kyle puts his arm around my shoulders. "What can I get you?"

Maybe this is just his manner outside of work, I tell myself. But after a half hour or so, I do notice he seems to focus all of his attention on me and ignore the rest of the group. I like Kyle—he's super smart, has a bit of a deadpan sense of humor that I appreciate, and he's definitely cute. Not lose-the-ability-to-speak cute, but cute nonetheless. So, after my first drink and a half, when I've loosened up a bit, some of my natural shyness wears away and I think maybe I don't really mind the attention. It's certainly not something I'm used to; I had a boyfriend pretty much as soon as I turned into a girl in college, and I've only been single for a few months since he and I broke up. I tell myself that Kyle is a good catch and that I should be excited he's infatuated with me, but all I can think about, even after two strong margaritas, is the sexy stranger with the arresting stare.

I hope Kyle doesn't ask me out tonight. I have the guiltiest conscience imaginable and wouldn't feel right saying yes when I've spent half the day going over and over how I will "accidentally" run into Owen tomorrow. I do—or at least did—have a little crush on Kyle, but if something is going to start between us, I want to be excited about it. I think I could be at some point, but right now it would seem like settling, which certainly isn't fair to him. Perhaps leading the conversation back to work will make it a little tougher for him to find an opening to ask me out. We've been talking about movies, and even I can tell it would be a perfect opportunity for him to suggest a movie date. Maybe he's not as smart as I think, though, or maybe my head is so in the clouds after meeting Owen that I'm completely misinterpreting Kyle's signals.

"So," I say when there's a lull in the conversation, "how have your sample collections been going? I've had almost fifty in the past two days, and if I never see a cup of urine again, I'd be a happy girl."

Kyle laughs. "They've been okay. I've had maybe twenty-five, and I only had to ask my boss for help finding a vein on one of them, so I figure that's not bad. Thanks for helping me practice."

"No, thank you. I was super nervous for the first few. I have no idea what I would have done if we hadn't practiced. Probably get arrested for inadvertently killing a patient with a thousand tiny needle wounds."

"Let me see your arm." He takes my hand in one of his and turns it over so he can see the inside of my elbow. There are still a few marks, but they're just little pinpricks now. He runs his fingers over the inside of my elbow. "Glad I didn't do too much damage. Looks like you'll pull through."

I laugh and take my hand back. Maybe my plan to bore him out of asking me out isn't working. Another question occurs to me. "Does your boss run any confidential studies? We had a subject come in at the wrong time today, so I tried to squeeze him in. Turned out he was from a confidential study, and Strickland flipped the F out." My stomach twists just mentioning Owen in this innocuous way.

"Not that I know of. My boss seems pretty straightforward. I will say, though, he thinks Strickland is a raging douche bag, so maybe flipping the F out is just the normal course of business."

People must really dislike Strickland if other researchers are willing to talk to their research assistants about him after less than two weeks. He could be right, though — Strickland is a weird guy. Maybe it didn't really have anything to do with Owen after all.

After a few more minutes of chatting, I manage to excuse myself tactfully, leave some money on the bar for my drinks, and I'm out the door before Kyle has a chance to say anything other than "See you at work."

I enjoy the warm evening air on my walk home. I can't remember if Maddie said she'd be home tonight or not, and I cross my fingers that she's there. There's nobody else who would indulge me in, let alone enjoy, a play-by-play analysis of a ten-minute, mildly flirty conversation that really didn't lead to anything other than my complete fascination with a man I may well never see again.

It's about nine o'clock when I walk into my apartment, and I can hear Maddie's computer. She must be watching a DVD in her room.

"Madison Williams, get your butt out here. Today I met the perfect man, and we need to discuss."

July 20th

Friday drags. I'm at least glad that Strickland isn't too pissed to let me see subjects throughout the day. He's been in reception with me the whole time, though, presumably to make sure I don't try to hijack one of his secret study participants.

I've been very careful to check each person in the computer as they come in to make sure I'm allowed to work with them. I don't like Strickland, but he is my boss, and I'd rather have him trust me than not. The one time a subject for a restricted study came in a few minutes early while Strickland was still with another, I waited in reception for him to return and told him the second he walked through the door. By lunch, it seems like he has largely cooled off.

I start to get pretty nervous as three o'clock rolls around. I tell myself that it's ridiculous to get this worked up over a guy I don't know at all, a guy who probably flirts with every girl he encounters, who I can't have anyway, but of course it doesn't work at all. I'm usually a very practical person, but something about Owen Becker has me all out of sorts.

I have a subject scheduled for 2:45, but, luckily, Owen is the only one in the book for 3:00 p.m. My 2:45 gets in right on time, and I'm glad to have had three days of practice at getting people in and out quickly. I only need two vials of blood, and by 2:52, the subject is on her way. Strickland is in the reception area, and I tell him I'm going to grab a coffee. For a moment I think I register a slight look of surprise on his face that I'm not waiting around for Owen, but maybe I'm projecting.

I head out to the hallway, and stand where I can see the elevator bank. I bury my face in my phone, only looking up when I hear the elevator. It's like I'm a complete middle-schooler, but I'd rather feel silly than pass up the chance to see Owen again, even if it's just for a minute.

At 2:57, the elevator dings, and I look up. I think I half expected to be underwhelmed, like somehow I had completely inflated Owen's image in my head over the course of the last twenty-four hours.

That could not be further from the truth.

As Owen steps out of the elevator, I immediately wish I had stopped at the bathroom to at least put on a little more mascara. He's in chocolate-brown linen pants and a pale blue button-up shirt, and he has just a bit of stubble that wasn't there yesterday—maybe it's casual Friday. He looked sexy and put together in his navy suit, but today he looks just as attractive in a slightly undone, rugged way.

I have a moment to ogle him before he notices me. He walks with a powerful fluidity that makes me think he must be an athlete. He's looking at his phone, tapping out a message, and something in the way he holds his bold features—a little tension maybe—reminds me of the flash of melancholy from yesterday. When he does look up and catches me eyeing him, his eyes brighten noticeably, the gloominess dissipates immediately, and the corners of his mouth turn up. He walks straight for me and drops the phone into his pocket.

"Charlotte," he says, his voice liquid steel flowing over me, and kisses my cheek when he gets to me. Kisses my cheek! Every hair on my body stands on end when his lips make contact with my skin, my breath catching abruptly. His lips are soft, but there's the slight scratchiness of his stubble against my cheek as he lingers there, just for a moment. My stomach takes a tumble, and my heart begins to pound.

"Hi," I breathe. It's all I can manage. I've spent pretty much all available down time since yesterday afternoon thinking through what I'd say if I had the chance to speak to him again, but it's all gone. My mind is silent, save for the crackle of electricity radiating inward from my cheek, and all I can do is stare when he pulls back from the quick kiss.

"I was hoping I'd run into you."

My head buzzes, and Owen's eyes burn into me with that same overwhelming power, pulling me toward him. "Me too," I force after a beat. His eyes sparkle, and he moistens his lips with the tip of his tongue, momentarily catching my gaze.

"When can I see you again?" he asks, and I stop breathing. "Outside of this building, I mean."

This is certainly not a scenario that I've prepared for. All the time I spent rehearsing exactly what to say to him has been a glorious waste. My cheeks flush hotly, and I struggle to come up with something.

My job. I can't.

"I…I can't tell you how much I'd like that," I stutter, "but it would be against company policy." I look down at the floor, unable to bear the intensity of eye contact. "I really can't lose this job." This is almost worse than just assuming that he was completely out of my league. Apparently my flirt-dar was working just fine, but now I have to turn down my fantasy man. My heart is thudding against my ribcage, trying to escape.

Owen hasn't backed up much since kissing my cheek, and his face is only maybe a foot from mine. He tips my chin up toward him with the side of his bent index finger, and my skin sears pleasantly at the contact. I have nowhere else to look. He stares down at me, unflinching. And when he bites the inside of his bottom lip, the movement only draws my attention to that heavy, strong jawline.

"How about just your number, then? Maybe I won't be a subject forever." His tone is steady and even, his voice rumbling through me to the core. Is he suggesting that he'd back out of his study to date me? After all these years? That would be crazy.

If we exchange numbers and he asks again to see me, I don't know how I will possibly muster the willpower to turn him down a second time, but I find my head nodding against my better judgment. For the first time, I see his full, toothy smile. This man really has a lot of teeth. It's adorable.

Owen gets out his phone, and I recite my number to him. After he has typed it in, he reads it back to me. I nod.

"A six-one-seven number," he says. "Boston? You don't sound like you're from Boston." He's still standing quite close to me, and though I'm not sure it's possible, I think I can feel the heat radiating from his body.

"From college," I say, hoping he won't ask me where I went. I'm not embarrassed, in fact, I'm quite proud of my alma mater, but

Owen doesn't really know anything about me, and I don't want that to be the first thing he learns. He doesn't seem like the type to be intimidated by a smart woman, but sometimes mention of the H-bomb brings with it a whole host of assumptions, and I want to make my own impression on him.

Just as he opens his mouth to speak, the door to subject reception clicks open behind me, and my heart leaps into my throat at the thought that it could be Strickland about to catch me being "accommodating" again with an off-limits subject. We both turn, and relief floods my system when I see that it's just Strickland's 2:45 leaving. Owen's eyes soften as he looks at me, clearly noticing my nervousness.

"Okay, I better go in before Strickland gets his panties in a bunch, but you'll definitely hear from me. I…I must see you again." He kisses my cheek again—slowly—and turns to walk toward subject reception.

I stand dumbfounded for a moment, my body still floating and my mind blank save for the hum left in the wake of Owen's words. Then a million thoughts stampede through my head all at once. Owen's absolute straightforwardness and confidence have come as a complete surprise. It didn't occur to me even in my wildest dreams that he might just out and ask to see me like that, and now I'm really not sure how we left it. Is he going to call me even though we can't go out? Is he going to quit his study and then call?

I watch him disappear through the door to subject reception, then I get in the elevator and head for the lobby. I walk into the Dunkin Donuts across the street, thinking that caffeine might not be the greatest choice given the adrenaline still pumping through my veins. I did tell Strickland I was getting a coffee, though—I'll just get an iced decaf.

As I'm waiting in line, I send Maddie a text.

completely freaking out.
dreamy mcperfectface asked me out.
i said no but gave him my number anyway

I feel silly typing out Dreamy McPerfectFace, but during our hour-long conversation about him last night, Maddie started calling him that, and I thought it was pretty funny, and also pretty fitting. Before I even see that the text has gone through, I can't help myself and tap out another.

let me reiterate: COMPLETELY FREAKING OUT

I have a message back from Maddie almost immediately.

HOLY SHITBALLS. I'VE NEVER BEEN SO PROUD.
i will be home tonight to discuss

I giggle to myself and pay for my coffee. My head is still buzzing with excitement when I walk back into the Garrison—so much so that I completely forget to hold up my badge for the security guard standing by the door. I don't even hear him when he calls after me; he has to grab me by the elbow as I'm walking away, which startles me out of my reverie.

In the elevator on the way back up to the lab, I begin to really wish I'd been more prepared for Owen to directly ask me out. Though I'm still ecstatic that this gorgeous specimen is interested in me, I wish I'd had time to be a little more specific about how we left it. I don't even know if I'm waiting for a call now. For all I know, Owen could be tied up in this study for who knows how long, and I don't have his number, so I'm completely at his mercy. Maybe I should have just said yes and gone out with him anyway. I've never had a secret relationship before, and that might even add a little extra excitement.

I scold myself for going down this path again. I already have a difficult boss; the last thing I need is to lay something easy like a direct violation of company policy in front of him to jump on. But I just know I'm going to obsess until I hear from Owen. If I hear from him. This could be a long weekend coming up, but at least I can distract myself with something fun rather than sitting at my station running lab tests for hours on end.

When I step out of the elevator on my floor, I'm completely startled to find Owen waiting in the elevator bank. I shouldn't be—I've probably only been gone about fifteen minutes—but I was so focused on orchestrating the meeting before his appointment that it didn't even cross my mind that I might see him on the way out too. His eyes meet mine, and a smile crosses his face. He has his left sleeve rolled midway up his bicep, and there's an adhesive bandage over a little piece of gauze on the inside of his elbow. My heart, still pounding from before, is now fluttering erratically around my chest.

"I hope Strickland didn't rip your arm up too badly," I say, looking at his bandage. There's a little bit of blood that has seeped through the gauze. And I can't help but notice how well-muscled his arms are. He's not bulky, but I can tell he's strong, and when he bends his elbow, I see the rolled-up fabric of his shirt strain against the bicep beneath.

"I think I'll survive." He glances at the bandage and then back at me. "I'm really looking forward to our date." He gives me an absolutely smoldering look, his eyes shading with something like naughtiness.

"Owen—I—you know I…" I have to take a deep breath before I can bring myself to finish the sentence. "Can't if you're in one of my pod's studies, which you are." The look he's giving me is testing my resolve, so I have to avert my eyes.

"It seems to me," he begins, and I can't keep myself from looking back up at him. "That you've already been removed from my study, and if my recollection of Genesis policy number thirty-eight is correct, whether or not a subject is dateable, should a researcher be removed from his study for unrelated reasons, is really quite ambiguous."

I'd guessed yesterday that he was probably a lawyer, and now I'm pretty sure of it. How did he manage to even find a Genesis policy manual in the last fifteen minutes? I bite my lip and think about what he's said, but just then he steps toward me and puts one hand on my cheek. Before I know what's happening, his mouth is on mine.

His kiss is gentle and light, but I can feel the heat of his body as his chest just brushes mine. I produce no coherent thought, but some muscle I'm not sure I've ever been aware of before clenches deep in my core. When he pulls back, his eyelids are heavy, and he's looking at my mouth. His gaze shifts to my eyes.

"Now you don't have to be nervous about our first kiss." His confidence is almost shocking, and if I weren't so absolutely smitten, I might be irritated that he went ahead and kissed me after I'd turned him down for a date twice in the span of twenty minutes. But all I can think about is how much I want his mouth on me again. It's like all my senses are heightened—my skin is tingling and my insides are flitting around my abdomen. We're in the elevator bank, though, and I break eye contact to look around. I don't see anybody.

"What…what about our second kiss? I could still be nervous about that," I whisper, and my eyes drift to his slightly parted lips. Heat is pooling quickly in that unfamiliar place deep within me.

This time his kiss is not so gentle. His lips press against mine, and he leans into me, pinning me against the closed elevator door behind us. One of his hands cups the back of my head, protecting it from the steel door, his other on my hip. My lips part instinctually, and when his tongue softly circles my own, my free hand moves to his back to pull him even harder against me. Every nerve in my body is trembling, screaming at me for more—for this to never stop. His body is warm and firm up the length of mine, but then he releases my mouth.

"I better go," he breathes, reaching around me to press the down button. "I don't want to get you in trouble, and if I stay any longer, I'm pretty sure I will."

I hear the ding of another elevator door opening. Owen takes a step back and straightens his shirt.

"I'll call you," he says as he walks toward the open elevator across the bank. Our eyes lock until the doors close.

It's 3:20 when I return to subject reception. That whole interaction took less than five minutes. Somehow I still have my iced coffee in my hand. There are two subjects waiting, and Strickland is at the desk. I feel like everyone is staring, like they can somehow tell from my face what has just happened. My lips are still hot and tingly, and I wish I had stopped in the bathroom to check that my hair isn't looking too crazy.

"You two can come back with me now," Strickland says to the women in the waiting area. Nobody is looking at me, thankfully, and I'm glad that I'll be alone momentarily to calm down.

For a good few minutes, all I can do is sit and try to breathe normally to bring my rapid heart rate back under control. When I'm a little bit calmer, or at least calm enough to form a coherent thought, I catch a glimpse of my reflection in the computer screen. I run my hands over my hair to smooth it, but otherwise I look pretty normal.

I debate texting Maddie again, and just as I'm thinking I'll just wait and tell her the whole story tonight, my phone buzzes on the desk. I pick it up. It's a number I don't recognize with a 215 area code—Philly. My heart pounds.

"Hello?"

"How about tonight?" He hasn't even introduced himself, and his voice sounds urgent. Like he *has* to see me.

"Owen, hi," I say. He just left the Garrison. He can't even be back in his office yet—I hear a car horn in the background. "I…I haven't even had time to think through what you said about the policy."

Every fiber of my being is screaming at me to just say yes.

"You have my number now. Call me back as soon as you decide." There's no question in his tone.

"Okay, Owen." I close my eyes, willing him to just say good-bye and hang up. I need a few minutes to think and his presence, even over the phone where I can't see him, is making it difficult.

"Bye, Charlotte," he says, and the call drops.

I glance at the schedule on the computer. It should be at least five minutes before another subject arrives, so I quickly dart back to the lab to grab the Genesis policy manual from my lab station. I'm back in subject reception and have just opened it to the page with the subject dating policy when my phone dings. A text from the same 215 number.

Say yes.

I save his number and put my head in my hands. I can't do anything that would put my job in jeopardy, but I have never in my life felt such an immediate attraction to someone. I part my fingers just enough to look at the book on the desk in front of me.

Genesis Life Systems Policy #38: A Genesis researcher may not date a subject of a study from his or her lab pod. Should a researcher begin a relationship with a subject, he or she will be immediately removed from that study. Any inappropriate behavior by a researcher toward a subject could qualify as grounds for termination with cause.

Owen is right — it is definitely ambiguous. While he's certainly a subject of a study from my pod, the rule doesn't address whether there's an exception for studies that are not only confidential but that a researcher has been specifically barred from. As removal from the study is the outcome of Genesis finding out about a researcher/subject relationship, it seems I already have that base covered. It's the last sentence that worries me.

Could saying yes to a date count as "inappropriate behavior"? I wouldn't think so, but it's really not clear. I think the chance is quite slim that they would actually have grounds to fire me, but it could certainly cause trouble with Strickland. If he's looking for something to pick on me for, this would be some pretty low-hanging fruit. But maybe Strickland doesn't need to find out. If I don't think it's likely I could lose my job over saying yes, and the worst-case scenario is a little more friction with a boss I already dislike, then maybe it's not a terrible idea. Maybe it's worth it to taste Owen's mouth again.

As soon as I let myself think this, my stomach flutters with excitement, and I know there's no turning back. I also wonder whether I've just talked myself into doing something against my better judgment, but when the image pops into my mind of Owen pinning me up against the elevator door, I decide I don't care. I've spent twenty-two years exercising good judgment.

YES. But please don't tell anyone at Genesis.
Agree there's ambiguity but no reason to test.

I send the text and lean back in my chair. Tonight. A shiver of excitement and nervousness runs up my spine.

I'm still alone in reception when my phone buzzes again.

"How about seven thirty?" Owen asks as soon as I pick up. "I'll make us a reservation."

I'm a little surprised he called rather than just texting back, but I remind myself that he's a good deal older than me. Maybe he actually prefers to speak on the phone.

"That should work," I say, and I can't believe I only have to wait a few hours for this date. Ten minutes ago I was wondering if I'd be waiting by the phone indefinitely.

"Perfect. What kind of food do you like?"

"I like everything. I don't really have a favorite cuisine." That's mostly true; I'd say I have a few favorite cuisines, but I'm interested to see what Owen picks.

"An adventurous eater, I like that. Okay. I'll find us a good spot and call you back, okay?"

"That sounds good. I'm looking forward to seeing you again."

"Me too," he says with a breathy urgency that makes my insides clench down.

"Oh, and Owen? Thanks for not making me wait to hear from you."

"I didn't want to wait to see you. I'll call you back in a bit. Bye, Charlotte."

"Bye, Owen."

I've only heard him say my name a few times, and this time I noticed there's something soft about the way he says it, like he's handling it gently. Maybe it's the contrast of hearing my unfittingly feminine name on such a masculine voice. All of Owen's taking charge has really made me feel like a girl today, and for a hopeless tomboy like myself, it's a nice change.

I look at the clock and it's almost 3:30 p.m.—I should have another subject any moment. I check the calendar and see that I have back-to-back appointments for the next hour, and then I should be able to speed through cleanup and get out of here by 5:30.

My 3:30 subject, a kindly older woman, is on time, and she comments to me in the middle of her appointment that it's "nice to have such a peppy young lady around here." I must not have stopped smiling since Owen called.

Just as my 3:45 is leaving, my phone buzzes again.

"Hi, Owen," I answer, doing my best to keep my voice at a normal pitch.

"Charlotte." There it is again. "I've made us a reservation for seven forty-five at Cochon. Have you been? It's my favorite French place in the city."

"I haven't. French sounds delicious. Should I meet you there?"

"I was planning to take a cab. Why don't you text me your address, and I'll pick you up at seven thirty?"

Hmm. My place isn't picked up, and as much as I'd love to show him off, I should at least have a first date before introducing him to Maddie. But I can just watch for the cab and run down when he arrives.

"That would be wonderful. I'll text it to you right now."

"See you in a few hours, Charlotte."

"Bye, Owen." I like saying his name. Somehow it feels like he's a tiny bit more mine when I do.

My last two subjects go relatively quickly. Between them, I send Maddie a text.

**date tonight. i caved. r u home right after work?
emergency wardrobe consult needed**

I get her response after my last subject appointment.

will be home, mark in tow.
he can help vote on an outfit. this is huge, charlie.

Charlie is a nickname I've had since I was little. Only my family, Maddie, and a couple of other close friends use it. It was cute, apparently, when I was tiny and still being dressed in pink frilly things by my mom. In my short-haired grade school phase when I legitimately could have been confused for a boy, I hated it, but in the past few years, I've started to come around.

I finish up at work in record time, leave at 5:15, and practically speed-walk home. What's normally a twenty-five-minute walk goes by in seventeen, and I turn on the shower the second I walk in the door. Maddie and I live in a small two-bedroom apartment that occupies the entire third floor of an old row house in South Philly. The bedrooms are at the back of the apartment, facing the overgrown alley behind. A tiny bathroom is tucked next to my bedroom, across from the small open kitchen with laminate countertops and builder grade cabinets. The front half of the apartment is a bright living room with exposed brick walls. Maddie says our decor is "shabby chic," which sounds a little generous — we've done our best with our hand-me-down furniture and mismatched prints, but we're not exactly going to win any interior design contests. But there is something charming about it, and it's starting to feel like home.

I have just about two hours to get ready for Owen, which should be way more than enough time. I don't think I've ever spent two hours getting ready for anything. But I know I'll spend half the time yapping with Maddie and Mark, so hopefully I can at least get showered and blow-dry my hair before they get home.

I have my hair just about dry when I hear the door open. My hair is naturally a dark blond — so says the guy who did my hair in college — but I always thought it was more of a weird non-color, with none of the richness of brown and none of the brightness of blond. But one of my friends in college convinced me to try highlights, and I've stuck with it since. For all intents and purposes, my hair is blond and a few inches beyond shoulder length, with some soft layers. I rarely see it down, and I'm a little bit impressed with myself that I've been able to blow-dry it smoothly while still leaving some body in it. I walk out of the bathroom in my towel, and Maddie basically starts squealing.

"A blank canvas, I love it! Okay, let's pick your outfit first, and then we'll do makeup after that. Your hair looks great—did you spray it? You should spray it so it doesn't flatten out over the course of the night."

All of the girliness that I never had growing up somehow made its way to Maddie. I wave hello to Mark as she basically pulls me by my arm back into the bathroom, makes me flip my head over, and sprays my hair with something that I'm pretty sure I don't want to breathe in. Mark is already seated on our couch with a beer in his hand; he must know it's going to be a while before anybody pays any attention to him whatsoever, but he doesn't seem bothered. Before I've even flipped my head back up, Maddie has me by the arm again, drags me into my room and throws open my closet.

"Okay," she says as she flips through my clothes, "you can't really go wrong with a little black dress, though maybe red would make more of a statement."

"The only red dress I have is way too formal—that strapless long one from a dance at school. And I don't really have a little black dress."

Maddie stops and turns to me. "You know, you'd think after sixteen years, I'd start to expect this kind of shit, but seriously, no little black dress? How are we even friends."

She rolls her eyes and grabs me again by the arm. "Come on," she says as she pulls me to her closet. Maddie is a little slighter than I am, but we wear the same size. Anything that's cut to be snug in the shoulders and fits her will be too tight on me, but otherwise we can usually trade clothing. Though for some reason, even though I'm only two inches taller than her, anything that's a little short on her looks positively indecent on me.

"This, this, this, and this," she says, producing four dresses: two black ones, a red one, and a flowy silk one with a small pattern of gold chains set on a purple background. Very pretty, but probably not me. "Okay, how are we on shoes?"

That's one thing we can't trade—my feet are a size and a half bigger than hers.

"I have those nude pumps you like, and the black peep-toe sling-backs I bought the day we went to that sale at Bloomies a few weeks ago. Would one of those work?" This really isn't my area of expertise. The nude pumps have been worn exactly once—on my first day of work.

"Yes. Okay. You start trying stuff on, and while you're at it, tell me exactly what happened today." My best friend is in the zone here. I smile apologetically at Mark before I close the door to her room. He nods and holds up his beer in a mock toast.

While I try on each of the dresses, I give Maddie a play-by-play of the afternoon's Owen-related events.

"Wow," she says. "I can't believe he kissed you in the elevator bank! That is seriously bold."

"Twice. He kissed me twice," I say. "Before I even agreed to go out with him."

She bites her lip and shakes her head. "You said he's in his thirties, right? What does he do?"

"He's thirty-four. That much I know from his file. And I think he's a lawyer, but I'm not positive. I suppose I'll find out tonight."

After much deliberation about the dresses, we decide on the red one. Maddie argues that Owen is probably surrounded by drab lawyers in dreary black clothes all day and that our best bet is to go with some color. My first instinct was to keep it simple and go black, but when I put on the red dress, I do feel feminine and a little sexy, so I take her advice. It's cut just a few inches above the knee and is fairly form-fitting with a tank-style top, so I can wear a normal bra, which is a relief. The last thing I want to do on my first date with Dreamy McPerfectFace is yank a strapless bra up every two minutes.

I put on the nude pumps with the red dress, and Maddie sends me to the living room for the Mark stamp of approval. He gives me a thumbs-up.

"Hot," he says.

"I know, right?" Maddie calls from the other room.

It's nice to have a best friend you're close enough to that there's no competition. We both always want the best for each other, so there's never any jealousy. I'm just as comfortable telling her a story about me doing something idiotic as I am telling her one about something I did that was really great. She'll never judge me, and she'll never get mad at me for bragging — she'll just be proud. Whenever I hear stories about best friends stealing each other's boyfriends or sabotaging each other one way or another, it never really computes. Any guy Maddie dates is so completely off-limits that I wouldn't even think about having the beginnings of any kind of rumblings that could lead to boyfriend stealing. It's like any boyfriend of hers instantly becomes my brother; I can recognize if he's good-looking or charming or whatever, but it would never dawn on me to think any more of it than that. It works both ways too — at least I know if I ever bring Owen home, she'll be wildly impressed and proud of me, but that's it.

"Okay," she says when I walk back into her room. "I'm thinking we don't want to go too bold on the lips with the red dress, so maybe we do a smoky eye and keep the lips neutral."

I nod and sit down in Maddie's desk chair as she gets out a big, clear plastic box of makeup. I know how to put on eye shadow and mascara, but a smoky eye is a little beyond my capabilities, so I don't stop her when she gets out two palettes of eye shadow and a black eyeliner and comes straight at me. A few minutes later, she hands me her eyelash curler and shows me how to use it.

After a couple of coats of mascara, I look in the mirror, and I have to admit I don't look too bad. She hands me a pale pink lip gloss and instructs me to put some on and then put it in my purse for touch-ups. I'm not sure I've ever done a touch-up while out before, but I'll try to remember to use it if I go to the bathroom.

Once my makeup is done, Maddie determines that we can go light on the accessories because of the bold color and smoky eye, so she puts a few gold bangles on me and some small gold dangly earrings. She then hands me a nude clutch to borrow and tells me what to put in it. I'm used to carrying around my big orange purse that can hold everything I could possibly need. Tonight, I'll have the bare minimum.

It's 7:25 by the time all of this is done, and Maddie stands back to look at me.

"You look hot, Charlie, really. Dreamy McPerfectFace is going to be blown away. And the dress is simple enough that you won't be overdressed if the place is pretty casual."

"Maddie, thank you. I hope I didn't ruin any big Friday night plans you guys had."

She smiles. "Luckily, Netflix isn't really on a schedule, and if I know my boyfriend, I bet he's already ordered our Chinese."

We make our way to the living room where we can see the street outside. At 7:29, a cab pulls up outside.

"That must be him." I pick up Maddie's clutch.

She runs to the window and looks out. "Oh, he's getting out to ring the bell." She goes silent for a moment. "Good God, Charlie, you lucky bitch!"

I hug her and turn for the door. "Thanks again, Mads. I'll see you guys later tonight."

I open the door and pull my keys out of the clutch.

"That's debatable, looking like that!" Mark calls after me.

"Mark!" I hear Maddie whack him playfully.

I lock the door and start down the stairs.

"I meant that as a compliment!" he yells through the door.

I smile and shake my head as I walk down the last few stairs.

When I open the door to my building, Owen is right on the other side. My skin tingles just at the sight of him. He's in the same linen pants and light blue shirt, but now his sleeves are rolled up just below his elbows. He's waiting with his hands in his pockets, and he looks almost ridiculously handsome. Like I've stepped into some romantic comedy and he's been styled meticulously and lit professionally.

"Hi," I manage, my voice weaker than I expected. He looks me in the eye for a moment before his gaze wanders slowly down and then up my body. It's the kind of look that might make me uncomfortable if he were someone else. But I *want* Owen to see me.

"Charlotte," he says softly. "I…You look…you look gorgeous. Sublime." I made him stutter. I made this beautiful man stutter.

I can't help a smile from spreading across my lips and find myself taking a step toward him, my feet operating on their own. "I'm so glad you're here."

"Me too." He puts his hands on my waist, which sends a little current down through my core. I tip my head up toward his—he has a couple of inches on me even when I'm in heels, and he seals his mouth softly over mine. His kiss is warm and intimate, heating me from the inside out, but he doesn't linger too long. Which is fine with me since I can practically feel Maddie's eyes on me from the living room window and the cab is waiting.

Owen opens the door for me, and I scoot to the middle, noticing there's a small canvas bag next to me on the seat. He sees me looking at it.

"Cochon is a BYO," he says. "I brought wine."

I lean over and peek into the bag.

"Two bottles. Trying to get me drunk on the first date, I see."

He picks up my hand and holds it in my lap, and I lose my train of thought. "I don't know if you like red or white, so I brought both. I was planning to save getting you super wasted for date two." He grins at me, kidding. But he made reference to our second date—is he saying he already thinks this is more than a one-date thing? Maybe it was just part of the joke. Either way, I smile and squeeze his hand.

Owen moves a millimeter closer so he's right up against me; the heat of his thigh warming mine. I can tell by the way his pants hang over his knees that his legs are strong and he's in good shape. He has that thick ridge of muscle that runs from the top of the knee, then tapers as it meets the quad.

"Do you run?" I ask him.

He cocks his head slightly to the side and looks at me quizzically. "I do, actually. Why do you ask?"

I free my hand from his and trace the muscle with my fingers, pleasantly surprised with myself for this boldness and enjoying the feel of his taut flesh under the thin linen.

"This," I say. He closes his eyes for a moment when I touch him. "I think it's called the *vastus medialis*, if I'm remembering my anatomy. Always seems to be prominent on men who run a lot."

God, I've just pointed out the scientific name for a muscle—not exactly sexy date conversation. Oh, well.

"Were you a biology major?" he asks.

"Close—biomedical engineering." He knows I work at Genesis, so my being an engineering dork should not come as a surprise. "What did you study in school?"

"Economics. Though I suppose that's a while ago now."

"Are you a lawyer?"

"That obvious, huh?" There's a little disappointment in his face, and I'm not sure why.

"No, actually, you just told me yesterday that you'd have to rearrange a case meeting to make it to your appointment today. What kind of law do you practice?" It's nice to get some of the getting-to-know-each-other stuff out of the way. The intimacy between us is building at a breakneck pace, but I don't even know, say, where he's from or where he went to school.

"Corporate law. I've been staffed for the past few years on cases related to the financial crisis. It's interesting, but I don't love it. I'd always planned to work for a while in corporate to make some money, and then move to something a little more interesting like criminal law. Have you always wanted to do research?"

"I'm not completely sure what I want to do at this point, actually. I took the job at Genesis hoping that it would help me figure out whether I should apply to medical school or a PhD program in a bio-related research field. So far all I've learned is that taking samples and running blood tests all day is not the most exciting thing in the world. But I'm told it gets better." I'm dying to ask him what Genesis could possibly want with him for twenty-seven years, but it seems too early, too personal.

"Brains and beauty," he says with a silly smile.

The cab slows, and out the window I see a little restaurant with a sign that has an outline of a pig next to a wine bottle. "Cochon," I read. "French for 'pig'?"

"Exactly. They have other stuff on the menu, but they specialize in pork. I hope that's okay?" he asks as he pays the driver.

"I've never met a cut of pork I didn't like."

As soon as I've said it, I worry that it makes me sound like, well, a pig. But Owen smiles at me, reaches for the wine, and gets out of the cab. I scoot to the edge of the backseat, and he extends his hand to help me out. I'm not used to wearing heels, so I'm actually glad for the support, and I relish the feel of his hand as it tightens around mine.

"You'll love it. Come," he says as I step up onto the curb. He holds the door for me and then follows me in. "Two for Becker," he tells the hostess.

Two for Becker. I like the way that sounds.

She seats us at an intimate table near the back of the restaurant. It's a little dark, and there's a candle between our water glasses. Romantic, but not in a heavy-handed way. The restaurant has an easy vibe; people seem to be enjoying themselves.

"I like it, cute place," I say, and a waitress carrying two plates walks by us. One of the plates catches my eye—I think it's a thick pork chop that has been breaded and fried, and it looks amazing. When I look back at Owen, he's laughing quietly. I cock my head to ask him what's funny.

"It's just, well, the way you watched that pork chop go by…It was like seeing a teenage boy watching a supermodel."

Not my most feminine moment. He doesn't seem to be making fun of me, but I'm a little embarrassed. I look down at the table.

"No, no," Owen says, and he reaches across the table to pick my arm up out of my lap so he can grasp my hand. "I love a girl who likes to eat. It's sexy." As he rubs the back of my hand with his thumb, any embarrassment drains from my mind, replaced with the heady buzz of physical contact.

If Owen is somehow turned on by my salivating over fried pork, then we might just be an ideal match. I've always had a big appetite and truly love food. I do have to watch myself—I'm entirely capable of loving food right into a bigger pair of pants—but I don't really worry about it on the weekends and plan on ordering whatever sounds good to me tonight, and probably finishing it.

I turn Owen's hand over on the table.

"You have nice hands," I say, running my fingers over his. An image flashes into my mind of where else he might put those fingers, and it's startling. Meeting Owen has awoken something a little bit animal in me, and I think he notices. He looks me dead in the eye with that look that threatens to drag me right over the table and onto him.

"I hope to put them all over you," he says. Not a trace of teasing is in his voice. He's just telling me, in plain English, what he wants to do. My heart starts to pound, and a fire ignites in my abdomen.

"I…" I start, but just then, our waitress walks up to the table.

"I see you've brought wine," she says. "I'll grab two glasses and the corkscrew. Anything else to drink?"

"I'd love some water, please," I croak, parched, like my building want for this man has actually dried out my throat.

"Two, please," Owen says, and the waitress disappears. "Should we open the white or red? The white is a nice chardonnay from Napa, and the other is my favorite red—it's a cabernet merlot blend I bring back from Argentina. I've never seen it in a store in the States."

"Well, with that description," I say, "obviously I'd like to try the red. Do you go to Argentina a lot? My parents went to Buenos Aires last year and loved it, but I've never been." I pick up the bottle from the table. "Saint Felicien," I read, trying my best to pronounce *Felicien* correctly. I took Spanish in high school and for a few semesters in college before my engineering course load got too heavy and I had to drop it.

"*Muy bien*," he says, smiling. "I try to get down there once a year. I have family in Buenos Aires, my father's side. He came to the States when he was a teenager, but I have aunts and uncles and cousins there. It's a really wonderful city."

The waitress is back, and Owen hands her the red.

"So you speak Spanish?" I ask. I've always thought it was sexy to hear a guy bust out another language.

"I do. I'm lucky; my parents sent my sister and me down for a few summers when I was young to spend time with my cousins. They didn't speak English fluently then, so we pretty much had no choice but to learn."

The waitress pours our wine and disappears.

Owen picks up his glass and holds it toward me. "To meeting someone lovely where you least expect it."

"Cheers." I clink my glass against his, then take a sip. "Wow, Owen, that's really delicious."

He looks pleased. "I'm glad you like it. Every time I go down, I pretty much have to bring an extra suitcase for wine, leather, and dulce de leche."

I want to say I'd like to go with him sometime but catch myself before I start talking. This is a first date — that would be a ridiculous thing to say.

"So," I say instead, looking down at the menu for the first time. "Do you have any recommendations? Have you been here many times?"

"I've been a few times, but they change the menu often. The fried pork chop is always there though, and I'd be a little surprised if you didn't order it," he says with a playful half-smile.

I wonder for a moment whom else he's been here with, and then I stop myself. I tend toward jealousy, but Owen is thirty-four. If he hasn't been out with other women, that would be pretty weird.

He looks back down at the menu. "I don't recognize any of these appetizers, though I've had something similar to the gnocchi here before and it was fantastic, and I just watched the spareribs get delivered to that table over there—" he glances at a table to my left "—and they looked pretty serious."

I close my menu. "That makes it easy. Herb gnocchi and the pork chop Milanese it is."

The waitress comes back a few minutes later, and Owen orders for both of us, looking at me after he says my order to confirm that I haven't changed my mind. It's nice—he's taking charge, but in a considerate way.

While we work on our wine and wait for our appetizers, we get some more of the basics out of the way. I learn that Owen grew up outside of Philadelphia, went to Stanford for college, and then moved back to Philly for Penn Law. He learns that I grew up in New Hampshire, went to Harvard, and currently live with my childhood best friend.

As the appetizers come out, we finish our first glasses of wine, and the waitress refills them. My gnocchi is amazing, and I ask Owen if he wants to try it. He nods, and in a moment of confidence—the date is going really well, I think—I skewer a piece with my fork and lean toward him. He opens his mouth, and as I feed him the bite, a little of the rich Parmesan cream sauce drips onto his lip. I put my fork down and wipe it from his mouth with my finger. There's a brush of stubble under his lip, and just the brief touch seems to awaken my body. I notice him watching me, and another wave of boldness courses through me. So I put the saucy finger in my mouth, pursing my lips as I pull it out slowly. It's really not the kind of thing I would ever think to do, but Owen has me feeling sexy and brave.

He stares, entranced. After a moment, he closes his eyes briefly and runs his fingers through his hair. He takes a deep breath and seems to have regained his composure when his eyes blink open. He offers me a taste of his ribs, and I'm sure to lick my lips slowly after I take a bite. He seems a little bit flustered again, and my heart pounds. I have the ability to turn this man on. *I* do.

We get back to normal conversation as we finish our appetizers, and the waitress brings our entrées. Owen has ordered short ribs, and when I tell him they were my second choice, he asks if I want to split both entrées. I do, of course—not only do I get to eat both dishes, but it's also intimate and comfortable. I'm pretty full after that, so we split a dessert, both of us leaning forward over the plate in the center of the table. Even being a few inches closer to him seems to have heightened my senses, my nerves humming with the proximity.

The waitress comes over to clear the dish and thanks us. Somehow Owen has paid the bill without my noticing.

"Shall we?" he asks. I thank him for dinner, and we leave the restaurant, Owen's hand wrapped firmly around my own.

I realize when he flags down a cab that I'm not sure where we're going. I haven't thought at all about what I'd do at this point in the evening. Every impulse I have is telling me to spend the night with him, to get him to a private place and get his clothes off as quickly as humanly possible. But while the cab pulls up, I resolve to go home. Unless I have absolutely no ability whatsoever to read him, he enjoyed dinner and will hopefully want to see me again, and I don't want him thinking I sleep with any old guy on the first date. Plus it's 11:30, and I'm actually pretty tired — keeping my brain functioning in the presence of this gorgeous human has been no small feat.

When we get in the cab, Owen doesn't say anything to the driver but looks at me. He's letting me decide. This is him telling me that he's up for whatever I am, but he's not going to push me.

"Two stops," I say to the driver. "First, Nineteenth and Carpenter and then—" I look to Owen.

"Then the Hutchinson on Rittenhouse."

I don't want Owen thinking I didn't have fun, or that I don't want him, so in another moment of unprecedented bravery, I reach up and turn his face toward mine, my heart beating out of my ribcage. I feel a little pang of relief when he takes the cue before I have to do it myself and kisses me. Hard. One of his hands finds its way to my face as our tongues swirl around each other, and the other runs down my thigh, leaving a tingling trail along my skin. I want to touch more of him, want more of his body against me, and I find my hands pulling at his shirt, drawing him closer to me by his chest.

Owen leans into me, pinning me against the seat with the weight of him, the hand on my thigh now nudging under the fabric of my dress to trail over my hip. His entire body tenses against mine as his kiss becomes deeper, more insistent, and mine responds in kind, heat building quickly in my abdomen and making me question the directions I've given the driver. But just as he slides a finger under the lace of my thong, the cab slows to a stop. We're already back in front of my apartment.

I pull my mouth from Owen's, and he slowly removes his hand from under my dress. I straighten and take a deep breath, trying to regain some semblance of composure. He opens the door and gets out, and again holds his hand out to me. I take it, smoothing my dress back down with the other hand as I step out of the cab.

Once we're standing, he pulls me close to him, so our faces are only a few inches apart. His breathing is a little heavy. "I need to see you again." He looks from my eyes to my lips and back to my eyes. "I have to go to New York for a case Wednesday morning. Tell me you're free before then."

I think for a moment. "Tuesday. I have a friend coming in to visit from San Francisco tomorrow, and she's staying three nights. I shouldn't ditch her."

"There will be more weekends," he says, and he kisses me again, quickly and deeply. "Tuesday."

He watches as I unlock the door and go inside, and then he gets back into the cab, and he's gone.

I close the door behind me, leaning against it for a few seconds to catch my breath. I have never, *never* had a date like that. My body is still buzzing, but I slowly regain my wits enough to tackle the stairs. As I work my way up to the apartment, I wonder if Maddie and Mark will be awake, and what I'll say to them if they are. I half hope they're in bed already; as much as I absolutely want to tell Maddie all about it, I wouldn't mind having a night to savor the date all to myself.

I open the door and find them on the couch. She's dead asleep with her head in his lap, and he's fast-forwarding through commercials on the TV. He pushes play right as I close the door behind me — *SportsCenter*.

"Mark, you know you're just going to have to watch that again in the morning if you finish it without her." Maddie has one particular non-girly quality that isn't really in keeping with the rest of her — her absolute obsession with New England sports, and anything related, which for her applies to pretty much all professional sports teams. She has to know all about the Ravens, for example, to know what to expect when the Patriots play Baltimore, and I'd guess she could tell you what day that particular game is going to happen this year, even though preseason hasn't even started. Football is really her specialty, but she's still more knowledgeable than almost anyone I know on basketball and baseball too.

"I know," he says. "She'll probably be up before me, though, so maybe she'll finish it while I'm in bed."

He presses pause, puts the remote down, and looks up at me.

"So?" he asks. This actually works well. I get to gush about Owen, but I won't have to rehash all the tiny details until tomorrow.

I know I'm blushing already.

"It was…He's…" Clearly my ability to speak the English language has not been completely restored. I kick my heels off next to the coffee table and slump down in the old armchair that Maddie brought from her parents' basement. "I mean, he's just so…I don't know. I don't think I've ever met anyone like him, and I'm not sure why, but it seems like he's pretty taken with me."

"I have to say, I did take a peek when he came to pick you up. He's not really my type," he says as he runs his hand over his girlfriend's hair, "but that, my dear, is one sexy-looking man."

I can really see why Maddie likes Mark, and I'm glad he's around. He's funny and sweet, one of those guys who's confident enough in himself to, say, wear a pink shirt or point out when another man is good-looking.

"You say that like you're surprised," I tease, and when he starts to protest, I cut him off. "Mark, it's okay. *I'm* surprised."

He smiles. "So, are you going to see him again? I see you've made it home in one piece."

"I can't even tell you. I think I used up a year's worth of self-control coming home tonight. And yes, Tuesday. I think he'd have wanted to see me earlier, actually, but I wasn't going to ditch Maddie and Rachel this weekend."

"Wow, a night picked out and everything. Smooth going, Kane."

"That's me, smooth as silk." I take off the borrowed earrings and bangles and lay them on the coffee table. "Okay, I think it's about that time," I say and get up to head toward the bathroom.

"Good night, Charlie. I'm glad your date went well." I haven't known Mark all that long, but people who know me exclusively through Maddie tend to call me Charlie too.

"Thanks, Mark, me too. Sleep well."

I wash my face and brush my teeth quickly. When I look in the mirror, I realize I've only gotten maybe half of the eyeliner off, but I don't care and head for my room. I toss Maddie's dress in my dry cleaning bag, change my thong for cotton undies, and pull on a soft old tank top before climbing into bed.

As ecstatic as I am about how the date went, the nerves before seeing Owen this afternoon and then before the date must have really tired me out. I'm thinking about how long ago it seems that I was worrying about what I'd say to him in the elevator bank when I drift off to sleep.

July 21st

When I wake Saturday morning, I almost wonder if my date with Owen was a dream. I check my dry cleaning bag just to be sure I'm not crazy, and there's the red dress. An image pops into my mind of Owen's hand pushing up under the hem, and something flutters deep in my abdomen just replaying the memory in my head.

I pick up my phone from my bedside table. It's 7:45 a.m., and there's an alert that I have two new text messages. My heart starts to beat a little faster.

The first is from Rachel. She must have sent it just before I went to sleep — just a quick one to let me know she was getting on her red-eye from San Francisco, and that we should expect her around 10:00 a.m., after her connection through DC.

The second is from 6:30 a.m., and it's from Owen:

> *I woke thinking about you.*
> *Tuesday can't come soon enough. O*

My stomach takes a tumble. I wonder what he sleeps in. Probably just underwear. I sit back down on the bed and indulge in a few moments of picturing Owen waking up in tight gray boxer briefs. Before I can get too far into my fantasy, though, I hear the TV turn on in the living room. The *SportsCenter* theme song. Maddie is up.

I pull on some yoga pants. I should text Owen back before I go talk to her, I think, as she's going to want to hear every detail, and it could take a while. I start typing on my phone:

Likewise. I can't wait for Tuesday. CK

Boring. I erase it and try again.

**I woke scared I'd dreamed you entirely.
I checked my hamper for the dress I wore last night
to make sure I hadn't imagined you.**

I hit send before I've really thought about it and immediately regret it. It's too much — absolutely true but too much. His text was sweet and flirty. Mine, when I go back and read it, seems juvenile and sappy. But before I have too much time to beat myself up about it, my phone dings.

*I assure you I'm very real.
You looked amazing in that dress.
Though I bet you looked even better
putting it in the hamper.*

Flirty texting Owen. I wasn't really expecting that, but I like it. And at least he wasn't completely disgusted by my lame text. He wants to watch me take my clothes off. A tremor runs through my body. I consider enlisting Maddie's help to come up with an appropriately sexty response but decide I want it to really come from me.

**It was hard to unzip by myself.
Maybe next time you can help.**

I read through this one twice before I send it, and I'm a little proud of myself for coming up with something flirty but not desperate.

The ding, right away.

I'll help in any way you'll let me.

Sexy and vague. I respond:

**You were very helpful during our short cab ride.
But I do think your nice hands
have some more exploring to do.**

Honestly, I have no idea how I'm going to make it to Tuesday. He responds:

They haven't even gotten started.

I have to get out of my room, or I'm going to end up spending half the morning in here, texting with one hand. I don't think we're quite in a place where I can make a joke about *that*, so I decide to let him have the last line here and think of something flirty to text him later.

I swing open my bedroom door, which leads right to our living room.

Maddie is on the couch in an old, faded Exeter tee and a pair of boxers. She has a cup of coffee in one hand and immediately picks up the remote and turns off the TV with the other.

"Spill."

I rehash the major things I learned on the date — that he's a total gentleman, that he went to Stanford and then Penn Law, that he's half-Argentine and speaks Spanish fluently, and that he has good taste in wine and is totally into food. When it comes to talking about how I felt about the date, I once again lose my grasp on the language.

"Maddie, he's just…I'm…I'm totally smitten. I've never…He's just…he's just so…There has to be something really wrong with him, right? There has to."

Maddie looks at me. "Well, I mean it's been one date, so definitely be careful, but he does sound pretty great. And from what I could see from up here when he picked you up…I mean, obviously he's absurdly good-looking, but the way he kissed you, he certainly looked pretty smitten too." She smiles. "Charlie, I'm really happy for you. If he ever thinks about hurting you, I'll cut his balls off, but for right now, I totally approve. So, how did you leave it, though? Is he going to call you?"

I tell her about the end of the date — how he let me decide where to direct the cab, how we kissed on the way back, and how we settled on Tuesday. I also tell her about the flirty little texts this morning, and she of course demands to read them.

"Well," she says, "this first one may not be your finest work, but the rest of this is pretty hot, I have to say. Sounds like your 'kiss' in the cab got a little grabby, huh? I hope you gave the driver a good show."

She pauses for a second and then shakes her head.

"What?" I ask.

"You are absolutely going to die waiting for Tuesday to come around. Die!"

"Oh my God, I know. I'm glad you and Rachel will be around to distract me or I really might go insane."

"Oh, we'll do our best, but you're still going to go insane." Maddie is not one to sugarcoat, and she's totally right. "But at least we can help you get prettied up for Tuesday. Maybe we drive to the outlet mall this afternoon and do nails and brows tomorrow?"

"Yes and yes." I've never gotten my eyebrows done; I've always just plucked anything that shows up between them. I doubt I'll look that much different, but Maddie says that it "really opens up your eyes," whatever that means. Hopefully it won't hurt too badly.

We spend the next half hour picking up the apartment and getting ready for Rachel to arrive. Now that we're not in college anymore, it doesn't seem like a great plan to just assume everyone will pass out wherever, so we pull together a couple of clean towels, sheets, a blanket, and a pillow and pile it neatly at the end of the couch. It's all mismatched, and we only have the couch and not a spare bedroom, but it seems better than nothing. At 9:45, Maddie and I walk the three blocks to where her Jetta is parked on the street and head to the airport.

Rachel, Maddie, and I have been friends since grade school, and it's been a few months since we've all been together. After an adequate amount of hugging and squealing at the curb, we pile into the car and head back to our apartment.

We spend the morning relaxing and catching up. Rachel is excited to hear about Owen and Mark, and she's just moved in with her boyfriend, so Maddie and I pelt her with questions about it, everything from who buys the groceries to whether or not she ever gets tired of coming home from work and knowing he's going to be there. She seems to be adjusting to her new living situation quite well. I get the sense that Maddie is thinking about going that route with Mark eventually, and I'm happy they're doing well, but I hope it's not too soon.

When we get to the outlet mall in the afternoon, Maddie is on a mission. As she practically speed-walks toward Neiman Marcus Last Call, she explains the severity of the situation to Rachel.

"Rachel, this guy Charlie met—it's like every cologne ad in *Vogue* got mashed together and coughed up this delicious lawyer."

"Mads," I butt in, "let's not get too carried away. He's hot, but it's not like he's a model or anything." And I mean it. I think if I had seen a picture of Owen before we met, I would have thought he was really handsome, but it's really how he moves, how he carries himself, that makes him so attractive. Masculinity just drips off him.

Maddie rolls her eyes at me. "Fine. He's not *technically* a model. That doesn't change the fact that you desperately need some clothes you can wear on a real date." She turns to Rachel. "She doesn't even own an LBD. Can you believe that?"

The next two hours are spent playing dress-up in various stores, and I do end up with some good stuff. My job doesn't pay particularly well, but I have a little money from graduation gifts. While I'd never go and blow all my savings on clothes, I convince myself to at least dip into it a little bit. I'm not in college anymore, and I'm going to need to look presentable, not just for Owen. So I find a little black dress that fits like a glove, a patterned flowy one that the girls convince me looks good, a fire-engine-red shift that shows a lot of leg, a pair of dark skinny jeans, and a few silky tops that could be worn with said skinny jeans. It's probably the most clothing I've ever bought at once, but it was all on pretty significant sale, so at least I don't feel like I overpaid.

I really am distracted by the girls, and other than a stop at the apartment to drop off our loot and get dressed up, we spend the rest of the evening out. We eat at a trendy new Mexican restaurant and then hop in a cab to Rittenhouse Square.

I eye the Hutchinson from across the park before we head to the spot that Maddie picked out for us, wondering if Owen is on one of its many floors right now. Lights are on in a few of the highest windows, and I manage to get lost picturing him pulling a beer from a fancy refrigerator and settling in to watch the end of a baseball game before Rachel tugs on my arm and snaps me out of it.

It's been a hot day, but by 10:30 when we get to the bar, it's become a nice, breezy summer evening, and all of the big French doors that make up the outer wall of the place are open. The three of us stake out some room just inside around a high bar table. Maddie says she has the first round, takes our drink orders, and disappears toward the bar.

When she returns a few minutes later, she looks stricken.

"What happened?" I ask.

She takes a deep breath and blinks slowly. "I think I just saw Owen eating at a table over there." She points to a section of the restaurant where people are still eating and the tables haven't been cleared for bar space. "With a woman."

To say my stomach drops is a gigantic understatement. I wonder if I actually might need to run for the bathroom. I know from the way the girls are looking at me that all the color has drained from my face, and it seems like even Maddie doesn't know what to say, which never happens. A clammy wetness starts to build around my lower back. I've never in my life had such a physical reaction to a piece of news like this, and I try to reason with myself. For one, I *just* met this guy Thursday. I barely know him, and, two, I have no idea who this woman is—she could be a friend or relative. So I ask the natural question.

"What did she look like?" I'm practically whispering.

"Pretty redhead," she says. "I mean, she definitely has nothing on you, but if you were asking if she's cute or not, which I assume you were, unfortunately the answer is yes."

My head spins. I take a long gulp of my vodka soda. This is ludicrous, I tell myself. I cannot possibly be getting this upset.

"I mean, I don't really have any excuse to be mad," I say. "It's not like I have any reason to think we're exclusive after one date."

Maddie puts her drink down. "Well *fine*, he didn't technically break any rules, but it still sucks, and you can still be upset."

She's right. I'm not sure if I can be mad at him, but I can definitely be disappointed. "Did it look like a date?" I ask.

"Well, they weren't making out or anything, but any man and woman eating dinner at eleven on a Saturday night kind of looks like a date, right?"

I take another big gulp of my drink, and it's half gone already. I also had two margaritas with dinner, and though they were spread over some time and we ate plenty, I'm certainly feeling a little lightheaded.

"I'm going to go to the bar for a glass of water," I say, "and to make sure it's even him."

I can tell from their looks that Maddie and Rachel don't think this is the best idea, and they offer to come, but I don't want company. They don't try too hard to stop me.

The bar is crowded, so while the bartender is distracted with other customers, I scan the dining room. Right in the middle, at a little table with a candle, is Owen. And Maddie was softening the blow—the redhead is *very* pretty. She looks to be in her thirties too, fueling my growing fear that I'm too young and inexperienced for

Owen. He's just playing with me, and I bet it's so *easy* for him to get someone like me into bed. He'll probably give it another go on Tuesday and then give it up if I don't put out.

As anger and disappointment start to spin out of control in my mind, the bartender has to tap my arm to get my attention.

"Miss? What can I get you? Looks like you need something strong."

I need to work on my poker face.

"Just a glass of water," I say. He nods and fills a pint glass. I slide a few dollars across the bar to him and take a sip as I turn back to Owen and his mystery redhead.

They are sharing a dessert.

I'm starting to wish I had taken the bartender's advice and gotten another drink. My head is positively spinning when I notice that the redhead is eating with her left hand. And that there's a petite gold band around her ring finger.

Good God, the fucker is married.

I wonder if I'm going to vomit, and I slam my glass down on the bar a little harder than I mean to. The bathroom is past the dining room, so I have to walk in Owen's general direction. I don't want him to see me freaking out like this, but I can't look away as I walk by, and just when I'm almost out of sight, he lifts his head and his eyes meet mine. I look at the redhead and then back to Owen, who looks surprised, maybe almost fearful, and quickly pushes his chair back and jumps to his feet.

I tear my eyes from his and make a beeline for the bathroom. He's upset he got caught, and I don't need to indulge that or hear any excuses, at least not while I'm literally worried about losing my dinner.

There are a couple of girls touching up their makeup at the bathroom mirror, so I go into one of the stalls and close the door behind me. I'm leaning against the door and trying to catch my breath when one of the girls from the mirror calls to me. "Hey, you okay in there?" I must really look like a wreck.

"Yep, thanks for asking," I manage, but my voice is *shaking*. An obvious lie, but she did the nice thing already by asking, and I'm glad she drops it.

After a few minutes, I finally get my heart rate under control, no longer seeming in any immediate danger of vomiting. I open the stall door slowly. Finding nobody is at the mirror, I go to one of the sinks to inspect my face. My hair looks a little crazy, so I smooth it as well as I can with my hands. My face is still pale, but I'm not sure what I can do about that, and with a little effort I can make my expression look somewhat normal.

I decide on a plan. I'm going to put my head down, not even glance at Owen, and get back over to Maddie and Rachel as quickly as possible. I'll leave some money and tell them I'm heading home and that I'll see them in the morning. They will of course offer to go with me, but I'll encourage them to stay out — I don't want to talk about it, and I'd rather be done crying myself to sleep by the time they get back. I take a deep breath to steel myself before stepping out into the hall.

Owen is standing a few steps outside the bathroom door. I didn't expect this, but I put my head down and keep walking. I really can't hear him apologize or make excuses or, God help him, ask me not to tell anyone.

I've only taken a couple of steps when he blocks my path with his body.

"Charlotte." It still sounds sexy to hear him say my name, and I hate myself for thinking that. He's right in my face, and I'm tempted to physically push him out of my way, but I don't want to make a scene. So I don't say anything. I don't look at him. I can't get caught in that magnetic stare. And seeing his gorgeous face, even more exquisitely stubbled than it was yesterday, could be my undoing. He can't see me cry. Then I'll have not only lost the man I've so aggressively convinced myself is perfect, but also humiliated myself in front of him, and proven to myself that I am exactly as immature and silly as I feared.

It makes complete sense now that I think about it — the urgency, Owen's calling me right after I saw him at Genesis, his needing to see me *that night*. He made me think that was all because of me, because he wanted me so much. His wife was probably away for the night. I'm sure he does that every time she's out — find some just-pretty-enough, young, and impressionable girl, make her feel like she's special, like he *must* have her, and then try to screw her before his wife comes home. I am such an idiot.

"Charlotte," he says again. "I think you've misunderstood." He puts one hand on my shoulder, and I can't muster the willpower to shake it off. His hand is heavy and warm against my bare skin, and the image of him pinning me against the seat in the cab pops unwelcomed into my mind. I force it kicking and screaming from my head.

"Misunderstood that you're married?" I say. "That seems pretty straightforward to me."

"What?" he asks, and there's genuine shock in his voice. I lose my nerve and look up into his face, immediately caught in that pulling intensity. His eyes search mine, looking concerned, earnest. Or he's at least doing a good job of feigning concern. "No. I absolutely am not, and have never, been married. The woman I'm dining with is, though. She's also my sister."

My heart soars and sinks at the same time. Relief washes over me, but so does embarrassment. How could I be such a foolish girl? I was just in the bathroom, ready to puke over this, ready to tell him he deserved an Oscar for the facility with which he duped me, and it's his sister. If he didn't already think I'm too young and immature for him, he will now.

"Your sister…" I say. "I thought…I'm sorry." I'm mortified and can't hold his gaze. I look at my shoes instead.

We're still standing so close that the heat of his body radiates up the length of mine. He puts his hand under my chin, angling my head up toward his. I have nowhere else to look so fix my eyes on his, his stare sucking the breath from my lungs.

"I knew what you thought the second I saw you, and I was worried I'd missed you." He kisses me gently on the lips, and the tension in my gut starts to loosen.

"I'm sorry. You must think I'm a lunatic."

He shakes his head immediately. "Look, if I had seen you out tonight with some guy I didn't know, I'd have been the same way." A moment passes, and he kisses me again, a little deeper this time. His hands have made their way to my waist. "Speaking of, who are you here with tonight? Your friend from San Francisco?"

"Yes, and my roommate, Maddie."

He takes my hand in his. "Come. Meet Isabelle, and then I'd love to meet your friends, if you're comfortable."

I nod and run my thumb over his palm.

"Just let me send Mads a quick text so she knows I didn't die in the bathroom." I pull my phone from my purse and type as quickly as I can:

all good, redhead is sister, coming back in a min

I put my hand back in Owen's, and he holds it firmly as he leads me to his table.

"Charlotte, this is my sister, Isabelle. Isabelle, meet Charlotte."

Isabelle is even prettier close up, and she extends her hand to me. I drop Owen's so I can shake it, and she has a firm handshake just like he does.

"What a nice coincidence," she says. "Owen spent half our meal gushing about you, so it's nice to get to put a face with a name so quickly."

She's smiling, but it doesn't quite seem genuine. Her mouth is in the crescent shape of a smile, but her eyes are a little dark. A protective big sister. I'm a little intimidated, but it's also endearing and makes Owen seem a little younger. I look at him. The corners of his eyes crinkle as he smiles at me. I'd be mortified if one of my siblings had just told him that *I* spent half a meal gushing over *him*, but he appears unfazed.

"It's really nice to meet you," I say. I remember Owen telling me last night that she lives in the suburbs with her husband and two kids. "You live in Gladwyn, right?"

She smiles again, but it seems a little more genuine. "That's right. I hate to run out when we've only just met, but I should actually leave in a minute. Paul's been on baby duty all evening." She pauses. "Look, I'm sorry you thought—"

I shake my head. "No, no, I was just being silly. I'm sorry I disturbed your meal." It's embarrassing enough that Owen saw me freaking out, and of course his sister had to be a witness too. Great first impression.

"Listen." She looks me right in the eye and touches my arm. "I'd have thought exactly the same thing. I mean, it's past eleven and we're sharing a dessert at Parc. It's not our usual MO, but when your little brother calls and says he met a girl, you show up for dinner." This does make me feel a little better. A *lot* better, actually—did she just imply he asked her to dinner because he was so excited about meeting me and couldn't wait to talk about it? "I really should go. It was lovely to meet you. Hopefully I will see you again soon."

"You too, Isabelle."

She gives Owen a kiss on the cheek and heads for the door.

He turns to me and smiles. "At least you don't have to be nervous to meet my sister."

"That's true, though I'm not sure it's worth the ulcer I gave myself."

He picks my hand up again. "Shall we get you back to your friends?"

"Let's go. But don't be surprised if there's blatant gaping."

The girls have clearly moved on to another drink by the time Owen and I get to the table. When Maddie spots us walking over, I see her elbow Rachel and nod in our direction. Rachel's jaw practically hits the floor. They both watch us, completely still, as we snake around the bar tables and other patrons. I expected Rachel to be surprised, but both of them are gawking at us like we're fifteen and I just brought Harry Styles home from the mall.

He still has my hand when we get to the table. "Owen, this is Maddie and Rachel. Guys, this is Owen."

Rachel at least closes her mouth when she shakes Owen's hand, and composes herself enough to notice that he doesn't have a drink. "Owen, what do you drink? I'm heading to the bar," she says as she downs the last sip of her gin and tonic.

Owen of course protests and offers to go himself, but Rachel insists, and he finally tells her he'd like a Scotch. Even his drink order is sexy and mature, and I'm once again reminded that I'm a lot younger than he is. But he's standing right against me, and as he chats with Maddie, he's charming and sweet, and all I can think is how glad I am that the pretty redhead was his sister. Rachel comes back with another round, and after a little more drinking, the conversation becomes easy and comfortable. The girls seem to have shaken off their initial awe of Owen, which I'm not sure he even noticed in the first place. Or maybe he's just used to it.

Around 1:30 a.m., the bar starts thinning out, and Maddie and Rachel are pretty clearly drunk. I'm definitely tipsy, but I've been conscious to keep a lid on my drinking, as I know my self-control is already in question when it comes to Owen, and I don't want to end up going home with him and sleeping with him drunk.

Rachel suggests that we call it a night, and nobody protests. She stops in the bathroom on the way out, and as the three of us wait for her, Maddie scrunches her nose and looks at Owen.

"You…" she starts, squinting up at him and poking him right in the chest. "There must be *something* wrong with you. I can't see what it is, but there has to be something." She's toeing the line between coherent and word-slurring.

I giggle and squeeze Owen's hand. This is a compliment.

But he wears a serious expression, his wide mouth flat and the little vertical lines between his brows visible and deep. "I'm not perfect," he says, his voice low and soft. "I'm really…not."

Maddie doesn't seem to notice his tone. "Okaaay, McPerfectFace," she says in a singsong voice. She gets five years younger when she drinks too much.

Owen seems to cheer at this and laughs, but I know there was something pained there, something real and…specific, maybe, behind his look. Before I can analyze it further, Rachel rejoins us, and we walk out into the breezy summer night. When we're across the street from the Hutchinson, Owen exchanges good-byes and nice-to-meet-yous with Rachel and Maddie, and I walk him across the street to the door of his building.

I'm aware of my drunk friends watching me, so I don't do what I really want, which is to pin him against the brick wall of his building and run my hands all over him. I've never been a PDA person, but I'm not going home without at least a kiss, so I grab him by the hips and pull him against me. His mouth is hot against mine, and I can faintly taste Scotch. After a few mind-blanking moments, he frees his lips and looks into my face. He pushes a stray piece of hair from my forehead.

"Charlotte," he says, in a low whisper. I melt. "Do you want to come up?"

Willpower. I had a reason before that I didn't want to go home with him tonight, didn't I? For a moment, my body tries desperately to convince my brain to just throw in the towel and screw him already, but then I remember. I didn't want to sleep with him drunk, and while I'm not wasted, I'm certainly not sober either.

"Owen…" It's going to be hard to get the words out. That jawline is inches from my face, and I'm momentarily distracted by the idea of licking slowly along that scratchy, stubbled edge. "I…Yes, of course I want to, but I…I shouldn't ditch my friends, and…" The alcohol makes me bold. "I'm a little tipsy and I want to have all my wits about me the first time I watch you take your clothes off." His eyes move to my lips.

"Or the first time you take them off me."

I close my eyes. I can do this. I am going home. I hug Owen tight against me for a moment, nuzzling my face into his chest. I kiss him quickly when I let go, then turn and walk back toward Maddie and Rachel.

"Tuesday," I say over my shoulder.

"Tuesday." The low heat in his voice almost makes me turn around.

July 23rd

onday morning is spent running the same basic blood tests—a metabolic panel—on blood from over fifty subjects. It is excruciatingly boring, and I really can't figure out why we do the tests ourselves rather than send them out to a lab that processes thousands a day for area hospitals and can probably blow through the results four or five times faster than we can. I guess that's what the "assistant" means in research assistant—total bitchwork.

I'm about to take a midmorning coffee break when Hannah, the only other girl in the lab, stops by my station.

"Yikes," she says. "Metabolic panels. The worst." I finish the glucose test I'm in the middle of before I look up at her. The only thing worse than running these tests is screwing them up and having to run them twice.

"Eyebrows?" she asks. "Looks good."

Much to my surprise, I thought the eyebrow threading that Maddie convinced me to do actually did make a noticeable difference—my eyes look a little bigger and brighter. Confidence in how I look has never been a strong suit of mine; for most of my adolescence, it didn't really occur to me to worry about my appearance. It wasn't something I had the time or energy for, so having a sense of my looks and how I might feel about them just didn't really happen in either direction. As a result, I'm not particularly self-conscious, but I'm also not particularly confident. A tiny compliment like this, though, makes me a little more comfortable about how I stack up next to Owen.

"Thanks for noticing," I say. "First time. Now I can justify paying somebody thirty dollars to torture me for fifteen minutes."

Hannah smiles and opens her mouth to talk, but shuts it quickly and looks over my head.

Strickland, great.

"Charlotte, a word in my office, please?"

That's never good.

I follow Strickland back to his office, and he shuts the door behind me. He motions for me to sit in one of the two metal chairs in front of his desk. As I get seated, I see that there's another door in his office, one without a clouded glass window in it like most in our lab area. Maybe the lucky shit has his own bathroom. He notices I'm staring at the door.

"That's my private lab," he says. "Where I conduct my research on confidential studies. I know you have an…an interest in working on studies above your clearance, but you're *not* cleared, and that door stays closed. I keep it locked, but you should not try to open it."

I nod in understanding. A simple "That's a high-clearance lab" would have done, but Strickland is again treating me like he thinks I'm trying to sneak a peek at his confidential information. I do notice, though, that the door doesn't have the standard-issue Garrison barcode reader on it. On the knob is a standard key lock.

After a long and somewhat awkward pause, I raise my newly shaped eyebrows, hoping I can prompt him to speak without actually having to ask why he brought me in here.

He takes a breath, and his tone changes.

"Charlotte," he starts. "I wanted to say you did a nice job with the subjects last week. Most of our RAs take longer to get the hang of it, and several of the subjects we've been seeing for some time mentioned to me that you were efficient and pleasant. I suppose that we don't always…hire for people skills here at Genesis, so it's nice to see that you're both doing a good job and making the subjects feel comfortable."

He looks at me, seeming really awkward, like he's not used to giving compliments and had to really force it. But I'll take it—a compliment from him is not something I really expected at any point, and it *is* nice to hear that some of the subjects liked me.

"Thanks, Todd, that's very nice to hear."

"I also wanted to ask you," he starts, "you remember Owen Becker."

He pauses. Uh oh. Does he somehow know? He can't. I nod again, though, as I do indeed remember Owen Becker, and the two seconds before Strickland speaks again seem like absolute eternity.

"I know you spoke for a few minutes when he was here on Thursday. Did he…happen to mention anything to you that seemed strange? Anything about his study or how he was feeling?"

That's a surprise. Strickland is bringing up Thursday, which I hope means that he doesn't know we saw each other again.

"I don't think…I'm not sure I know what you mean?"

Strickland shakes his head. "Never mind. It's nothing. I just… Never mind."

All of a sudden, dread rushes through me, and I'm jumping to conclusions before I can stop myself. Owen has been coming in for practically his entire life, and Strickland is suddenly worried about how he's feeling. He must have some disease, something wrong with him, and it has just started to flare up after all these years. That's where his pained expression came from on Saturday night after Maddie joked about him being perfect—he's perfect, except that he's dying of some horrible disease. It's probably some rare cancer.

"Is he okay?" I eek out.

Strickland fixes his eyes on me and cocks his head. "I think so. I have no reason to think he's not. I just…I think I'm close to something in his case, and he's never been very open with me."

I really don't know what to make of this. The tangle in my stomach loosens slightly. Maybe he's not sick. But what is he talking about?

"Like something has changed recently?" I ask.

"I don't know, just—never mind. He just seemed chummy with you, so I thought I'd ask. Forget it."

Well, forgetting it is one thing I'm not going to do, but I can't say I'm not relieved to be dismissed from Strickland's office.

July 24th

Tuesday at work, I can barely sit still. The work is actually somewhat more interesting than usual — Strickland has asked me to help him design a study to test one of Genesis's new thyroid drugs. It is by no means my dream workday, but it's not complete busywork, and I probably would even enjoy it if I could think about anything other than my upcoming date with Owen. And Strickland's odd questions make me even more eager to see him. It might be prying to ask him about the study right away, but maybe if there's an opportune time, I'll try to bring it up.

Strickland finally leaves at 5:45. Genesis has no rules about how late to work or when to get there in the morning, but I've been trying to get in before and leave after my boss. I'm not sure he'd say anything if I left before him, but Strickland seems like the kind of guy that would hold that against me, and I'm still working on my good impression. As soon as the door closes behind him, though, I'm up from my station and heading for my locker. Owen has suggested that he swing by my place to pick me up at 6:30, so I should have just enough time to rush home, change, and throw on a touch of makeup before he gets there.

It's 6:28 when the buzzer rings. I run across the living room to the gray plastic intercom on the wall that I really hope was never supposed to be white. I hold down the talk button and shout hello.

"Hmm, hi, Charlotte, is that you? It's Owen." Even over an old crappy intercom, he sounds sexy. His voice is low but not too low — maybe he's a baritone. When he trails off or pauses, there's a graveliness that creeps in, like at the end of *hmm*.

I buzz him in and can hear the door click open.

I cleaned up the apartment last night in case he wanted to come up, but I'm still nervous as I listen to his footsteps up the stairs. Owen is over ten years my senior and is a successful lawyer. I'm proud that I have a job and that Maddie and I are able to rent this apartment without help, but it's not in the nicest part of town, and it's not exactly a luxury rental either. Owen didn't grow up with a ton of money and has been independent for a long time, so I know he won't judge me for my, say, lack of dishwasher, but I just hope it doesn't emphasize to him that I really am a lot younger. I can keep up with him on a lot of levels, but I don't want to give him any reason to doubt my maturity, especially after the nonsense at the bar on Saturday. I briefly wonder if I've chosen the wrong outfit too — he said to dress super casual — so I'm in my new skinny jeans with simple flats and a black tank top. I'm not sure I'd have picked it out on my own, but Maddie was insistent last night that it "highlighted my toned shoulders" and gave off a "casual but sophisticated" vibe.

I hear his footsteps stop, and I know he's on the landing, just on the other side of the door. It's only a moment before he knocks, but in that brief time I have to keep myself from throwing the door open like I'm just standing there, holding my breath. Which of course is exactly what I'm doing. He knocks twice, and I open the door.

He has flowers.

It's a small bouquet of those tight little roses that are maybe half the size of normal ones. They're orange but tinged with pink around the edges of the petals — beautiful. I stand on my toes to give him a kiss, and when our lips touch, there's that same electricity as at the end of our last date. His lips are soft but somehow strong, and after a gentle first few seconds, the kiss becomes more passionate and his tongue searches my mouth. My mind gets cloudy, and my free hand wanders up Owen's back. All of a sudden, there's a hand in my hair and one gently cupping the side of my face.

As the heat starts building in my belly, some distant voice of reason in the recesses of my mind points out that this is the beginning of the date, not the end, and that, again, I've only just met this man. The apartment door is still open, for God's sake. And he's brought flowers — thank him for the flowers! My body resists, but I manage to free my mouth and lean back slightly. I haven't really gotten a good look at him until now. He's in particularly flattering jeans and a cream-colored polo shirt. Simple, but he looks hot, *really* hot. I feel better about my outfit choice.

"The flowers," I stutter, "they're lovely. Thank you."

His eyes still look a little dazed from our kiss, and he just smiles, close-lipped, and pushes the apartment door closed behind him.

"Can I get you something to drink?" I turn toward the kitchen and open a cabinet that I really hope has some sort of vase in it. I certainly don't own one, but Maddie comes through, and I start filling a simple glass cylinder with water. "These are too pretty to let shrivel up while we're out."

"Just a glass of water would be great," he says. "The cab I caught over here had no AC, and this humidity is just not letting up." He does have just a few droplets of sweat around his hairline, and he wipes one with his thumb. "Maybe I should have worn a darker shirt. I'm not sure if date number two is the correct point in a relationship for sweat stains to make their first appearance."

I laugh. His simple but self-deprecating joke somehow makes me feel more worthy. Sure he's successful and impossibly handsome, but he's just a guy, and he'll be just as much of a sweaty mess as any other if he's stuck out in the heat. He also said *relationship*—I know he was just making a silly comment, but does he think this is the start of a relationship? I guess gushing about me to his sister is a clue in that direction also, but after my utter despair on Saturday when I thought he was married, I don't want to make any assumptions.

"Eh, might as well get it over with," I say, handing him a glass of ice water. "It's bound to happen sooner or later."

He smiles and takes a sip.

"So," he begins. "Is your roommate still at work? What does she do again?"

"Maddie's an accountant. Well, I guess I should say she's an aspiring writer who happens to be working as an accountant. She's probably left work by now, but she's staying at her boyfriend's place tonight."

"Ah, right," he says, with a glint in his eye that makes me think he was more interested in whether she's coming home than what she does. "So, I was thinking about your, um, unfortunate predicament and thought we might correct it tonight." There's that gravel in his voice again when he says *um*. I'm distracted by his inadvertently sexy tone, but he has a serious look on his face.

"I'm not sure…" I say. "Which predicament are we talking about?" Everything has gone so well so far, but I really don't know what he's talking about, and I'm scared he's about to say something weird.

"Charlotte. If I'm thinking about this correctly, you've been in Philly for almost a month now. On Friday, when I asked you which cheesesteak joint was your favorite, you informed me that you have indeed never had one. Before you embarrass yourself further by letting anyone else in on this shameful secret, I thought we should do something about it."

"You jerk, I thought you were serious!"

He licks his upper lip as his mouth curves into a smile. "Charlotte Kane, it appears you need to get to know me better."

Not a second later, Owen has me in his arms and his mouth covers mine again, his kiss deeper and more urgent than the last. My back is against the fridge and his hands are on my hips, his fingers under my tank top. When he pushes his hands under my shirt and up my sides, my skin is so sensitive that it tingles under his touch. Heat builds within me as his kiss intensifies, and soon his mouth is moving down to my neck. I tip my head back and to the left to open my neck to him, and when he takes my earlobe into his mouth and begins to gently suck, the sensation shoots straight to my groin. I can barely think—it's like all the blood that should be in my brain is headed straight south, and my want for him, my need for this man, takes over. I grab for the hem of his polo shirt and begin to lift it up. He pauses his exploration of my midsection just long enough to hold his hands up so I can pull the shirt over his head. He jerks my tank top up and off in similar fashion, and I don't even get a good look at his shirtless form before his body is pressed up against mine and I'm pinned against the fridge.

His growing erection presses against my hip, and it excites me even more to know that he wants me as much as I want him. Suddenly, he takes a small step backward and his eyes search my face.

"Are you…" His breathing is ragged. "Do you want—"

"Yes. Yes, I want this. I want *you*," I pant. The thought passes through my mind briefly that I haven't even known this man a week and that it might not be wise to sleep with him so quickly, but when I look into his face and see the way he's looking at me, any doubt is erased. There's something more than just lust there, and every molecule of my being is screaming at me to take him to bed.

I take his hand from my side and pull him after me into my bedroom. I've never done something this impulsive, and it feels wonderfully free. I back him up against the bed and kiss him hard as I reach my arms behind me to unfasten my bra. I let it fall to the floor.

When Owen touches my breasts for the first time, the feeling is so unexpectedly powerful that I let out a gasp. He rumbles a low "mmm" in response. As he's massaging each of my breasts and rubbing my nipples between his fingers, sending unfamiliar ripples of sensation down through my core, I run my fingers over the front of his pants. His tongue stills in my mouth for a brief moment when I first touch his erection through the fabric of his jeans. His package strains against his fly, large and rock hard under my hand. I rub slowly up and down, and Owen flexes his hips forward into me. I'm still rubbing him when he releases my breasts and quickly unbuttons my jeans, unzipping my fly to push them down over my hips. I didn't intend for him to see my underwear—I told myself I'd make it to date three—but I'm glad I had the good sense to change into a lace thong just in case.

I step out of my jeans, leaving them in a pile on the floor with my thong. Owen pulls me toward him as he topples backward onto my bed, and I end up straddled on top of him, on my knees and sitting on his thighs. It occurs to me that I'm absolutely naked, but before I have time to develop any self-consciousness, Owen sits up and pulls me closer into his lap. He's still wearing his jeans, his erection pressing through them. As I lean into him, he takes one nipple into his mouth, licking slow circles around the tip, and I'm almost overcome with sensation. Each movement of his tongue shoots pangs of pleasure straight to my clit. Pleasure is building deep in my body, and as I begin to rock my hips and grind myself against his hard cock, I wonder how long I'm even going to be able to hold on.

Realizing that I'm already exceedingly close to the edge, I stand up on my knees to both ease the pressure and pull my nipple from his mouth. I reach down and fumble with Owen's belt. It takes me a moment to undo the buckle and reach the button on his jeans below. As I unzip his fly, he reaches into his pocket and removes a condom. I'm still kneeling above him when I push his jeans and boxer briefs down over his hips, and his erection pops free. Straining upward, it's even bigger than I expected, and I wonder how I'm going to accommodate his full size, my breath quickening with excitement and nerves.

Just then, Owen rolls to his right and flips me over, and I end up on my back, with him next to me, his bare member pressing into my hip. He bows his head and resumes his slow but intense assault on my nipples, taking first my right and then my left into his mouth. He flicks his tongue back and forth across each hard point, and I feel myself getting wetter and wetter, my legs trembling as my body tries to manage the overpowering sensation.

Owen's hand glides down my stomach, and I find myself holding my breath in anticipation. As the long breath hisses slowly out of me, he spreads me apart with his thumb and ring finger and gently runs his pointer and middle fingers over my clit. My body jerks as sharp pleasure ricochets around my pelvis, and I press into his hand as he begins a slow rhythm with his fingers, drawing the wetness up from my entrance with each devastating stroke. I begin to moan, focusing on the warm sensation spreading in slow waves from my center.

When Owen pushes two fingers deep inside me, his guttural moan of delight almost startles me.

"Charlotte," he whispers into my ear. "You. Are. So. Wet." He takes a breath before each word, and his hard cock presses into the flesh of my hip in a faster rhythm.

"It's for you," I murmur. "I want you inside me." I don't recognize my own voice. "Right now."

Owen has the condom rolled down over his pulsing cock within seconds, and he's on top of me. Still supporting his weight on his elbows, he kisses me slowly and passionately, teasing my mouth with his lips and tongue. I've regained a small amount of control over my senses with the brief hiatus, but I've never felt such a carnal want, such an animalistic need as my desire now to have this man inside me.

Our mouths are still locked together when I reach down, take hold of his erection, and guide the tip to my opening. He lets some of his weight fall on me as he pushes slowly inside, and I quiver around him as he parts the sensitive folds. I can't help myself and grab his butt to pull him closer, pressing the full length of his erection deep inside. He remains there for a brief moment, fully embedded in me, and I watch a shiver run the length of his body, shaking his cock and rippling pleasure through my core. Then he draws out of me slowly, deliberately, until just the head of his penis remains inside, taking a moment to massage the slick entrance of my body before slamming forward, his hips bumping mine as I stretch to accommodate his still-growing cock.

Owen begins to really thrust. His face is now a few inches above mine, and when I look up at him, his eyes meet mine for a moment before his gaze trails lower to my chest. My breasts are bouncing and jiggling with each thrust, and as he watches them, his pounding becomes less controlled. The thought that a part of my body, a part of me, turns him on so much fuels my own fire, and as he pushes faster and faster, I feel like I'm coming apart at the seams, ready to explode under him. Tension builds, coiling like a spring through my center.

A slight shift in the angle of Owen's hips causes his base to brush over my clit with his next thrust, and I am catapulted over the edge. Rhythmic pulses of pleasure rip through me, and I arch off the bed as every muscle in my body pulls tight, my fingers digging into Owen's back and wrenching him closer. He groans audibly as three more pounding thrusts plunge his erection even deeper inside me, and then he stills his hips, his cock jerking inside me as he comes.

It takes me a good few minutes to come back to Earth. My body is still buzzing when I open my eyes. Owen is collapsed on top of me, the weight of him on my chest, but his breathing has slowed to a more regular rhythm. His face is nuzzled between my shoulder and neck, his warm, wet breath against my collarbone. I turn my head a little and rub my cheek and nose against his hair. It's very slightly damp with sweat, but he smells clean and sweet.

I enjoy the closeness for a few moments. I've known this man less than a week, but somehow it feels right to have this intimacy with him. I don't mean the sex—the sex felt *really* right—but this calm after the storm where our bodies are still joined and we've just come down together. My revelry, however, is interrupted by a more practical thought.

It's 7:30, and we're already naked in bed. We never made it to dinner, and I'm hungry. If it were later, maybe I could ignore my growling stomach and drift off to sleep in my post-orgasmic daze, but there's no way we can go to bed at this hour. What do I do? I don't want to disturb the intimate moment, but at some point I think we have to get up and get dressed. Does he want to sleep over? I guess we could order some food. My stomach drops when the next wave of doubt hits me. What if this was all he was after? I gave it up *before* dinner. It doesn't seem like sex is all he wants from me, but what if I'm reading it completely wrong? It's not like I have any experience with this sort of thing, and I'm pretty sure Dating 101 would not recommend taking the guy to bed on the second date, let alone *before dinner* on the second date.

As if he's been listening to my ridiculous inner monologue, Owen pushes himself up onto his elbows. He kisses me gently on the lips.

"How about those cheesesteaks?" he says, looking from my mouth to my eyes. His own are shining with excitement, like our romp has given him a second wind. "I'm starving. You've really worked up my appetite, my Charlotte."

My panic abates. *My Charlotte.* He called me his Charlotte.

"Let's go," I say.

"We have a few stops to make. You can't very well have a favorite cheesesteak if you've only ever tried one, so I'm taking you to my four favorite spots so you can try them all." Still on top of me, he smiles. "I'm glad we have a lot of eating ahead of us, because I fully intend to do this again later tonight, and we're going to need the energy." I think I see a quick flash of doubt cross his face. "If you're interested, that is."

Okay, so he's not going to run out of here, and he at least liked the sex enough to want to do it again. And he planned a cute date and brought me flowers. My insecurity fades.

"I think I could stand to enjoy an encore performance."

We're up, dressed, and out the door ten minutes later. We take a cab to the first destination, Jim's Steaks on South Street. From there, Owen says it's a twenty-minute walk to Pat's and Geno's, the two most famous cheesesteak joints in Philadelphia, and then a short walk to Owen's favorite, a less well-known dive in South Philly.

Jim's has a line out the door, but Owen tells me it should move quickly. He holds my hand while we wait, and he wants to hear about how I ended up at Genesis. I explain that I've always been interested in science and math and have known since high school that I wanted to do something involving biology and the human body.

While studying biomedical engineering in college, I had an internship at a hospital with an infectious disease specialist, and I'd loved it—loved the combination of science with what felt like detective work in diagnosing exotic diseases. But I'd also enjoyed research, and I wanted to have some exposure to working in the industry before deciding on medical school over a PhD in a field like biophysics.

"My father was a biochemical engineer," says Owen when I've finished explaining. "He couldn't really talk about what he was working on, and he died when I was young, so I never had a great understanding of what he did." His face darkens slightly at the mention of his father.

"I'm so sorry to hear that. How old were you?"

"I was six," he says, and I'm about to ask him where his dad worked, but we've gotten to the front of the line, and the moment passes.

Within minutes, we're seated at a table that has just been vacated by what appear to be drunk teenagers, armed with a plastic knife and a stack of napkins.

Owen watches me as I take my first bite. "So?"

It's good. It's *really* good. Though I'm not sure why, exactly; I watched the guy make it behind the Plexiglas, and I'm pretty sure it's just thinly shaved steak and onions cooked on a griddle, then piled onto a roll and smothered in Cheez Whiz—actual Cheez Whiz from a big tub. I didn't even know they still made that.

"Whoa," I say as I wipe a drip of grease from my chin. Owen smiles triumphantly while he chews a big bite of sandwich. We finish our halves quickly and head out the door—we have three cheesesteaks left to procure.

A few blocks into our walk to our next stop, we come upon a Walgreens. Owen slows as we get to the door.

"Do you mind if I stop to…I just need to pick up a…" He's actually starting to blush a little. "I only brought one condom."

"You underestimated yourself, huh?" I squeeze his hand. "Actually," I say, and I'm sure I'm starting to flush a bit too, "I'm on the pill. And I hope you're not mad, but on Thursday when I tried to check you in to collect your sample at Genesis, I flipped open your file to see which tests they normally run." I eye Owen, and he's fully focused on me, listening intently. "And they run everything—I mean *everything*—on you, and I didn't mean to, but I did see the page with your results from last month, and you were negative for everything. I am too. When Strickland taught me to run the tests at work, I was scared to waste subject samples if I messed up, so I practiced a few times on myself." I'm really not sure what to expect for a reaction—it does seem like an invasion of privacy, but I didn't know at the time that he'd be any more to me than a subject, and I also didn't know I wasn't allowed to work on his study to begin with.

"That's good," he says. "I haven't slept with anyone since then, and I certainly don't intend to now."

"Me neither."

Did we just become exclusive? Here I am, worried that he'll think I was snooping through his file, and he tells me he's not going to see anybody else. That seems fast, but I can't even imagine wanting to be with any other guy at this point, so I make the conscious decision to just be happy about this development and move on. The thought of going to bed with Owen without even the small barrier of latex sends a little flutter down through my core, and though I'm still hungry for more cheesesteak, I'm also looking forward to getting back to my apartment and having my way with this lovely, confident man.

By the time we finish at Pat's and Geno's, I'm pretty full. I'm glad we have a little walk to get to the next spot, since a cheesesteak and change plus some fries from Pat's are starting to weigh me down a little. Owen holds my hand as we walk down Passyunk Avenue, getting farther into South Philadelphia. It's dark now, and as the blocks get a little sketchier, I'm glad to have a man by my side.

On a particularly poorly lit side street, I notice a man stumbling on the sidewalk up ahead of us. He's in jeans and a gray-hooded sweatshirt, and he's swaying from side to side.

"Do you think he's drunk?" I ask, but the way the man is moving tells me something else might be wrong. Owen is watching him too. "Seems strange," I say. "Maybe he's hurt."

The man is moving very slowly, and as we're coming up behind him, he falls to his knees.

Owen drops my hand and whispers, "I'm going to see if he needs help. Why don't you hang back just in case."

As I watch Owen take the last few steps toward the figure, I have a growing sense that something isn't right. Why is he in a sweatshirt in this weather? It's a warm summer night. I'm about to step forward and grab Owen's arm, but I'm just a moment too late. It's like I'm watching the next few moments in slow motion, and there's nothing I can do to stop it.

Owen reaches the man and bends to ask him if he is okay. As he leans toward the hooded figure, the man seems to lose his balance and falls forward. Owen instinctively grabs for him, but as soon as they touch, the hooded man yells something incoherent and twists away. I see a small flash as something shiny and metal catches the light from the streetlamp on the corner, and the man lunges at him.

Owen cries out before he hits the concrete sidewalk.

The hooded man turns toward me and scampers away. I'm frozen for a moment, and I see as he passes me that his hoodie is unzipped in the front and his undershirt is soaked in blood. I don't get a good look at his face.

Absolute panic sets in as I fly the few steps to where Owen is hunched on the ground. There's blood—a *lot* of blood. The knife is still in his abdomen—only the handle is showing.

"No, no, no," I shriek. I'm kneeling in a pool of Owen's blood, digging around in my purse for my cell phone. It seems like eternity before I finally find it at the bottom of my bag, and my hands are shaking so badly, I'm not even sure I'll be able to dial 9-1-1. I take a deep breath and focus all my energy on keeping my hands steady. I glance at his face—his features are twisted into a grimace, but at least I know he's still conscious.

I have 9-1-1 typed into my phone and am about to hit the call button when a hand locks around my wrist. I just about jump out of my skin, and it takes me a moment to realize it's Owen's.

"Don't," he whispers. "You can't…you can't call for help."

He's delirious—he must not know what has happened. I try to twist my wrist free, but his grip is strong and he's not letting go.

"Owen, listen to me, you've been stabbed, and you're losing a lot of blood. We have to get you help, and it has to be now. You're going to be okay, but we have to get you to a hospital right now." I of course have no idea if he'll be okay. I have no way to know if the knife, lodged a few inches under his ribs in the center of his torso, has hit his stomach or perforated his intestines or damaged any number of other important organs in the general vicinity. I have no way to know if the blood pooling on the ground is coming at such a rate that he'll lose consciousness even before an ambulance can get here.

I try again to free my wrist, but he won't let go. When I try to take the phone with my other hand, Owen grabs that wrist too. At least he hasn't lost enough blood yet to lose his strength, and he pulls me toward him with both hands.

"You don't understand," he says, and tears spring to my eyes. If I can't get him help and he bleeds out here on the sidewalk, I will never forgive myself. The adrenaline starts to pump through my veins, and I put my face right in his.

"Owen, you're delirious, and if you don't let go of me right now, you are going to die. That can't happen. You need to let go of me, and it has to be right now."

Nothing.

"Charlotte, listen to me. I am not delirious. You're not going to understand this now, but I'll explain everything later. I'm going to be fine. I am not going to die. You can't call for help, though." He certainly doesn't sound delirious; he has that tone a movie hero has during an emergency while everyone else is freaking out. "I need you to do something, and it's going to be hard for you, but it's very important. You need to pull out the knife." He's looking me straight in the eye and seems as lucid as ever.

"Owen, you'll bleed out, I know you will. You're already bleeding so much, moving the knife will for sure make it worse. We really need to get you an ambulance." Tears run down my cheeks.

"Charlotte, I know you can do this. I promise you I won't die. I'm not…I'm different, and I'll be fine, but we have to get the knife out so I can heal." He's staring me down.

"What we need to do is stop the bleeding, and we need to get you to a doctor." I'm starting to sob now, but he squeezes both wrists firmly, and I can see in his face that at least he believes what he is saying.

"I need you to trust me. I know you haven't known me for long, but I need you to trust me, *right now*."

My gut tells me I should, but reason tells me I'm letting him die.

"Calling for help would be the most dangerous thing you could do for me. I'm not normal — no one can know. You just have to get the knife out." Owen's jaw is clenched, and his eyes squint tightly against the pain.

I take a deep breath and give in to my instinct to trust him. I nod, and he releases my wrists. Then I grab the handle of the knife and pull gently. It doesn't move. After another deep breath, I yank the handle—and a six-inch blade pulls free. It's dripping dark red blood and must be at least two inches wide at the base. I drop it beside me and press the heel of my right palm over the wound—which is bleeding even faster. My mind clouds over with panic again as crimson blood seeps between my fingers.

I press my left hand over my right and lean in with as much of my weight as I can, willing the flow of blood to stop, willing Owen to survive.

After a few moments, I notice through tear-blurred vision that the bleeding is slowing.

As the bleeding tapers off, I look back up to Owen's face. His expression is somewhat less pained.

"Charlotte, thank you," he says. "Thank you for trusting me. You can stop holding pressure. It won't bleed anymore."

It occurs to me that I've just put my own fingerprints all over the knife, and that the story of what happened—that an injured and possibly crazy man got frightened and stabbed Owen when he tried to help—sounds seriously fictional. He really better be okay.

I frown at him skeptically, but he nods to reassure me, so I remove my hands. His polo shirt is soaked with blood, but it's still in one piece save the cut from the knife. I can't see the actual damage, though, so I pull the shirt up toward his chest. There's blood all over his abdomen, but the wound itself doesn't look nearly as bad as I would have expected. It's not bleeding at all, and it doesn't appear to be more than an inch or so deep. How is that possible? I bunch as much of my tank top together as I can and lean forward to use it to wipe some of the blood from around the wound. It really doesn't look that bad. I glance down at the knife again—still six inches—and then look at Owen's face.

His expression has relaxed; he doesn't look in pain any longer. "I…I don't know how to explain this to you, but I'm different. I…I heal."

I search his face, hoping for some further clarity, but he's just focused on me, waiting for my reaction. He heals—what is that supposed to mean? We all do, but nobody can heal on their own from a six-inch knife wound to the gut. That's the kind of thing that happens in superhero movies but obviously not in real life.

I tell myself to calm down and think this through, but then I look back at the injury. It looks more like a fresh scar than a stab wound. Running my finger back and forth over the raised pink flesh, I just can't get my mind around what I'm seeing. My head is foggy with confusion, and after a minute I realize I can't feel the raised scar anymore. When I remove my fingers and look where they were, I see only Owen's smooth skin below.

There is still some blood smeared across his abdomen, and I frantically wipe it away with my already blood-soaked tank top. Where is it? This can't be happening; I don't believe in this. It doesn't seem like the kind of thing he would do, but maybe Owen put something in my Diet Coke at Geno's. That must be it. This is all in my head, and I'm having some sort of psychotic episode.

I stand quickly. "I…I'm sorry…" I'm backing away from Owen. "I think I'm…" I look down at my hands. They're still stained glossy red with blood. I don't remember anything else, but I'm pretty sure the next thing that happens is I hit the concrete.

I wake up in my bed.

A dream. Relief floods my system. It was all a bizarre dream. Maybe the most vivid dream I've ever had, but at least I'm not crazy.

"You're up." A warm hand touches my cheek. Owen is here—that's a surprise. "Thank God. How are you feeling?"

"I…I don't know." I feel strange, and there's a bit of throbbing at the back of my head. Did I fall? No, we must have fallen asleep after our early evening romp. I'm glad at least that part wasn't a dream. I look at the clock. It's 11:15 p.m. Ugh, poor Owen. I must have fallen asleep at 7:30, and he's been sitting here for almost four hours, unsure of whether to wake me. The covers are pushed to the bottom of the bed, and I'm in my bra and underwear. I guess I managed to get those back on and then fell asleep? Odd. I can't believe I did this on our second date. At least he didn't leave. He's lying on his side next to me, propped up on his elbow.

"Owen, I'm sorry. I must have fallen asleep. I wish you'd woken me. Have you just been sitting here bored all this time?"

"Charlotte…" Owen furrows his brow. "Do you remember what happened on the sidewalk after Geno's? You fainted. I hope you'll forgive me for going through your purse for your keys. You hit your head on the sidewalk when you fell, but it doesn't look too bad. You'll have a little bruise, but I'm pretty sure it wasn't bad enough for a concussion. I'm glad you woke up, though. You've been out about fifteen minutes, and after another five I was going to take you to the emergency room." I notice he's propped my feet up on a few pillows.

Okay, so I fainted while we were walking, and Owen got me home. And in the fifteen minutes I was out, I had a bizarre dream. I've never fainted, so that's pretty weird, but I guess there's a first time for everything, and Owen has had me feeling a little lightheaded since we met.

I sit up. "Thanks for getting me—" I completely lose my train of thought when I see what's draped over the back of my desk chair. My jeans—and the knees are stained dark maroon. They still look wet. My vision dims slightly, and an uncomfortable heat rushes through my body. I lower my head slowly back to the pillow and look up at Owen.

I hadn't noticed before but he's in an old, gray Exeter T-shirt—my brother's shirt that he forgot when he visited a few weeks ago. Owen is also wearing a pair of mesh gym shorts of mine from high school. Good thing I was a tomboy then and all my clothes were a few sizes too big.

Owen notices me inspecting his clothes, and his cheeks flush. "I hope you don't mind I borrowed these. I found them in your top drawer. I just pulled out the first thing I thought I could possibly get on. My clothes are in your bathtub. I didn't want to stain anything with the blood, and I didn't want you waking up with me naked after the fright I just gave you. I'm sorry."

I can't tell whether he's apologizing for opening my drawers or for the "fright" he gave me. My mind is completely numb, and I'm not sure if I'm even going to be able to form a complete sentence.

"You…got stabbed." It's the best I can manage, and I look to Owen, hoping he'll say something that can make all of this make sense. Or at least help me understand what's real and what's not.

He takes my hand and holds it to his face, the back of my hand against his cheek.

"There was a man stumbling on the sidewalk," he starts. "When I went to help him, he stabbed me in the stomach and ran off. I noticed right before I saw the knife that he was hurt — there was a lot of blood on his shirt. My best guess is that he was delirious and mistook me for whomever it was that hurt him. Or maybe he was just crazy." He looks to my face as if to ask whether he should keep going. I nod.

"You wanted to call nine-one-one, but I convinced you not to. My healing, it's…Nobody knows. Just my mother and my sister and now you. If you'd called an ambulance, either the EMTs would have seen what I do, or it would have been healed by the time they arrived, and we'd have had no explanation for all the blood. I asked you to pull the knife out and you did. Thank you for that. I couldn't heal until it was out."

I pulled the knife out. I do remember that. I remember all of it; I am just having trouble believing it.

"How can…" I don't know how to ask. "What…what are you?"

His face darkens. "I don't know."

"Why didn't you pull the knife out yourself? You had a pretty good grip on my wrist, you probably could have gotten it out on your own."

"I knew the bleeding would get worse before it got better, and I thought if that happened, I wouldn't have been able to keep you from calling an ambulance. I'm sorry; I know this is all crazy to you." He still has my hand against his face, but he's looking down at the bed.

"So you manipulated me into pulling the knife out…so I'd be too distracted to call for help?"

"I…yeah, I guess so. I'm sorry, Charlotte. I'm sorry for laying this on you. Do you want me to go?" He closes his eyes, and his expression is almost as pained as when he still had the knife in his gut. My heart breaks. The hand that was holding mine goes slack.

I cup his cheek with my hand, running my fingers along his jaw. His eyes open.

"Why would I want you to go? You were right. I would have called nine-one-one if you had done that on your own, I think. What you can do…it's…I don't understand it, but it's amazing."

He closes his eyes again, the creases between his brows softening. I have a lot more questions.

"How did you get me home?" I ask.

"I put you over my shoulder and hailed a cab. I told the driver you'd had a little too much to drink."

He put me over his shoulder? Owen is in great shape, but I'm no waif, and a limp body is not exactly the wieldiest thing in the world. That much I know from trying to move my sleeping niece to bed after she's passed out.

"That's…You're strong."

"I guess," he says.

"But what about the blood?"

"It was pretty dark, and your legs covered most of my shirt. The driver must not have been paying too much attention, thankfully."

"Good thing Maddie isn't home," I say, and Owen smiles. My head is still absolutely spinning.

"Charlotte, I'll answer any questions I can, but this has been a lot for you, I think. Why don't you try to rest? I have to go to New York in the morning to work with a couple of witnesses on one of my cases, but I'll be back Friday. Can I have another go at taking you on a proper date?"

I nod. I want to ask him more, but my head swims and I do still have a little bit of a headache. Owen kisses me lightly on the lips and then reaches down to pull the covers over us. I roll onto my side so that I'm facing away and inch myself back toward him. He drapes his arm over me and pulls me tight against him. It's just too much. I clutch Owen's arm to my chest as he spoons me, and within seconds, I'm asleep.

July 25th

When my alarm goes off Wednesday morning, I'm alone in bed. I reach my hand out and touch the other side of the mattress, and it's cold. There's a note on my desk.

CHARLOTTE—

I'M SO SORRY TO LEAVE BEFORE YOU'RE UP. IT'S 5AM NOW, AND MY TRAIN TO NEW YORK IS AT 6, SO I NEED TO RUN HOME AND GRAB SOME CLOTHES. I DEBATED WAKING YOU BUT DECIDED THAT AFTER WHAT I PUT YOU THROUGH LAST NIGHT, YOU'D BE BETTER OFF RESTING. I STILL HAVE YOUR T-SHIRT AND SHORTS—I'LL WASH THEM AND GET THEM BACK TO YOU NEXT TIME I SEE YOU. I HOPE WE'RE STILL ON FOR FRIDAY. I GET BACK FROM NEW YORK IN THE AFTERNOON, SO WHY DON'T YOU JUST COME TO MY PLACE WHEN YOU LEAVE WORK? I'LL TEXT YOU THE ADDRESS SO YOU HAVE IT AND MAKE US A RESERVATION FOR DINNER. I'LL MISS YOU.

OWEN

P.S. YOUR JEANS ARE HANGING IN THE BATHROOM—I WASHED AS MUCH OF THE BLOOD OUT AS I COULD. SORRY, AGAIN, FOR RUINING OUR DATE.

I allow myself a brief moment to marvel at the fact that even Owen's handwriting is somehow sexy—all capitals, written with a heavy hand—and then I can no longer evade the truth barreling at me like a freight train.

It was real. All of it.

Owen healed from what should have been a potentially fatal stab wound in what could have only been a few minutes. I feel a little crazy even just going over it in my head. These things don't happen in real life—they happen in comic books and big-budget summer blockbusters. A slight twinge at the back of my head tells me a headache is brewing. I can't tell if it's from my fall or if trying to reconcile what I saw last night with the reality I've always known has actually made my brain hurt. I shuffle toward the bathroom and shake two Excedrin from the bottle in the medicine cabinet.

I'm tempted to just get out my laptop and spend my morning workout time Googling to come up with some kind of explanation for what I've seen—for what Owen *is*. But thinking forward to the hours and hours of lab tests I have over the next few days, the titrations, the pH strips, the endless waiting to see what color some solution turns, I think I'd better put that on hold and get some of this nervous energy out.

My workout does seem to clear my head, but the lab is every bit as boring as expected. The events of last night have been playing on a constant loop in my mind, and I'm pulling my hair out by the time noon comes around. I still haven't had a chance to poke around on the Internet, so I run outside to WaWa to pick up a hoagie, and I eat as slowly as possible while trying desperately to find some kind of information that could help me understand.

My first inclination is to find a textbook that goes further into depth on the human body's healing process than my college biology books did. An Amazon search for "healing" is met with a slew of self-help books, books about healing through prayer, yoga, miracle diets, and a variety of other types of healing that are decidedly not what I'm looking for. "Biology of healing" finds me healing with essential oil or the power of the human spirit, mind-body healing, and hope and healing for those who feel trapped. "Wound healing" gets me a little closer—but all the books that come up there seem to be about wound management, not what's going on in the body on a cellular level. By the time I get through all the combinations of words to search that I can come up with, my sandwich is gone, I've found nothing, and it's time to get back to my titrations.

The afternoon drags slower than I even thought possible, and knowing I won't see Owen again for two whole days is absolutely not helping. At about three, I hear the little text ding from my phone. Thank God. I don't even care whom it's from; I just need a moment of distraction.

It's Maddie.

u have plans tonight? let's go see the new bond

Perfect. Maddie is always a great distraction, and seeing a movie in a theater means I won't have to spend as much time trying not to tell her about Owen's…unusual ability. If we were watching a movie at home, we'd just end up talking over the whole thing as always. I text her back immediately.

popcorn and 007 for dinner—ur on.
i'll be home around 630—meet u at the apt

Before I can force myself to get back to the lab tests, I debate sending a quick text to Owen too. I don't want to be too needy, but what happened yesterday *was* pretty crazy. I think about the last part of the note he left me and decide to go for it.

Owen, just wanted to say hi. Hope your mtgs in NYC
are going well. I'll see you Friday,
and FYI you did not ruin our date.

I put my phone down and start to get back to work, but the ding comes before I can even pull my second rubber glove on.

Charlotte, I'm glad we're on for Friday.
I've made us a reservation for 8 at the Dandelion.
Hopefully we'll have time for a drink first.
I live in unit 2803 at the Huntington.
The doorman will have your name.

I tell myself the next two days will go by quickly, but I know I'm full of it.

Looking forward to it. The one thing last night's date
did lack was the encore performance—
but I'm sure we'll have plenty of time
to make up for that on Friday.

He texts right back.

We most certainly will, and I intend to do
a VERY good job making it up to you.

July 26th

Thursday afternoon, Strickland calls me into his office to go over the study I've been working on for the past week. Two subjects had some unusual test results, and he shows me how to evaluate whether those outcomes are statistically significant.

Strickland determines that one of them needs to come back in for reevaluation, and he's in the middle of explaining the subject callback procedure — everything in this place has some specific procedure in some rulebook somewhere — when the door behind his desk catches my eye.

That door.

Behind that door is something about Owen, something about why he's different.

Does Strickland know? Owen said nobody does other than his sister and mother, but Strickland has been running all sorts of tests on him for fifteen years — he must know something. Or maybe he doesn't, but he's close to figuring it out, and that's why he was asking me about him on Monday. Could he really have been drawing Owen's blood for that long without ever noticing that the little needle stick heals immediately? I'm deep in thought about all of this when I realize Strickland is still talking to me.

"Charlotte? Hello?"

"Sorry, Todd, I…Maybe the Dunkin Donuts guy gave me decaf by mistake. You were saying?" I try my best to concentrate on what he's telling me, but I only absorb maybe two-thirds. I'll have to ask Hannah about some of this later.

When he's done explaining and I have a page full of incomplete notes in my notebook, I rack my brain for a way to bring up Owen to see if I can get any more info out of Strickland. I'm surely more curious than I'd have been if Owen had just remained a subject to me and I hadn't seen him again, but wouldn't I be curious anyway after Strickland's awkward questions on Monday?

"So, did you ever figure anything more out about that guy… Owen was his name, right? Twenty-seven years, must be something significant." I hope I sound believable.

Strickland has gotten distracted by his computer, and he responds before looking up. "Significant all right…" he says, and then his eyes snap to my face. He takes a formal tone. "I appreciate your curiosity, and thanks for following up, but there isn't anything about that study that I can share with you."

I nod, put my pen through the spiral binding of my notebook, and stand to leave. I've clearly been dismissed.

July 27ᵗʰ

I finally finish my last lab test at 6:15 p.m. on Friday and type the results into the database as quickly as I can. Hanging my lab coat and goggles in my locker, I pull out my faded red duffel bag and head for the bathroom to change.

"Have a good weekend, Hannah," I call. Hannah is the only researcher left in the lab and has her face buried in a microscope. She doesn't look up but swings one arm up behind her to wave.

I'm a little nervous to see Owen. It's been three days, and the monotonous lab tests I've been doing on autopilot at work have given me all the time in the world to think about him. In that time, I've been everything from ecstatic that I've met the perfect man to despondent, thinking that I slept with him too quickly and he won't respect me, to just completely confused about what happened Tuesday night. Since I've only ever dated one other guy, and Jeff and I were friends before we were anything more, I don't really have any experience with this kind of fast-moving romance. It's amazing, but this will only be date three, and I'm nervous that I'm already in too deep.

The older man at the front desk of Owen's building points me toward the elevators, and I ride it to the twenty-eighth floor. I take another deep breath before I knock on the door.

"Charlotte, you look beautiful." Owen is in dark gray suit pants and a pale pink button-up. His shoes are a little shiny, and he kind of looks like he's stepped out of one of those magazine ads that also features a half-naked female model from Brazil with smudged eyeliner looking angry and sexy at the same time. I feel momentarily inadequate, but when my eyes finish their survey of his body and wander back to his face, the way he's looking at me gives me a slight boost of confidence. It's like he's seeing that hot Brazilian model.

"Hi," I manage. "You look —"

His lips are on mine, and he pulls me into the apartment by my hips. He reaches behind me to slam the door without coming up for air, and all of a sudden my back is against the door and the length of his body is hot and hard against mine. His kiss is deep and aggressive, like he's releasing days of pent-up want. I'm glad he cut me off. I don't know what I was going to say, but it was probably something idiotic.

After a moment, he pulls back and looks at me intensely. His breathing is a little ragged, and he's silent a few seconds. I think he's regaining his composure. My heart beats out of my chest. His eyes soften.

"What can I get you to drink?" he asks. As much as every cell of my body is telling me to find his bedroom and drag him to it, I'm relieved that he's putting on the brakes. There's a lot we need to talk about, and if we start down that path, I don't think there is any way we'll make it to dinner. "I have beer, wine, vodka, gin."

"Just a beer would be great, actually." I'm tempted to go with something a little harder but am having enough trouble keeping my wits about me already.

Owen heads toward the fridge, and I take a moment to look around his apartment. It's spacious with an open floor plan — the front door opens into the main living area, which has the kitchen, an island, and a large living room. The far wall of the living room is all glass, affording a spectacular southern view across the park. To the left is a short hallway with three doors: a bedroom, a bathroom, and a master suite, I'd assume. The apartment is spotless and gorgeous with an industrial vibe. His aluminum barstools would be at home next to a workbench, and his coffee table is an old metal trunk that looks like it must weigh a ton. Two faded, rivet-studded, chocolate-brown leather couches form an L in the living room, and the table between them is really a small cart with a rusted iron wheel and beat-up wooden top. The entire apartment is shades of brown and gray save the two large paintings hanging on the wall above one of the couches. They're both street scenes that I assume to be in Buenos Aires, but they are frameless, painted on huge pieces of plywood, and covered entirely in a thick, clear lacquer. The scenes are sandwiched between thick bars of fire engine red running along the top and bottom of the paintings, and the overall effect is quite arresting. A perfect combination of classic and modern.

I look back at Owen, who's pouring a bottle of beer into a tall glass on the island. He pours a second and hands one to me.

"Cheers," he says. We clink glasses and each take a sip.

"So, how was your trip to New York?"

He tells me a little about the case he's currently working on, then asks me how my last few days have been at work. It has been excruciatingly boring, so I don't have a ton to say about it, but I do tell him a bit about the cast of characters—that Strickland is not the world's most ideal boss, that I'm starting to look to Hannah as a mentor instead. I want to tell him about the strange conversations I've had with Strickland about him, but it doesn't seem like the right time yet, so I file that away for later. In a way, it's nice to have a little small talk with Owen, and I'm learning things about the normal parts of his life. For example, it's becoming clear to me that despite being extremely successful as a young lawyer, he keeps a real distance between himself and his work. It's like being an attorney is something he's chosen to do to support himself but is not part of his identity.

While it's nice to learn about Owen in any way I can, I'm dying to get to what happened Tuesday night. Some small part of me also wants to confirm that I haven't had some sort of psychiatric break where my imagination has run wild and morphed the new guy I'm dating into some sort of undiscovered superhero. It occurs to me that I've never questioned my own grasp on reality so often as I have since meeting him. He seems to have something on his mind too. Having kept his healing secret for so long, it must be strange to have someone new find out in such a sudden and unexpected way.

I haven't eaten anything since lunch, so by the time I finish my first beer, I'm loosening up a bit. Owen offers me another, and I nod. As he pours it down the inside of the glass, I muster the courage to raise the subject.

"So," I say tentatively, looking down. "I've been wanting to ask you about what happened Tuesday, but I keep wondering if the whole thing was some crazy dream." I hope that will be enough to get him talking and look up at him expectantly.

He hands me the beer. "I've thought a lot about it too, and I'm sorry I didn't explain it better on Tuesday. I know it was quite a shock to you." He looks down at his hands. "It's…bizarre, and I don't want you to be afraid of me."

This is the first I've seen of any real lack of confidence on his part. This and the moment Tuesday night when he asked me if I wanted him to go, which I'm sure was the same issue. He's afraid I might judge him because he's different.

"Owen," I begin. He looks up, his stare clouded over by an uncertain hopefulness. My stomach flutters when I realize he's looking to me for approval. "You've given me no reason to be afraid of you. Confused, yes, curious, absolutely. Scared that I might be crazy for believing what I saw, maybe, but not scared of you." I'm also afraid of how I feel about him and how easy it would be for him to back a steamroller right over my heart, but that has nothing to do with his ability either, and while I certainly want to reassure him, that's not something I'm ready to say.

Owen closes his eyes briefly in what I can only assume is relief. "Okay," he says. "My mother and sister have known for over twenty-five years, so you're the only person I've ever had to explain this to. Forgive me if I'm not very good at it. I don't have any practice."

I take his hand. "If you're not ready to talk more about it, that's okay. You don't have to tell me anything you don't want to. I know what happened was an accident, and curious as I may be, I have no right to demand to know anything more. It's not like you're barging in on my life and demanding all my secrets."

"No, no. It was actually a relief when it happened. I don't want to hide anything from you." He looks at me, his eyes markedly brighter. "I'm glad I know you're not afraid of blood."

He unbuttons and removes his shirt, and for a moment I have trouble maintaining any coherent thought at all. This is the first time I've really gotten a good look at him shirtless, and I am absolutely gaping. He's not Thor—he's thin and toned and has a sprinkling of light brown hair across his chest and down his abdomen. His shoulders are broad and square, and he has those lower-ab hip lines peeking out above his belt. But before I can sink further into my ogling, he grabs a knife from the block on the counter. A shiny and very sharp-looking chef's knife with a couple of Japanese characters on the blade.

"Try not to look away if you can. It happens pretty quickly." He's visibly excited and seems much younger, like a kid showing off a new toy. It's hot and endearing.

As easy as it is for me to admire his naked torso, though, it does take quite a bit of self-control not to look away. He motions for me to come around the island and join him. He lays his left forearm, palm up, along the narrow strip of granite in front of the sink. Placing the knife against his skin about halfway between his elbow and wrist, he glances up at me to make sure I've braced myself for what he is about to do. I nod hesitantly.

The muscles in Owen's right arm tense as he presses the blade into his left. With one swipe, he has cut through skin, muscle, veins, everything—all the way down to the bone, which I see gleaming white for a fraction of a second before the blood comes.

So much blood.

He flexes his wrist backward slightly so the gash opens, and blood fills the opening and pours over into the sink. And it keeps coming. My eyes flash to his face for a moment—is this supposed to be happening? He wears a tight grimace and my heart sinks. Something is wrong. He's in pain and the blood is still coming—it must not be working. Panic sets in as I realize he must have cut all the veins people are looking for when they slit their wrists. He could bleed out before I can even get help. As I turn and reach over the island toward my purse, his right hand clasps around my elbow.

"Watch," he whispers through clenched teeth.

I turn back toward him. There is still blood everywhere, down the side of the sink, and a bit has dripped onto the floor, but it doesn't seem to rush from the wound quite as quickly. I stare at the deep gash, and within maybe thirty seconds, the flow of blood trickles to a stop. Owen releases my elbow to turn on the water.

"It's kind of hard to see with all the blood," he says, leaning over the sink to put his forearm under the faucet. The blood coating his arm rinses away, and I lean over to get a better look. He flexes his wrist back again, and the gash opens slightly, enough for me to see that it no longer goes all the way to the bone. It's still pink and raw, and very deep. It's kind of like watching the minute hand on a clock—you can't really discern any movement, but if you keep watching, you realize things are different than when you started. After what seems like a few minutes, the cut is only about a half inch deep, and some of the pink inflammation around it has faded. Another few minutes go by, and it's just a puffy and angry-looking red scar, about three inches long.

A few more, and it's gone. Completely gone.

I run my fingers over his arm in disbelief. His skin feels normal, smooth and warm. I pick his arm up and turn it over in my hands. There is blood smeared across the other side, but that must just be from resting it on the wet granite. I run my finger through the red smudge, and it leaves a clean trail on his skin.

I'm not even sure what to say. "That's amazing. It's like you've been through the entire healing process in, what, ten minutes?" I manage to squeak. The sink still has splashes of blood in it, and there's a fair bit on the counter as well. It looks like he's butchered a small animal, poorly, in his sink.

Owen turns the water back on and wets a paper towel. He crouches down, his upper back muscles tensing as he wipes the few drops up from the floor. "It was actually only about two minutes," he says. "I guess it seems like longer when you're really seeing it for the first time."

I grab a paper towel and start to mop the blood on the counter into the sink. Soon enough, every trace of Owen's self-inflicted injury is either down the drain or in the trash.

"Wow," I say, my heart still pounding. "You know, you really scared me there for a second. It looked like you were in real pain. I thought it wasn't working."

"I know. I'm sorry to have startled you. It did hurt. I do feel pain. I just heal unnaturally quickly before it can become too unbearable, I guess."

"Owen, this is more than just unnatural. It's superhuman." His eyes drop from mine to the floor. I put my hand under his chin and lift his face to mine. "That's not an insult, and I am not judging you. Actually, maybe I am…I think it's amazing." I kiss him lightly on the lips.

He wraps his arms around my middle, and I put my hands on his bare shoulders, feeling them relax. He pulls me closer into a hug and nuzzles his face into my neck.

"Thank you," he whispers.

"For what?" I run one of my hands along his shoulder, up the back of his neck, and into his hair.

"For not running."

It's just a block and change to the restaurant from Owen's high-rise. When we have both regained our composure after his display, it's already eight o'clock, so we get ourselves out the door as quickly as possible. Before we leave, I ask him if I can leave my gym bag so I don't have to deal with it at the restaurant, and I think I see a flash of wickedness in his eyes before he nods. I hope it's not too forward, though I suppose he doesn't have to know that in addition to this morning's sweaty gym clothes and today's work outfit, I've packed a toothbrush and some clothes for the weekend.

Owen holds my hand tightly as we walk through Rittenhouse Square and head for Eighteenth Street.

"I'm really looking forward to dinner," I say. "I'm starving."

"Me too." It's a warm night, and the sleeves of his pink dress shirt are rolled up almost to his elbows. I eye his exposed forearm.

"You really did lose quite a bit of blood," I say softly. "Do you get lightheaded or anything? I usually give blood a few times a year and don't really get back to full strength for a week or so. Do you feel any differently?" I have a million questions that I don't want to bury him in, but this one seems timely and straightforward enough.

"I've never noticed feeling weak or lightheaded, but I'm not sure I've ever tried to do anything strenuous just after. The only thing I have noticed is that I get super thirsty, and I'm hungrier than usual. I guess my body needs to replace the fluid, and maybe the energy it expended fixing the wound? You know a lot more about biology than I do." He looks to me.

"Well, I don't know that what you do can be explained by any biology I've ever learned, but healing certainly consumes a lot of energy, so that makes sense. I have no idea how it's possible for your body to go through that whole process so quickly, though. Maybe we shouldn't assume that your healing even follows the same rules as a normal person's."

We cross Walnut Street and head up Eighteenth. "Have you been like this for…" I trail off and start again. "Have you always had your…ability?"

"No. I was six when it first happened. I skinned my knee playing in the driveway with Isabelle, and it was gone before I could even get inside. I guess I can't know for sure when I…when I changed, but that was the first time I healed. Before that, I was normal. See this—" He holds out his right hand to me, and there's a faint scar running from the bit of webby skin between his thumb and pointer down almost to his wrist. "I caught it on the top of a chain link fence I was trying to climb when I was five." He smiles at me, maybe a little wistfully. "I don't scar anymore. Here we are."

He has chosen a cool spot, a gastropub called The Dandelion. The restaurant is housed in two old Philadelphia homes that have been joined and renovated but still have lots of cozy separate rooms. I may not have had any way to research Owen and his extraordinary abilities these past few days, but he did tell me what restaurant he was taking me to, so I might've gotten a little overzealous in reading up on it. I've gone over the menu a few times and already have my eye on the pickled beetroot appetizer.

It's 8:09 when we get to the host. "Two for Becker," says Owen. "Reservation was for eight. Sorry we're late."

He's polite. I like that.

"Not a problem, Mr. Becker," says the host. "Let me see what we have."

"A quiet table would be great if you have one," Owen adds. I was thinking the same thing; it'll be impossible to avoid the obvious topic, so it would be better if we could talk without fear of half the restaurant overhearing.

The host leads us up the stairs to a corner table in a room where half the seating is couches or plush armchairs instead of regular din-ing chairs. Owen ends up on a bench along the wall, but I'm in a crimson velvet armchair that looks like it belongs in a period movie set in the eighteenth century. It's a little dark and quite intimate. I put my hand on his knee under the table and lean over to kiss him softly and quickly on the neck, just below his jaw. His stubble is rough against my lips, and need starts brewing in my core. When I straighten, he's looking at me a little quizzically.

"I just…" I mumble. "It's…really good to see you. I don't know if I said this at your apartment, some of that is a bit of a blur, but I've been really looking forward to this these last few days."

Owen's eyes get soft and the corners of his mouth turn up slightly. "I couldn't wait to get back from New York. I usually like going. I have a lot of school friends there, and I love to run the loop in Central Park, but this time all I could think about was getting back here to see you."

My insides somersault, and my cheeks flush. Luckily, before it's obvious that I've become completely tongue-tied, our waiter appears and asks if we've decided on drinks. I manage to focus on the menu long enough to select a beer from the list.

Studying Owen's face as the waiter walks away, I notice a faint line maybe an inch above his lip on the right side, just a thin light patch where he seems to be missing stubble. A scar. I reach out and run my ring finger along it gently. He closes his eyes when I touch him, and a pained expression flickers across his face, vulnerable. I don't want to push him, but he's waiting for me to say something.

"A scar?" I ask.

He nods slowly and opens his mouth to speak. "It's...I was six. It's from a piece of glass." He takes another long pause, seeming to decide whether to go on. "It's from the explosion at Genesis Life Systems that killed my father."

I learn quite a bit over the course of our meal. At first, Owen seems hesitant to talk about the accident, but after a few minutes, he calms and fluidly recounts what he remembers about the day his father died. It seems almost therapeutic for him to get some of this off his chest. Quite a heavy burden to carry around for nearly his whole life.

Owen grew up in a suburb called Wayne, about a half hour outside Philadelphia. His mother, Gail, was a businesswoman but gave up her career to raise Owen and Isabelle, who's two years his senior. Owen's father, Eric, had a PhD in biochemical engineering and worked at the Genesis campus in Malvern, another town about twenty minutes farther from Philly. Eric had the highest level of security clearance at Genesis.

When Owen was six, he convinced his mother to take him to Genesis to surprise his father at work on his fortieth birthday. They baked a cake in the morning, and after much pleading from Owen, Gail agreed to wait outside Genesis while Owen brought it in to surprise his father. Isabelle was away for the day at music camp, though the family had plans to have a birthday dinner for Eric that evening.

Eric's unit at Genesis had stringent security rules, so Owen waited in the reception area as one of the security guards went to find his father. Completely surprised, Eric teared up at the sight of his young son, so eager to wish him a happy birthday. When one of the guards tried to stop him from bringing Owen back to the lab to meet his coworkers and share the cake, Eric argued.

"He's *six*, Charles, *six years old*. Give a guy a break here. It's my fortieth birthday, and my son is here to surprise me. You're really not going to let him in? I know Genesis has to keep up security, but *come on*. It's tough enough that I can't say I'm in my thirties anymore, don't make me turn away my son too."

The plea worked, and Eric led Owen into his lab for the first and last time. His coworkers sang "Happy Birthday" and ate cake. Eric showed Owen around the lab, pointing out different machines and explaining what they did. At the center of the lab was a large glass case with a thick metal frame.

"This, my son, is the most important thing in here, which is why we have to keep it very safe." He pointed to the six small vials of clear liquid inside, each no bigger than a shot glass. "This, Owen, *this* could change the world."

They were back near the cake when it happened. Eric must have seen something, because just before the blast, he shouted and threw himself between Owen and the glass case. Just one word — *no*. The explosion was so fast and so powerful that Owen and his father were thrown back into the four-foot thick, blast-proof concrete wall behind them. Owen got the wind knocked out of him and felt a searing pain above his lip but wasn't seriously hurt. Eric managed to roll off his son and onto the floor.

Eric's left leg was broken, and he was bleeding from a small wound on his back, but he didn't appear to be critically injured. He begged his son to get out of the lab and stay with his mother somewhere safe, but Owen wouldn't leave his side. Owen could see that most of the other men in the lab were injured, but only one appeared to be dead — an unlucky lab tech whose neck was broken. The rest were moving — limping out of the lab, making frantic calls from the lab emergency phones, pulling shards of glass from their skin. A few minutes before the EMTs arrived, Eric told Owen he felt like something was stuck in his back and asked him to pull it out. Six-year-old Owen pulled a curved, two-inch shard of glass from his father's back just before pulling a similar but smaller one from his own upper lip. Both pieces were faintly etched with a repeating pattern of the Genesis logo. The only place Owen had seen glass like that was in that big case in the center of the lab.

When the EMTs arrived, Eric was completely lucid as they loaded him onto a stretcher. Owen stayed by his side as they walked him out to one of the many ambulances that had arrived out front. His mother met them outside, hysterical but relieved, and rode with them in the ambulance. When they arrived at the hospital, Eric was whisked away to have his leg set, and Owen held his mother's hand while an ER doctor put four stitches in the gash above his lip and checked him over for other injuries. After a CT scan showed no hidden damage from the impact, he was released.

Owen and his mother were in the waiting room when the doctor who took Eric away came in looking stricken. While they were setting his leg, Eric had begun bleeding badly from the gash in his back and within minutes was in multiple organ failure. They tried to revive him, but it was too late. Gail demanded answers — some kind of a real explanation — but there was none. The autopsy showed nothing they hadn't already known. His tox screen came back clear.

That day, eight Genesis employees died — Owen's father, the poor lab tech with the broken neck, and six others. Owen and his mother were never able to get a report from the hospital or from Genesis on what happened to the other six, but Owen always assumed their deaths were similar to his father's. He had seen several of them walking and talking while he waited with his dad for the EMTs, and, like Eric, none of them seemed at serious risk.

The gash on Owen's face healed normally. But three weeks later, Owen skinned his knee, and it didn't stay skinned.

We're about halfway through our entrées when Owen finishes telling me about the accident and gets very quiet. He puts his fork down and stares at his plate.

"I know it's weird to have kept a souvenir from the day my dad died, but I still have the two pieces of glass — the one from my dad's back and the one from my lip." He touches his scar with his hand. "I've never told anyone that. Not even Isabelle or my mom."

"Owen," I say tentatively. "That's not weird at all. You didn't keep a souvenir from your dad's death, you kept a memento from the last intimate moment you had with him."

He looks up at me, and his eyes are a bit less cloudy. "I've never thought about it in those terms before. I've always felt a weird sort of guilt about it, but maybe you're right."

"I am right. In fact, you'll learn I'm right about most things. It's probably better you come to terms with that now." I smile at him; maybe a little joking will lighten the heavy mood.

He laughs. "I'll keep that in mind."

I'm eager to know more but hope there are some happy memories in his past to balance out the tragic.

"That must have been fun, to discover at age six that you're basically invincible."

I laugh as he tells me about the two hours he spent with his dad's pocketknife in his room, making a bloody mess on his bed before presenting his new skill to his mom. Owen smiles too as he tells me about walking into the kitchen, cutting the back of his hand and watching his mom's reaction shift from worry to anger to amazement. She made him repeat his trick six times before she really believed it.

"It really was fun. Jumping out of trees, convincing my sister to hit me with my dad's old golf clubs. She actually broke my arm once and laughed for the four minutes I cried until it healed."

I'm glad we've moved on to something a little lighter, and as our desserts arrive, I want to keep it going in that direction.

"Is there anything else you noticed after the healing started? Any other changes in your body?" I ask. It just doesn't seem likely that *such* a drastic change could occur to one of his biological processes without affecting anything else.

"I guess there are a few other unusual things, yeah. I don't seem to need as much sleep as most people. I *can* sleep and I do enjoy it, but I seem to function just fine on two or three hours. I'd also say I'm…unusually gifted when it comes to particular athletic endeavors. Like I can do pushups indefinitely. I once did five thousand before I finally got bored and gave up on finding my limit. It got me through two episodes of the Wire. I can also run pretty much forever."

"So you're unusually strong. That's interesting. I wonder if your healing is not strictly macroscopic?"

"What do you mean?" Owen says with a bite of sticky toffee pudding in his mouth. "Ugh, this is delicious. You have to try it." He pushes the pudding across the table in my direction. We've ordered three desserts to share, but I've been so distracted by our conversation that I've yet to touch any of them.

"Well, I just mean your body might be doing less obvious healing too. Like in your muscles, maybe, which get stronger by actually getting hurt first. A strenuous workout causes tiny tears in them, but each time, they heal a little stronger. It's why overtraining can be a problem. If you don't give yourself time to recover and heal, you can't keep getting stronger. So if your body is healing your muscle tissue on a microscopic level the same way it heals injuries, theoretically, you could get really strong, *really* fast. It would be virtually impossible for you to over-train."

Owen puts his fork down and looks at me, his eyes sparkling. "Charlotte, that's really interesting. That's…You're…really smart."

My heart flutters. I've been told I'm smart for most of my life. But to hear it coming from this man, this gorgeous, complicated man — it sounds like something sexy rather than something that gets you good grades and no boyfriends in high school.

I want to test my theory about Owen's strength, so when we return to his apartment after dinner, I suggest that we visit the gym on the top floor of his building. It's almost eleven, but we both change into workout clothes to avoid suspicion. Experimenting with something so secret as Owen's extraordinary abilities seems almost illicit, and we don't want to draw any more attention to ourselves than is absolutely necessary.

A pang of self-consciousness flashes through me when I pull some clean gym clothes from my bag — by packing so thoroughly, I've not only assumed I'll be staying the night, but that I might spend the weekend. I wonder whether I should have just stashed a toothbrush in my purse instead and left my gym bag at work. Hopefully he hasn't noticed. Sitting on the edge of the couch, I slide my shoes on and push the bag out of sight.

After tying my shoelaces, I look up to find Owen hovering, staring down at me with his piercing blue eyes. He is wearing track pants and an old gray tee worn so thin that I can faintly see the muscles of his chest and shoulders. I lose my train of thought.

"I've never had a woman assume she'd stay over before. With anyone else I've ever dated, I think I'd have hated it, but with you I don't mind." The corners of his mouth turn up slightly in a kind smile, yet my stomach flips over, and I want to crawl out of my skin. He's just trying to be nice but really thinks I'm completely presumptuous. Which I am.

"I…I'm sorry, I wasn't thinking. I guess I just—"

He leans over, and his kiss is fast and deep.

"That didn't come out right. I mean I'm glad you're staying. I'm actually relieved we're on the same page," he says, never taking his eyes off mine. "Let's go upstairs and test your theory, okay?"

Relief streams through my body, and I'm once again elated. I've never had such extreme feelings about anything in my life. One second I'm floating, and the next I'm utterly terrified of scaring him away. I'm pleased that he wants me to stay, more than pleased, really, but I vow to be more careful with such things in the future nonetheless.

It's a short ride up to the gym on the top floor. Though we're only in the elevator for a moment, he still bothers to entwine his fingers with mine. He draws slow circles in my palm with his thumb, causing a flutter in my groin. I inhale sharply, startled at the sensation. He squeezes my hand in response, and the elevator doors open. He gives me a sweet smile before I step out of the elevator.

"Okay," I say, "so if I remember correctly from my high school lacrosse coach, common practice is to increase the weight you lift by ten percent once you can get through fifteen reps with whatever weight you're using. Having seen that gash heal in two minutes, I'm guessing your muscles will recover even more quickly." Hearing this out loud makes me realize that what I'm proposing sounds completely ridiculous. Any of my biology professors would laugh at me.

He takes a breath and clasps his hands together in front of his chest. "Which exercise should we start with?"

"It shouldn't matter. Are there any where you know approximately what you can lift?"

"Well, I usually do pushups and core after I run, but I've never been that into the weight room. The other day, though, there was a big guy in here benching two hundred pounds. He left the weights on the bar, and I tried to lift it after he left, just to see. I couldn't do it." He glances down.

"That's perfect. Let's start with one-fifty and see what happens?"

He nods and we gather the weight, placing it evenly onto the bar. Owen lays on the bench and positions himself underneath. "Spot me?" he asks, tilting his head back to look up at me.

"Of course. Though if anybody is going to drop a barbell on himself and crack a rib, you're probably the guy to do it. It'd be healed before I could heave the bar off you."

He smiles his big smile, teeth and all, and my stomach wobbles pleasantly. I've only seen that smile a few times; he seems to reserve it for when he means it.

Owen takes a big breath in and pushes up on the bar. The muscles in his chest contract under his thin tee, and the thick ridge of his triceps appears on his upper arm. I can tell it's hard for him — his breath whistles out as he strains to push it up. But he manages to lower the bar to his chest and push it up again. His face reddens, and I can see a hint of a vein along his temple that usually doesn't show. After six reps, his arms start to shake slightly. After eight, he guides the bar back over the rack, where it clangs back into place. He scoots out from under the bar and sits up, breathing heavily and leaning his elbows on his knees.

"How do you feel?" I walk around the bench to stand next to him and rest my hand on his shoulder.

"Tired. I don't think I could do that again right yet." He shakes his arms out and flexes them into the air. After a few seconds, he grimaces.

"Are you okay?" I ask, watching his face.

"Yeah. It's not too bad, just sore all of a sudden."

I glance at the second hand on the wall clock. It's only been about twenty seconds since he finished his set.

"Actually, it's gone. Weird."

Twenty-five seconds.

"Okay, let's try again, if you're up for it," I say, looking back and forth between Owen and the clock.

It's been about forty seconds when Owen is situated and presses up on the bar to begin his second set. Eleven reps this time.

"Same feeling?" I ask him.

He stares at the wall and moves his arms around again, focused on the sensation. "Sore again." Nineteen seconds. "And gone." Twenty-four seconds. "Strange right? It's like my muscles are tired for a few seconds, and then they hurt, and then it stops almost as fast as it started and my arms feel normal again."

My head clouds with nervous exhilaration. I try to temper my excitement, though — twice could still be a coincidence.

"I think I know what's going on," I say, "but let's do it a few more times to make sure."

Owen slides back under the bar. Fifteen reps this time. When he sits up, he looks at me, his eyes lit with excitement. I glance between the clock and him. Right at twenty seconds, he scrunches his nose. Sore. A few seconds later, he smiles. "Same feeling," he says.

"Again, then, and this time we add weight." I walk over to the rack and grab two ten-pound plates. As I load the weights on each end of the bar, I smile down at Owen, who is already back underneath, ready to go. "We're adding twenty pounds. It's a little more than ten percent, thirteen and a third to be exact, but they don't have plates in the right denominations to split fifteen pounds evenly on the bar. I think you can do it."

"My math whiz." That smile again. My heart pounds.

Owen strains as he presses the bar up. On the eighth rep, his arms get wobbly, and he guides the bar toward the rack instead of all the way up.

"We'll call that seven and a half," I say.

This time, he stays underneath the bar, excited to try again. After a squint around the twenty-second mark, he's ready to go. He starts the second set with one hundred and seventy pounds about thirty seconds after finishing the first. This time, he completes eleven reps.

Thirty seconds later he does fifteen.

"Oh my God," I say, and Owen wiggles out from under the bar and stands. He wraps his arms around me and pulls me tight against his chest. His face is buried in my hair, his hot breath on my neck.

"You were right," he whispers into my ear. "My very own scientist, you are brilliant and you were right." He pulls back just enough to find my mouth with his and kisses me urgently, his tongue exploring my mouth. After a few seconds, he releases me. My lips tingle. "Let's see if we can do some more."

"We! Really, all I'm doing is standing here watching you do this most unbelievable thing."

His eyes are on me again, pulling me toward him with that excruciating power. "They may be my muscles, Charlotte, but you figured out how to use them. *We* are doing this."

We add twenty pounds to the bar and repeat the same process. Three sets and we add another twenty.

Owen presses the two-hundred-and-ten-pound bar upward and breezes through eight reps. Then twelve. Then sixteen.

I look at the wall clock. We've been in the gym for twenty-three minutes total. In twenty-three minutes, Owen has increased his strength at the bench press by more than forty percent. And that twenty-three minutes included a bit of talking and a really fantastic kiss.

"I understand that I'm strengthening so fast because the microscopic tears in my muscles are healing really quickly. But what's with the wave of pain at twenty seconds?" Owen is looking at me quizzically, and I notice the beads of sweat that have formed on his forehead near his hairline. It occurs to me that he has probably never experienced, or at least never noticed, any kind of muscle soreness. I guess it would be pretty easy to overlook if it was gone in five seconds.

"You've never been sore after working out, have you?"

"I guess not, come to think of it."

"Well, I think what's happening is that you're experiencing typical post-workout muscle soreness. In normal cases, soreness peaks about forty-eight hours after a workout and then diminishes over the following day or two. So apparently you're experiencing three or four days' worth of muscle recovery in about thirty seconds. This is insane."

I start to walk toward the rack to gather more weight when Owen grabs my hand and pulls me to him. He's sitting at the end of the bench, and I don't even have a moment to think before he has his hands on my hips, pulling me onto his lap so his legs are between mine and I'm sitting on his thighs. Suddenly there's a hand in my hair under my loose ponytail, urging my face toward his. His lips are soft when they touch mine, and he kisses me tenderly. It feels like he is telling me something different each time he kisses me. His last was raw excitement. This time I think it's pride.

After a few moments of kissing me slowly, gently, his breath quickens and his kiss becomes harder, deeper, less controlled. His hands move to my midsection, and he pushes them under my shirt, running his fingers up and down my sides, leaving a shivering trail along my skin. When he slips his fingers under the tight elastic band of my sports bra, his thighs tense under me, his body stiffening with want. He pushes my sports bra and tank top up over my breasts just enough to free them and takes a breast in each hand, growling into my mouth as my nipples pucker under his touch. My skin burns with need, and I squirm in his lap, pressing myself farther into his body. He pulls his mouth from mine and trails lingering kisses down my neck while he teases my now erect nipples with his fingers. When his lips reach the base of my neck, where he runs into bunched fabric, he moves one hand to the small of my back and bends his head lower to take a hard nipple into his mouth, sending a trembling spasm up the length of my body. I'm about to pull my tank top and bra over my head when I open my eyes and am reminded that we are, in fact, in the gym in Owen's apartment building.

"Owen, wait…" I manage to whisper. "What if somebody comes in? Your whole building has access to the gym, right? That must be hundreds of people?"

He releases my nipple from his mouth just long enough to utter breathlessly, "Who works out at eleven thirty on a Friday night?"

While it might be unlikely, it's certainly not inconceivable that someone in a major city would work out at this hour. But just then, I realize that the incredible sensation in my nipples has stopped, and my body is screaming obscenities, willing me to get his mouth back on me. Fuck it. I bunch his short sandy-brown hair between my fingers and pull his head back to my chest. When his tongue touches my nipple, the twinge of pleasure shoots straight through me.

Owen's hand presses against my lower back, and he pulls my body closer to him, farther into his lap. My body shudders when his erection nudges that sweetest spot through my leggings. He flexes his hips into me and releases a breathy groan as he presses himself more firmly against the tight knot of nerves. The heat inside me swirls and multiplies, readying my body to accommodate his growing cock. He starts thrusting slowly against me as my hips grind reflexively into him. I wonder if I'm even going to last long enough to get my leggings off. I try for a fleeting moment to inch my body away from him and relieve the unbearably exquisite pressure on my clit, but his grip on me is too strong. I'm just about at the brink, barreling toward orgasm, when he stops abruptly and in one swift movement has me turned around so I'm sitting on his lap, facing away from him. He kisses the back of my neck as he pulls my hips toward him until I feel his chest hot against my back and his erection, huge and rigid, against my backside.

He's gently sucking my earlobe when he tugs my leggings down over my butt and pushes them halfway down my thighs. I turn my head toward him to find his mouth with mine, and he uses one knee to push my legs apart just a bit—as far as they will go with the restriction of my leggings. Then he pulls my hips back toward him as he guides himself into me, and his first thrust is so hard that I almost lose my balance. His mouth finds its way back to my neck, and I let out a low groan, the sensation building again as he pushes into me over and over, my core rippling along his length uncontrollably as I stretch around him.

I've again forgotten where we are, and Owen clasps one hand over my mouth to muffle my groans. His other hand moves down my lower abdomen to steady me against his thrusting, and one finger circles my clit as he pushes lower. I'm so close to the precipice that this tiny movement sends me over, the dam breaking inside me and flooding every corner of my being with searing pleasure. My entire body tightens against his as I lose myself to the sensation.

Owen's final few thrusts extend my orgasm, drawing it out nearly to the point of discomfort before he stills, losing himself in his own finish. His hand drops from my mouth, and he pulls both arms around me in a tight hug, his breathing in sync with mine as I sag against his chest.

As I regain coherent thought, still in Owen's lap, it occurs to me that there could be a security camera in the gym. I bolt up quickly and yank my leggings up and top down. My eyes dart around the edges of the ceiling. I can feel Owen's gaze on me as he slowly stands and tucks himself, still semi-hard and glistening with the evidence of what we've just done, back into his pants.

"There are security cameras in the elevators and one in the hallway outside, but there aren't any in here," he says. I let out the breath I didn't know I was holding. "That would have been quite the show for Arthur," he adds. He must mean the kind elderly man who was sitting at the front desk when we came back from dinner.

When we step back into Owen's apartment, a wave of fatigue courses through my body. Before I can suggest going straight to bed, he proposes we share a shower. "Just a quick rinse," he says. "I know you're tired. I just want to get this sweat off me before bed."

Following him to the bathroom, I realize that this is really our third date. Three dates and I've had sex with this man in a semipublic place, and I'm about to be completely naked in full light for the first time with him. I should be self-conscious—I've never been comfortable completely naked with anyone, not even my college boyfriend of three years. But for some reason, I'm just not. The thought of showing Owen all that my body is under the glow of his yellow bathroom lights seems oddly calming. I also wonder briefly if I should feel a little easy for sleeping with him so quickly. But how could something that feels so right be anything but? I put it out of my mind and watch Owen closely as he pulls the thin tee over his head. He catches me staring.

"I don't think your muscles have grown in size, do you?" I ask. "Do you feel any different?"

He runs his hand over his chest, outlining the musculature from his collarbones down to the bottom of his rib cage. Even through my haze of exhaustion, a stirring of desire springs to life within me watching him touch his own body. I wonder if I'll ever actually get to sleep.

"Feels the same to me. Which is good, because I don't want to have to buy all new suits every time I go to the gym." He smiles at me and reaches to turn on the water in the marble shower stall. I'm still watching when he pushes his pants down over his hips and they fall to the floor. He takes my hand and pulls me toward him, kissing me lightly before pulling my tank and sports bra over my head. I push my leggings toward the floor and we step into the stall together, my insides aching for him again already.

July 28th

When I wake in Owen's bed, I roll over to find his side cold. I'm still naked, and there's a note on the pillow.

CHARLOTTE, FORGIVE ME, I AM UPSTAIRS IN THE GYM. I WOKE EARLY THINKING OF YOUR DISCOVERY ABOUT ME AND COULDN'T GO BACK TO SLEEP. I HOPE YOU'VE SLEPT IN AND SLEPT WELL. COME FIND ME WHEN YOU'RE READY SO I CAN EAT YOU FOR BREAKFAST.

OWEN

P.S. THE COFFEE SHOULD STILL BE HOT. REMIND ME TO ASK YOU HOW YOU TAKE IT, OR IF YOU DRINK COFFEE AT ALL. I WANT YOU WAKING UP IN MY APARTMENT A LOT, SO I SHOULD KNOW WHAT YOU REQUIRE.

My heart pounds and my stomach flutters over his last sentence. Technically this is still our third date, and he's already planning for the future. He is just so straightforward with me, it's as if it doesn't even occur to him that saying things like this so early could scare somebody off. I envy his confidence, and I'm ecstatic at the idea of spending lots of nights in Owen Becker's bed.

But eat me for breakfast? Is he being silly or does he want a repeat of our gym experience from last night? It's nine on a Saturday morning, and there is no way I'm risking getting frisky up there at this hour. But a workout does sound appealing; maybe it will clear my head.

I sit up in bed and take a good look around the large room. I was so swept up in Owen last night—in the way he engulfed me, his body everywhere around me—that I haven't really seen his bedroom. Soft light from the floor-to-ceiling windows to my right peeks around heavy linen drapes in a color I'd bet was labeled something like *flax* or *latte* at whatever high-end store they came from. The bedding is all crisp white but feels almost like silk against my bare skin, and it contrasts sharply against the heavy wrought iron frame of the bed. His dresser and matching bedside tables are honed in a natural but slightly glossy red-tinged wood—probably some reclaimed something or other—and then framed in more black iron with heavy rivets and knobs. Everything is beautiful and comfortable, perfectly crafted and utterly masculine. Just like Owen.

I pull myself from the bed, digging my toes into the scratchy-looking yet very soft natural fiber rug beneath me as I stretch toward the ceiling. I find my bag in the living room and dig around for some clean underwear, and then find my gym clothes on a hook on the back of the bathroom door. Owen must have picked them up off the floor and hung them before he left.

I open cabinets in the kitchen until I find the mugs and pour myself a cup of coffee. He's left a little dish with sugar and sweetener out, and I find milk in the fridge. Once my caffeine fix is ready, I collect my phone and water bottle and head for the door.

As I step out of the elevator, a sweaty middle-aged man with a towel around his neck is just leaving the gym, and he holds the door for me on his way out. Owen is alone inside, standing near the weight rack with a bar at his feet; there must be at least four hundred pounds on it. When he spots me, that wide grin spreads across his face, and it's like his eyes are lit from within. His hair and T-shirt are both soaked with sweat, and I spot a few drops making their way down his forehead. He looks hot as hell.

"Whole milk and Splenda," I say, holding up the Stanford mug I've taken from his apartment.

He steps over the weighted bar and walks toward me, taking my coffee and placing it on an empty bench before he wraps me tightly in his arms and kisses me—a long, lingering kiss. After a few moments, he pulls back, his eyes closed for a second.

"I have much to show you, Charlotte," he begins. "I've been up here since five thirty, and with your insights yesterday, I've been making a lot of progress." He's very serious but clearly excited to show off. The wall of windows in the gym faces east, and sunlight pours in. Owen has a few days' worth of stubble, and in this morning light, his beard looks red, a sexy burnt orange. I sit down on one of the empty benches and take a sip of my coffee.

"Show me."

"This is four hundred and fifty pounds." Standing behind the bar at his feet, he grasps it with both hands and lifts it in one smooth motion until his arms are straight and the bar is above his head. The heavy metal bows under the weight of the plates on each end as he lowers it behind his head to his shoulders, does a full squat, and then presses it above his head once again, every muscle in his arms tense and defined. He lowers the bar to the floor in front of him, and looks up at me with a mischievous grin. My mouth is hanging open, and I have to tell myself to close it.

"Owen, did that guy who was in here before see you do that?" I'm beyond excited and impressed, but there is a little panic brewing deep within my belly, and I'm overwhelmed by the sense that there's something dangerous about this and I need to protect him. The only thing I can think to do at this point is keep it a complete secret.

"No, I was careful not to be obvious. He was on that recumbent bike over there, listening to music and reading. I'm not sure he'd have noticed if a marching band came through." He glances toward the ground. "I actually got a little overzealous adding weight about an hour ago and dropped a forty-five-pound plate on my foot. It made a hell of a noise and broke three of my toes, and that guy didn't even turn his head."

I'm not sure how to react to Owen telling me he hurt himself. My instinct is to ask if he's okay and express some sympathy, but I have to remind myself that for him, a major injury means a moment of pain and nothing more.

"How long did that take to heal?" I ask instead.

"I didn't time it, but the pain went away pretty quickly. Maybe two minutes or so? I'd say a minute of severe pain and then a minute for it to fade away completely."

"So that's pretty much the equivalent of stubbing a toe for us mere mortals."

He bites his lip. "I'm not done showing you what I've been up to." My eyes widen as Owen bends down to grasp the four-hundred-and-fifty-pound bar. With one hand. "This is what I was working on when you came in. It's not easy yet, but I'm getting there."

He straightens so the bar lifts off the ground, and with just one hand in the middle of it, the heavy steel bows even more than before. He's secured the plates with clips, but I'm still nervous that one of them is going to slide off and break his toes again—though it would probably take me longer to recover from the noise than it would for him to heal.

He takes a deep breath, and his arm shakes slightly as he curls the bar up to shoulder height and then back down. This is insane. Owen is doing a four-hundred-and-fifty-pound bicep curl with about the same difficulty that I'd have with a twenty-pound dumbbell. And I work out.

I blink at him. "Have you noticed any point where increasing the weight gets more difficult? Do you think there's a limit?"

"I've thought about that. Like unless what's happening in my body is straight-up magic, there has to be a limit to what my muscles can support, even if they're biologically different than normal muscles. I can't think of any way that my body could be stronger than, say, titanium or diamonds, or carbon fiber or whatever it is they're making airplanes out of these days. But I guess I just haven't approached that limit yet." He gently places the bar on the floor and starts to remove the weights.

I sip the last of my coffee, contemplating what he's said. It sure seems like magic. But I don't believe in that, and I'm too much of a science nerd not to at least try to come up with some kind of explanation.

"Have you ever had to give a muscle sample to Genesis?" I ask him. "I think something has to be going on with the way your muscles are structured. Maybe your body is producing some protein that normal people don't have or something. I'm not sure it can just be the healing." I realize that we haven't really spoken about Genesis's interest in him; I assume it started after the accident, but I don't know any of the details.

"Blood, urine, hair, nails, saliva," he replies. "I'm sure a few other things I'm forgetting, but never a tissue sample."

"Hopefully they won't ask for it. This is amazing, all of it, but it makes me nervous. Like someone would want to hurt you if they knew what you could do."

Owen nods. I had hoped he'd tell me I'm being silly, but he must think the same thing. He launches into an explanation of his relationship with Genesis.

After the accident, several investigations into the cause of the explosion turned up no wrongdoing on the company's part. Genesis continued to insist that it was just that—an accident—and that there were no neglected safety procedures, no extraordinary dangers that the company should have been aware of. With the sudden and unexplained death of her husband, Gail had always thought there was something amiss, something that had been swept under the rug by the company, but her attempts to find an attorney were unsuccessful—she was turned down by more than ten lawyers in the Philadelphia area.

"My mother has always been a deeply suspicious person. Maybe she wasn't that way before the accident, but she always suspected that Genesis had warned all the lawyers in the area not to take any case regarding it. Or maybe even paid them off. Given my legal background now, I don't know what to think. It's certainly possible there was more to it and that Genesis has preempted any attempts to investigate. It's also possible that we simply didn't have a case."

His mother is deeply suspicious. Great. I'm sure it will go over really well when he brings me home.

Owen notices that I'm deep in thought. "What is it?"

"Nothing. Just thinking that your mom's suspicion might not bode well for me." I smile sheepishly. And then my smile vanishes—I've once again put the cart before the horse. Maybe he doesn't have any interest in introducing me to her.

He grins, eyes sparkling. "She'll love you."

I feel better about my overstep, but not his mom. "Right. You keep your secret for almost thirty years and then it just happens to come out on date two with someone you just met…someone who just happens to work for the company she thinks, perhaps correctly, killed her husband. Not just the company, but the specific jerk who's been looking into her son's case for fifteen of the twenty-seven years since the accident. I'm sure she'll just be *charmed.*"

He presses his lips together for a moment. "I hadn't thought of it that way." He pauses. "Yeah, we might have a bit of an uphill battle on our hands there, but she'll come around. Maybe not right when

I tell her all the circumstances, but eventually." He smiles. "I did tell her about you after our first date, and she was really excited for me."

He told his mom about me. After our first date. My stomach can't help but flutter over that.

We're still in the gym, sitting face to face, both straddling the same bench. I lean forward and kiss him lightly on the lips.

"Sorry to sidetrack you," I say. "Go on."

The settlement that Genesis offered the Beckers was reasonable but not extravagant: a monthly stipend that was enough to cover the mortgage and food but not much else, and a promise that Genesis would pay for college and one graduate degree, if desired, for each child. In return for the settlement, Gail had to sign a release saying they would not sue the company over the accident at a later date, and that she would consent to monthly testing for Owen so the company could keep an eye on him in case any complications from his potential contamination manifested themselves later. Gail eventually came to believe that they wanted to monitor Owen for his own protection, and decided that her children's educations were worth agreeing not to sue, especially since no attorney would take the case anyway. She ended up going back to work part-time to fund extracurriculars like music and her kids' trips to Argentina, but she never thought she'd have been able to give them what they needed without the help from Genesis.

When Owen turned eighteen, consent became his issue, but he still had college and law school to get through, and Isabelle was halfway through college with medical school in her sights. While Owen would have been willing to take loans for himself, he didn't want to risk Isabelle's education or cutting off the stipend to his mother by refusing to keep on with the testing. And by the time he and Isabelle had both finished school, the testing had become so routine that it seemed like more trouble than anything else to make the stink needed to quit. Having hidden his secret for so many years, he didn't want to draw attention to himself, though by that point, Gail was back working full-time and doing quite well, and even if she hadn't been, Owen could have funded the stipend himself.

"What?" he asks. I'm focused on a spot on the floor.

"All these years of getting poked with needles by Genesis researchers, and not one of them has noticed that you don't stay poked? A wound that small must be healed by the time they can even get the needle out."

He smiles. "You, my sweet girl, are very smart and very thorough. The first time I went in for testing was about a week after I discovered my new…ability. My mother was particularly nervous, and the day before, she realized the same thing. She knew they routinely put a little piece of gauze over the needle while they drew blood, and then put a bandage over the gauze after removing the needle. We realized that if I insisted on holding the gauze on myself when they took out the needle, the bandage would go on before anybody ever saw the little wound, or lack thereof. There was usually enough blood to soak a small spot through the gauze, just enough to seem normal, and it was easy to pass off my insistence on holding the gauze myself as a little boy's eagerness to help. So after the first couple months, it was routine, and in all these years, nobody has ever questioned it."

The thought of six-year-old Owen practicing this act with his mom is both endearing and a little sad. "You must have been a pretty mature kid to understand the stakes."

Owen looks thoughtful. "I don't think I did at the beginning. I knew it had to be a secret, but I certainly didn't know quite how unusual I was. Or how dangerous it would be if someone else found out. I guess I still don't know that." He looks down.

Just then, I hear the gym door open, and Owen seems to snap out of his thoughts as an older woman wearing headphones walks in and heads toward the elliptical machines.

"Hi, Phyllis," Owen says loudly. She keeps walking, apparently unable to hear over her music. After she puts her towel and her *Us Weekly* on the elliptical, Owen catches her eye, and she waves excitedly, batting her eyelashes at him.

Owen smiles warmly and waves back, then turns to me. "I see you're in your gym clothes. Did you want to work out?"

A welcome change of subject. I'm still, of course, eager for more information, but I can tell it's a lot for Owen to talk about all this, and there's no hurry.

"Yeah," I say. "I was thinking I could use a quick run on the treadmill."

"Use some company?"

I give him a don't-be-silly look and hold out my hand to him as I stand and step over the bench. He smiles as he takes it, grasping my hand tightly.

"Charlotte, there's a lot I don't know about you, including whether you prefer to run alone with your thoughts."

"That's very considerate of you, but I think most of the things I used to like doing alone would be made better by your company." I look away, a little embarrassed at my own forwardness.

"Good," Owen says and softly kisses my lips. I think this kiss says, "Me too."

In the time it takes me to run five miles, Owen has run nine and hasn't been out of breath once.

During our jog on side-by-side treadmills, he tells me about how he's been running since he was young and that it calms him. It's always been easy for him, but to run fast enough for a challenge, he would draw attention to himself outside, and the fastest setting on a typical treadmill is just an easy jog. He runs the New York Marathon every year for fun, picking out the fastest four or five men that don't appear to be career marathoners and keeping pace with them. How he resists the temptation to win, to break a world record, I have no idea. Superhuman self-control seems to be included in his suite of special abilities. An unknown thirty-four-year-old lawyer with no history of competitive athletics winning a major event would certainly draw a lot of unwanted attention, I suppose, but he must, at *some* level, harbor some resentment that he receives absolutely no recognition for his extraordinary abilities.

When we return to his apartment, I offer to make breakfast while he showers. I noticed there were eggs in the fridge when I got out the milk for my coffee, and there is a loaf of bread on the counter.

"I'll shower fast," he says, "and I can finish up the food while you take yours. Use whatever you like." He shows me where the utensils and pans are. "One thing, though. Do you mind making a little more than you would normally? I get really hungry when I exercise."

"Sure. We talking like four or five eggs for you instead of two or three?"

He presses his lips together. "Actually, maybe let's make the whole dozen and I'll eat whatever you don't want?" He sounds a little embarrassed.

"Will do," I say. "You know that's nothing to be ashamed of, right? If your body metabolized food the way a normal person does, you'd need a lot more than ten eggs after the workout you did this morning."

"You think? I guess it just seems wasteful to me somehow."

"Well, I'm no exercise physiologist, but, yeah, I do. Your body must be extremely efficient to even keep you going through that kind of exercise without a break to eat in the middle of it."

He nods. It seems that guilt is a common theme in Owen's feelings about his unusual circumstances, and it pains me that it could overshadow the excitement and pride he clearly felt about this morning's progress.

I get to work on breakfast, cracking all twelve eggs into a bowl and beating them with a little salt and pepper. I've also found a half pound of bacon and some fresh berries in the fridge, and onions and a tomato in a basket on the counter. This man has a pretty well-stocked kitchen for a bachelor in Rittenhouse Square. I would think half a pizza still in the box, a couple six packs of beer, and a few condiments that expired a year ago would be more typical. He also has some raw chicken breasts, a variety of cheeses, a full vegetable crisper, several fresh herbs, and a bunch of Greek yogurts, among other things. I pull out some aged cheddar and a few chives and set them on the counter with the other ingredients. I've always liked to cook, and I'm glad I know my way around a kitchen; either Owen does too or he has a personal chef, and either way I don't want to make him something subpar.

His shower is quick, and he emerges from the bathroom with just a towel around his waist. He hasn't shaved, and his hair is still wet and messy. Gaping at him, I have just enough wits about me to stop slicing strawberries and put the knife on the cutting board. The ding of the toaster snaps me out my unabashed ogling after a few moments, and I pick up the knife and resume slicing strawberries, watching my hands carefully.

"You know, you shouldn't come around me looking like that when I have a knife in my hand," I say. "Not all of us can heal like you do."

Owen walks around the kitchen island and hugs me from behind. "You're brilliant and sexy *and* you can cook?" he whispers. "You just let me know when you're ready to get married, and I'll go buy a ring."

I laugh at his joke. It was a joke, right? Something shudders deep in my center at the possibility he's just a tiny bit serious. "It's just scrambled eggs," I say. "It's not like I whipped up a chocolate soufflé or something."

He kisses my neck. "Okay, go enjoy your shower and let me take it from here," he says, turning toward the stove and giving the onions a stir as they soften in a little reserved bacon fat. "Take your time."

I don't take my time. Though it feels good to let the hot water roll over me after a sex-filled night and a good run, I have no interest in being alone when the most incredible man I've ever met is in the other room in just a towel. When I'm done, I comb out and towel-dry my hair, then slip into a thin white, waffled robe that I find hanging on the back of the door. The thought that this fabric spends a lot of time against Owen's naked body is enough to get my mind wandering.

I walk back into the kitchen in just the robe, with a clean face and wet hair. Owen has piled the steaming eggs onto a platter with the bacon and set out plates and utensils.

"Iced tea?" he asks, removing a glass pitcher from the fridge.

"Please."

There are lemon slices floating in the amber liquid. I try not to make too many assumptions based on gender, but I can't help wondering if there's been another woman in this kitchen. I hesitate for a second, not sure I really want to know the answer, yet can't resist.

"Did you make this?"

"Yes," he says, putting a piece of toast on each of our plates. "It's just black tea. I like to have a pitcher around for after my runs. Anything hot gets me sweating again."

Relief tickles the back of my neck. "So do you cook a lot? I don't think I know too many bachelors who have standing mixers on their counters." I note that he didn't take a single bite while I was in the shower. He has waited for me even to have a piece of toast. I serve some eggs onto each of our plates.

"I do cook a lot. Growing up, my mom thought it was too risky for me to play sports, so she was determined to use that time to teach me things I wouldn't learn in school. Cooking, growing vegetables, that kind of stuff."

I look toward the windows and notice a neat row of small terra cotta pots lined up on a narrow shelf. Basil, parsley, and two African violets in full bloom.

"We grew up eating a lot of fresh food from our garden or the farms near us," he says, "so I'm used to eating that way. Cooking calms me too, and since I eat so much, I never really have the problem of cooking for one." Owen looks me in the eye. "Though hopefully I'll be cooking for two more often. Or hopefully *we'll* be cooking for two. You know your way around a kitchen too. Do you enjoy it?"

He's talking about the future again, and my heart begins to pound.

"I do, and I think I'll like it even more with you."

Owen's left leg is exposed in the gap between the ends of the towel, and I run my hand from his knee up his thigh. His eyelids droop until I take my hand away. I think I know where this is going, but he still has three pieces of toast and a mountain of eggs to get through, and I don't want him stuck eating cold eggs an hour from now. He seems to be thinking something similar, because he starts to eat faster.

Not wanting to distract him further, I explain how my mother is a great baker and how I used to help her bake pies and biscotti.

"I make a mean bagel too," I tell him. "There weren't good bagels near our town in New Hampshire, so rather than eat inferior ones from the supermarket, my mom and I fiddled with recipes until we had it down."

He gives me a surprised, open-mouthed smile. "Can I tell you that lack of good bagels is one of my chief complaints about Philly? I cannot wait to try one of yours."

"It's really not as hard as it sounds. I'll make them for you some-time. I can teach you."

Owen takes his last bite of eggs. I've been done for a few minutes.

"You know," I say, looking down at my hands, "when I read your note this morning, I thought for a minute you were looking for an encore in the gym. I'm glad you didn't try. I don't think I know how to say no to you yet. And I think eggs and bacon are a pretty good breakfast too."

When I look up at him, there's mischief in his eyes that I've yet to see. "Who says I'm done with breakfast?" He stands and, in one quick motion, picks me up off the stool.

Without thinking, I throw my arms around his neck to take some of the pressure off his biceps, but of course he's not straining in the slightest. It's only a moment before we're in the living room, but it's enough to notice the pleasant sensation of being so light in his arms and enjoy the clean scent of his hair.

Owen places me gently on the couch and stands above me. He bends over to kiss me, his lips soft against mine. His tongue traces my lips slowly and lightly and then runs along my top teeth. My eyes close as I focus entirely on the sensation. His mouth moves lower, and he's trailing kisses along my jawline when he tugs on the robe's belt. The knot gives quickly, and the robe falls open just enough to expose my breasts. He cups them with his hands, and my nipples harden. Letting out a breathy groan, I arch my back and press into his touch.

Owen is still standing above me and uses one knee to nudge mine apart. Then he drops to his knees between my legs and leans forward to take one nipple into his mouth. Pleasure shoots straight to my groin as he circles the hard point slowly with his tongue. When he runs his hands down my sides to my hips, the robe drops open the rest of the way. Fire builds deep in my middle, and my legs already tingle. I grip his shoulders and let my head fall back against the couch. Though firmly seated, I feel like I might float away if I don't hold on. When he releases my breast from his mouth and starts to lick and kiss down the center of my abdomen, I know where he's going, and it's like every nerve in my body is exposed in anticipation. He's moving downward so slowly that I'm not sure my body is going to hold up until he gets there. I try to concentrate on his skin beneath my fingers in an effort to stay in one piece. It's warm and smooth, and I trace the hard mounds of his shoulder muscles beneath.

He's only just past my navel when I reflexively open my legs farther, willing him to move more quickly. As I lift my head to look down at him, he must feel my stomach tense, because he tilts his head up to look at me. His eyes glint in the sunlight, and I can see a hint of a smile though his mouth is still on me.

"Faster," I whisper.

He shakes his head slowly from side to side and continues his slow assault. It's eternity — an agonizing, blissful eternity — before he's finally between my thighs. I'm breathing heavily when he uses one hand to spread me apart and starts tracing slow circles around my clit with his tongue. When he flicks his tongue over it for the first time, my hips jerk as my muscles try to handle the energy radiating outward. He begins to alternate slow flicks of the smooth and firm tip of his tongue with even slower strokes of the rougher top of his tongue. The combination of textures is like nothing I've ever experienced, and I instinctively run my fingers through his hair. For a few seconds, I try to focus on the softness of his short hair in a vain attempt to slow my body from barreling toward orgasm.

Owen is still holding me apart with one hand, my skin taut beneath his fingers, when he slides two fingers of his other hand deep into me. The sensation of his tongue moving slowly back and forth over my clit paired with this fullness is almost too much to bear, and when he bends those fingers toward himself inside me, my body gives in. My orgasm explodes around me, my back arching off the couch and my hands tightening in his hair as wave after wave of incandescent pleasure pulse through every inch of my being.

My body is exhausted, my muscles completely spent, when Owen climbs up to sit beside me on the couch. Somewhere in all of this, his towel has fallen to the floor, exposing his erection. I haven't gotten a good look at it in full light, and it's quite impressive. Long and thick and almost, but not quite, straight. I wonder for a second how it's even possible for my body to accommodate so much cock. Owen has his eyes closed like he's savoring what just happened, like he's savoring the taste of me. Taking in his naked form, the dusting of hair across his chiseled chest glinting red in the late morning sun, I am struck with an impulse I've never had before.

I want him in my mouth.

It's not that I've never gone down on someone before—I have, and I don't mind it. With Jeff, my college boyfriend, it was something I did because I knew he liked it, and I did want to please him. Sometimes seeing how turned on he got would get me going, but it was never the act itself. Sitting here, though, next to this extraordinary specimen, this invincible impossibility, I actually want to taste him; I want to feel the way his skin moves over the hard tissue underneath when I close my lips around him.

His eyes are still closed, and I slide off the couch as silently as I can. I lean down over him, careful not to touch him with any other part of my body, and gently lick, in one long stroke, from the base of him to the tip. I don't think he was quite expecting this, and his body jerks slightly as the muscles tense along his stomach and chest. His eyes open slowly, and I'm licking gently around the tip of his cock when his gaze meets mine. There's a fire behind his eyes, like it's taking every ounce of his strength to sit still while he watches me lick him slowly. I rest my arms on his thighs when I kneel down in front of him, and as I take him into my mouth, his quads tense and twitch under me.

I wrap one hand around the bottom of his shaft and move it up and down in sync with my mouth. As I continue faster and faster, Owen's body moves with me, and the twitching of his muscles becomes less and less controlled. Seeing him writhe beneath my touch has again ignited my desire, and as I suck and he grows even harder in my mouth, I let my other hand slip between my legs.

I can sense Owen getting close to the edge, so I suck harder and deeper. His erection pulses in my mouth, and my own sensation builds as I rub my middle finger back and forth over my clit. Owen inhales sharply.

"Charlotte," he whispers. Owen Becker is in my mouth, and he's whispering my name. "I'm…I'm going to come," he breathes haltingly.

I lock eyes with him for a brief moment, giving him silent permission. His hips tense forward, and he lets out a low sigh as he tips his head back in pleasure, his cock jerking in my mouth. When the warm liquid hits the back of my tongue, the thought that *I* did this, *I* made Owen come, tips me over the edge too, and a second finish, warm and electric, radiates through my body.

I'm still feeling a few aftershocks when Owen picks me up by my torso like I'm light as a feather, turns me around, and lays me down on the couch in front of him, spooning me tightly. He nuzzles his face into my neck, his breathing still heavy.

"That…Charlotte…You didn't have to…" I think he's trying to say I wasn't obligated to reciprocate.

"Shhh," I whisper. "I wasn't finished with my breakfast either."

We lay like this, naked and intertwined, on the couch for some time. After a few minutes of comfortable silence, Owen squeezes me tighter against him.

"Will you stay with me again tonight?" he asks.

Is he crazy? Of course I will. My stomach flutters at the thought that he's asked me to stay without plans—he just wants to be with me, regardless of what we're doing.

I turn my head toward him so I can see his face. He's looking at me expectantly, like he's not sure what I'm going to say. The trace of vulnerability is endearing, especially given my frequent moments of panic that I've said or done something that might hurt my chances with him.

"I'd love to stay here with you." I crane my neck so I can plant a soft kiss against his mouth, his lips still a shade redder than usual after their recent workout. A little tension in Owen's body releases; I hadn't noticed its presence until it was gone. "And if we have a chance to pick up ingredients for bagels, I'll make them for you in the morning."

He kisses my cheek. Even though the length of his body is pressed against mine, this little extra touch of his lips to my face sends a shiver down my spine, and I realize I'd better get some clothes on before I get too turned on again. He may have a superhuman ability to heal, but we *just* finished. Plus we have the whole rest of the day, night, and tomorrow morning for that.

I swing my legs over the side of the couch and stand quickly. I hold my hand out to Owen, and he takes it, letting me pull him up off the couch. But rather than head to the bedroom to get dressed, he envelopes me in a warm hug. My nipples harden at the skin on skin contact and slight roughness of his chest hair. A little groan leaves my lips, and he begins to stiffen against my lower abdomen.

"Again?" I whisper into his shoulder. "Already?"

But he doesn't answer. He's already trailing kisses along the side of my neck. And before I can muster any willpower for a futile protest, he swings me over his shoulder and carries me to the bedroom.

"Let's go grocery shopping," Owen says after we've managed to actually put some clothes on. There's something unexpectedly satisfying about hearing these words, something nice about the normalcy. Grocery shopping is something benign, but it's something real couples do. You don't go grocery shopping on a third date.

While I browse the flour and yeast in the supermarket a few blocks from Owen's place, he squeezes my hand and turns me toward him.

"I always cook dinner on Sundays. Sometimes Isabelle or my mother will come join me, but I cook regardless. Will you make dinner with me tomorrow?" The flash of vulnerability is again in his eyes, just for a passing moment.

My heart speeds slightly—he just asked me to stay for the rest of the weekend—and I manage a nod.

Owen launches into a list of entrée possibilities, and before we've left the aisle, we have a long list of ingredients we'll need to procure for tomorrow's short rib Bolognese.

Our grocery walk turns into a long and meandering stroll through Center City. We make it down to Society Hill, the oldest part of the city, and admire the historical architecture. Luckily we'd only picked up bagel ingredients and a couple of bottles of wine before we realized we were going to be out strolling for a while. Owen catches me eyeing him in front of an old row house.

"I was just thinking I should offer to carry the bags for a while," I say. "But then I realized your arms are not capable of getting tired holding a few pounds of flour and cabernet."

"Even if they were, I wouldn't let you carry them."

Some small part of me wants to tell him that I'm strong, and that I'm capable of carrying a bag too, thank you very much, but I've never had someone treat me like this—always opening the door, letting me go first, refusing to let me carry anything—and it feels good. He's just such a *man*. It's not that he thinks I can't open my own doors but that I shouldn't have to. It may take some getting used to, but something girly inside me is absolutely eating it up. Like if this smart and impressive man thinks I'm to be treated like a lady, then maybe I really am more feminine than I feel.

We settle on a bench in Washington Square Park with iced lattes and French macarons. When Owen shifts to put his arm around my shoulders, the wrinkles on his forehead catch my eye. I reach out and trace one of them lightly with my finger.

His eyes close when I touch him.

"You have lines," I say, realizing as soon as it's out of my mouth that it's not exactly the nicest-sounding thing I've ever said. "I just mean…" I mumble. "I mean, your body…You age."

He nods.

"I guess that means your body doesn't think aging is something to heal," I say. "It's sexy, actually. You look…manly. Like…a real man." Real articulate, great. He doesn't look insulted, but if somebody pointed out my wrinkles, I'm sure I'd be pissed even if he tried to make it into a compliment.

"I've had them for a few years now and don't really notice anymore. But I'm glad I age. My…uh, secret would be a lot harder to keep if I didn't. I'm pretty sure Strickland would have noticed that by now."

"That's true. I hadn't thought of that. He's definitely digging around for something, and that would be a pretty big giveaway. Also, do you think he knows what the original project was? The one your dad was working on? I keep dwelling on why he's so interested in you and what he thinks he's figuring out. If he didn't think it was something big, wouldn't he have ended the study years ago?"

Owen scrunches his brow, and those wrinkles deepen. "I'd have to think he would have access, right? Unless too much got burned in the accident. It was the eighties, so I can't imagine they had everything electronically. I guess it's possible that a lot of the study got lost after all those researchers died."

I nod, sipping my latte.

"Do you have any theories about what your dad was working on?"

"I've spent a lot of time thinking about that over the years. 'This, Owen, *this* could change the world.'" As he recites one of the last things his dad ever said to him, his eyes are somewhere else. He pauses, closes his eyes for a moment, and then when he opens them, he's back. "I think they were trying to create something, some drug that could give this, whatever it is that I have, to anyone. That—" He pauses again, his eyes bearing down on me. "That, Charlotte, would change the world."

It most certainly would. "Owen, that would be the most significant medical breakthrough — really, the most significant scientific breakthrough of any sort — of all time."

He's nodding. It's a lot to think about, like my brain can't keep up with itself and is just firing random consequences of that magnitude of discovery at me.

"So many things would change," I say, lowering my voice as a young couple with a schnauzer walks by. "I mean, firefighters, cops, athletes…I don't even know what it would do to sports, even jobs like nannies, teachers. Wouldn't you feel better if whoever was watching your kids would be willing to jump in front of a train for them? Hell, might as well give it to kids as well." I'm not making much sense, but then it hits me—the big one—and my eyes go wide. "The military. You can't lose a war if all your soldiers are invincible."

Owen twirls the straw from his latte between his thumb and middle finger. Then he nods and looks up at me. "That's my fear. That my dad was working on a drug that would essentially result in an army of…people like me." There's hurt in his eyes. I'm not sure he's ever talked about this before.

"Owen, even if the drug was intended to give your ability to others, we can't assume that the military had anything to do with it. It's an obvious connection, but so are a lot of others." I really don't know much about his dad, but from what he's told me, he doesn't seem like the type to knowingly work on something dangerous.

"I know," Owen says. "But I do remember my dad talking about grants, government research grants. And there are no pockets as deep as the military's."

Another thought hits me. "Even if it was for military purposes, I'm not sure that's necessarily a bad thing." Owen puts his latte on the bench and looks at me. "Sure, if one side is invincible and the other isn't, that's going to be a pretty uneven fight. But if eventually every side has the drug? No point of war if nobody can die, I don't think."

He looks at me thoughtfully. "That's really interesting. Charlotte Kane, you do make me think." He opens the little plastic box of macarons.

"I have to ask you, Owen, can you get sick?" This is another big one. If he's right about the project's intent, it would essentially have been a vaccination too—for *everything*.

He looks at me as he takes a green macaron from the box. "I don't know, actually. I know I haven't gotten sick, but that doesn't mean I can't." He takes a bite of the tiny confection, and his eyes widen. "You have to try this," he says, still chewing. "Pistachio. God, that's good." He hands me the rest of the macaron, and even after all the touching in the last day, a little current sparks when his fingers brush mine.

"Well, it can't just be coincidence that you've never come into contact with a cold or food poisoning in the last three decades." I pause to try the macaron. It *is* good. "I suppose your body could just be fighting any sickness so quickly that you would never notice being sick in the first place, like your five-second muscle soreness. Either that or you actually can't get sick."

"You're thinking maybe the drug was also intended to be some kind of universal vaccine?"

I shrug. "If Strickland is trying to revive your dad's old project, do you think it's on his own or with the backing of the company? Also, did anybody who worked on your dad's project survive the accident?" I can't seem to stop the questions from running out of me, so I take the pink macaron from the box and take a big bite, hoping a physical barrier might help.

"Honestly, I don't know what Strickland is up to. I wouldn't put it past him to be working on something off the record, but I really don't know if he's working on my dad's research at all, or for sure what that research even was. As for anybody surviving the accident, I'm quite certain that nobody who was actually in the lab at the time lived, other than me." Owen stares across the path at a squirrel working on an acorn. "Eight men died that day. But my mom was under the impression that my father was part of a nine-person team. So she spent a few years trying to find out who the ninth was and what happened to him, but Genesis claimed after the accident that there had only ever been eight. We never found out which was true."

All of a sudden, Owen is smiling, and a gentle laugh bubbles up from his chest. Ambiguity over the ninth member of the research team seems an odd thing to be happy about, so I give him a quizzical look.

"It's just…" he starts. "It's just nice to have someone to talk to about this. It's been a long time." His smile fades. "I'm sorry to dump this all on you, though." He searches my face. "I know it's a lot."

"Owen," I say firmly. "You don't get to take credit for dumping anything on me when I'm the one asking rapid-fire questions without even giving you time to answer in between. It's serious stuff. Maybe Strickland is secretly plotting to replace your bones with adamantium in his shady little lab," I add jokingly.

Owen looks confused. "What's adamantium?"

"You have got to be kidding me." Even as a tomboy, I've never been into comic books, but you'd think a kid growing up with a real superpower might have had a little interest.

He shakes his head.

"Wolverine? Heals in minutes? Bones replaced or enhanced or whatever with a made-up indestructible metal called adamantium?" He's still looking at me pretty blankly. "Okay, I'm not exactly an expert on Marvel Comics, or DC or whatever Wolverine is, but you only have to see maybe one out of every three summer blockbusters to have some idea about the big-name superheroes, right?"

"I guess I've always avoided them," he says. "My sister bought me some comic books one year when I was a kid. She thought I might enjoy reading about people who also have a gift—she always called it my 'gift.'" He makes quotation marks in the air with his fingers. "I agreed with her for a couple years maybe, before I started looking at it as a…an affliction. Reading about Superman or whoever always just made me feel worse. I've never seen any of the movies."

I don't understand. What about having this talent—this bona fide superpower—could make a kid feel bad about himself? Owen is looking at me, but his eyes are distant again, and it hits me. He's lonely. *Was* lonely.

"It's been very isolating for you," I venture. "Is that why?"

"Yes, I think that's a big part of it. It's also been hard for me to come to terms with the fact that I have this, this ability, and I'm not able to put it to any use. I was a kid who could have set world record race times at ten years of age, and I wasn't allowed to play sports. And now, as an adult, there's any number of ways I could be putting it to good use, and I'm a corporate lawyer."

No wonder he hasn't seen the *X-Men*.

"Owen, there is nothing wrong with being a corporate lawyer."

"I know," he snaps before taking a deep breath. "Sorry. It's just… I know there's nothing wrong with what I do, but shouldn't I be a firefighter or a Navy SEAL or something?"

"Not if being exposed would put you in danger."

He looks at me, and his eyes are shiny. There's a tiny rim of tears along his bottom eyelids. "Sometimes I think I don't care."

It breaks my heart that he's been alone with this for so long.

"Owen, I care. Maybe you could be exposed and it would be okay, but we don't know that. You have to protect yourself."

He closes his eyes, and a lone tear leaks out between his eyelids and rolls down his cheek. I take the cup and little box of confections from his hand, setting them on the bench so I can scoot closer against him. I run my hand along his thigh. He turns his face toward me, but his eyes are still closed.

I want to take his pain away, the hurt and loneliness of harboring this secret for all these years, all these years of unnecessary guilt. I run my thumb down over his face to wipe the tear away, and he opens his eyes.

"Owen," I say. "You know that you have nothing to be ashamed of, right? Absolutely nothing."

"I guess." He blinks the wetness from his eyes.

"No you guess. Remember how I'm right about a lot of stuff? This is not an exception." I smile, and the pain in Owen's face fades.

He puts a hand on my cheek. "Charlotte, where did you come from?"

I decide we've had enough serious talk and lean forward to kiss him, letting myself get a little more carried away than is probably appropriate for a public park. When I pull back, Owen shakes his head slightly, like he'd forgotten where we are. I stand and reach for his hand, pulling him up beside me.

"Let's go back to your place." I squeeze his hand. "Before we get ourselves in trouble."

By the time we get back to the apartment, I've convinced Owen that his healing is no reason to live a life deprived of superheroes, so he puts a bag of popcorn in the microwave while I order *X-Men: First Class* on demand. None of the major characters have healing powers, so it seems like a safe place to start.

Owen enjoys the movie. It seems my presence has at least made him comfortable enough with his gift, his affliction, to detach from it long enough to enjoy the fun and made-up world that these superheroes live in. I will say that watching a movie about people with all sorts of bizarre abilities is a different experience having met Owen. The vast majority of the characters still seem totally unrealistic, like it has to be a physical impossibility to shapeshift into different people or pull a submarine out of the water with your mind. But had Owen been a character in the *X-Men* rather than the lawyer with his arm around me on the couch, I'd have thought his ability was just as farfetched.

"You can't feel bad about yourself after watching a movie like that," I say as the credits are rolling. "At least you're not using your gift to start World War III or murder everyone who can't do something crazy like fly and spit fire."

"That's true." He squeezes his arm tighter around my shoulders. "For every superhero, there has to be a supervillain, I suppose. That would be a lot worse than corporate law."

"I'm thinking *Batman* tomorrow."

Owen looks at me, eyebrows raised.

"You'll like it. His only superpowers are fancy toys and extreme wealth. Though if you do decide you want to do something with your ability without exposing yourself, you could always take a card from Batman and go all masked vigilante all over Philadelphia." I smile and poke him in the side, hoping he won't be offended. Dating a guy with a veritable superpower is confusing enough, but dating a guy with a superpower he's ashamed of and has rarely spoken about is a whole different thing.

"Interesting idea, but there's no way I'm putting on a Spandex suit," he says, mock seriousness in his voice.

"Well, that's fine. Batman's suit is mostly rubber, if I'm not mistaken. I do have to say, though, you'd look hotter in Spandex than any of these actors anyway."

"Charlotte, is that so," he says as he swiftly rolls me onto my back by my shoulders and pins me under him. He kisses me hard and fast.

"My own Mister Mend," I say. His mouth falls open, which I take as encouragement. "The Indestructible Attorney…Professor Invincible…wait, no, Professor Invincible, Esquire!"

He laughs—more of a snort, really—and shakes his head. Before I can come up with another even more ridiculous name, my mouth is otherwise engaged, and his hands are pushing up under my shirt.

I'm still pinned under Owen on the couch, my legs quivering with the aftershocks of orgasm. I watch his body and can see the muscles of his shoulders and chest begin to relax. His eyes open and lock on mine, intense, searching.

"What would you say to some Chinese food?" he asks.

I laugh, and he gives me a funny look. "I just…It looked like you were going to say something serious."

He shakes his head. "Charlotte, my dear, I am quite serious about Chinese food."

I have to admit, as much as I'm enjoying the closeness, our bodies still joined, my stomach is grumbling.

"Well then, Owen, we shall have some."

We retreat to his bedroom to put on some clothes, and he gets out a white polo and some chocolate-brown shorts. I allow myself the indulgence of watching him dress, and when he notices, he slows down considerably to let me enjoy the show. He's biting his lip—being silly—and I get the sense he really doesn't know how attractive he is. Like I'm only staring because I like him, because I'm smitten. Which is absolutely true, but I'm watching him right now because he looks hot buttoning his shorts over his chiseled lower abs, and because the trace of his happy trail that peeks up over his shorts when he lifts his arms to pull the shirt over his head reminds me of what's hidden down there. He pulls a pair of faded navy Toms from the closet and slips them on.

"This style is from Argentina," he says. "I used to bring shoes like these back when I was younger, before they got popular in the States, and I'd occasionally get asked why I was walking around in slippers."

I smile. "You know, I haven't heard you speak Spanish yet."

"*Sos muy bellosa*, Charlotte."

Even hearing him say a short phrase is sexy. I think he's calling me beautiful. And Owen knows I haven't taken Spanish in a long time, so I think this gives me free rein to totally botch something.

"*Gracias*, Owen," I reply. "*Tu eres muy guapo y me gusta tocar tu cuerpo.*" *You are very handsome and I like to touch your body.* I think.

A smile spreads across his face, the big one that makes me think he might actually have more teeth than a normal human. "*Muy bien*," he says. "You remember something from your Spanish classes after all. *Me gusta tambien cuando me tocas.*" I think that means he likes it too when I touch him.

I step toward him and stand on my tiptoes so I can kiss him on the lips. His tongue wanders into my mouth. We just got dressed, which will really be a waste if we end up tearing each other's clothes right back off again. Which is what I desperately want to do, but I feel like I should try to exercise at least a little bit of restraint. I pull back.

"How about that Chinese food?"

Owen smiles, his eyes still closed. "I'm taking you to my favorite spot in Chinatown." His eyes open and shine with excitement, which makes him seem younger. "Best hot and sour soup you'll ever have."

When we leave Lee How Fook, it's about ten o'clock. It's a bit of a hike back to Owen's place, but after our lazy afternoon movie, a long walk seems just right. A few blocks from his place, he squeezes my hand.

"Maybe we should stop for frozen custard at Shake Shack," he says. "Too much?"

I'm still quite full of Chinese food, but I can always use something sweet after a meal. "Owen Becker, the chance of me ever turning down a Concrete or milkshake is really quite slim."

Owen pulls my hand, which turns me toward him, then he catches me by the shoulder and kisses me hard. I'm standing here on the sidewalk with his tongue in my mouth, but it only lasts for a second.

"God, I love that you like to eat. It's so sexy."

"If that's what gets you going, Owen, then you are really in for it with me." His face is still just inches from mine, and I hold his gaze while I run my hands down the front of him, tracing the muscles of his chest with my fingers.

He leans his head down to whisper in my ear. "You need to stop that, or I'm going to have to have you against that wall there, and we'll both be arrested for public indecency." His breath is hot on my skin, and though I know he's at least partially kidding, the thought sends a little wave of heat to my core.

I tip my head up toward him and pull his ear to my mouth. "Maybe it would be worth it," I tease, before standing straight again and putting a few inches between us. I can hear Owen take a deep breath and let it whistle out slowly between his lips.

We walk the last couple of blocks to Shake Shack in sexually charged silence. Owen's thumb paces across my palm and sends little tingling waves to my center.

We've just walked in and I'm looking up at the menu on the wall when I hear my name.

"Charlotte, hey!"

Kyle. He and two other guys from our program at Genesis have just gotten in line behind us. I turn, and before I know what's going on, he has both arms around me in a hug and is kissing me on the cheek. I can smell beer on him.

"Kyle, hi, uh…how are you? Hey, Justin, Dave." I nod at the other two guys as I detach myself from Kyle's embrace.

"What are you doing out here at this hour?" Kyle asks. It seems he hasn't noticed that I'm not by myself.

"Owen," I say, turning, "this is Kyle, and that's Justin and Dave. They're in the RA program with me at Genesis. Guys…this is Owen." I haven't had to introduce Owen to anyone other than Maddie and Rachel, and that was an unusual circumstance, but this is especially awkward.

"Owen Becker," he says, extending his hand to Kyle. "Nice to meet you." Kyle's face falls a little when he gets a good look at him, but by then Owen is shaking hands with Justin and Dave, so I'm not sure he notices. I feel bad—I do still like Kyle. But he's not Owen.

"Were you guys out somewhere fun?" I ask, hoping to keep it light.

"Just watching the Phillies game at Cavanaugh's," Kyle says, a little bit of an edge in his voice that's usually not there. "You're just out for an ice cream run on a Saturday night? How do you guys know each other?"

"We were out to dinner," Owen says. "I'm Charlotte's boyfriend."

He is absolutely matter of fact. He says he's my boyfriend—for the first time—in the same manner I'd expect him to, say, tell someone where he grew up or what he does for a living. I can tell Kyle was still holding out a little bit of hope that Owen was just a friend or cousin or something.

Kyle looks at me. "I didn't know you had a boyfriend," he says quietly.

Now I feel even worse, but I actually *didn't* have a boyfriend the last time I saw him, and even then, I don't think I led him on. But he's upset, and though I'm absolutely ecstatic to be with Owen—and pretty excited that he's made us official, whether or not it was appropriate to say in front of a friend before he said it to me alone—I'm sorry if Kyle thought something was going to happen between us.

"It's new," I say truthfully. Owen takes my hand in his, and I can't help but squeeze it, though I'm also hoping Kyle doesn't think I'm trying to rub it in. I still can't tell if Owen has picked up on the dynamic.

"Good for you," Kyle says through clenched teeth. He turns to Owen. "She's one of the good ones."

Owen smiles and nods at Kyle, and I'm relieved that nobody has time to say anything else because we're at the front of the line and the young girl behind the counter is asking our backs what we want. We turn around, and Owen motions for me to order first, so I ask for a vanilla Concrete custard with peanut butter and toffee, my usual.

"I was going to order something else," he says, "but that sounds way better. Make it two of those."

The girl rings us up and Owen pays, and our Concretes are done while she's still helping Kyle and the guys.

"Nice to meet you," Owen says toward them, and Kyle nods back.

"I'll see you guys at work," I say. "Kyle, maybe lunch one day this week?" I'm not sure if that makes it better or worse.

Kyle smiles, but it's the kind where you're just making your mouth into the right shape; his eyes still look defeated. "Sure, Charlotte. I'll text you."

I grab Owen's hand and pull him out the door as quickly as I can.

I have no reason to think Owen is a particularly jealous type, but I don't need to draw attention to Kyle's weirdness if he didn't already notice, so I don't say anything when we get out onto the sidewalk.

Owen starts talking a few steps after the door closes behind us. "That guy Kyle," he says. "He likes you."

So he did notice. "Yeah, I think he might."

"Should I be worried about this?" he asks calmly, turning to look at me.

"No." And before I can explain any further, he responds.

"Good." He puts a spoonful of the dense frozen custard in his mouth and rolls his eyes. "God, that's good. I'm glad I copied your order."

Just like that, we're done talking about Kyle. I've only said one word, but that's enough explanation for Owen.

<h1 style="text-align:center">July 29th</h1>

Given the tone of the weekend thus far, Sunday is a surprisingly normal day. I rouse late to find Owen next to me, awake and reading case notes. He kisses me lightly before disappearing into the other room, returning a moment later with a steaming mug of coffee for me—with whole milk and one Splenda. He finishes the case he's reading while I make bagel dough in the kitchen.

Owen is eager to resume his strength training to test his limitations, if there are any to test, but he's already exhausted the equipment in the gym, so I suggest he try some exercises that involve strength and balance. While the dough is rising, he teaches himself to walk on his hands. By the time the dough is ready to shape, he's running around the apartment on his hands, which looks exactly as ridiculous as it sounds. While I boil and then bake the bagels, he practices jumps on his hands. First over throw pillows in the living room, then a stack of books, and by the time I'm pulling the hot bagels out of the oven, he's jumping over the coffee table.

It's raining out, and over fresh sesame bagels, which Owen raves about to a nearly laughable degree, we continue his long overdue superhero education. We watch the old Michael Keaton version of *Batman* from the late eighties, enjoying it despite the wildly dated special effects.

"If I'm gonna be Batman," Owen says when it's over, "does that make you my Vicki Vale?"

"Ohh, no, no." I shake my head. "Batman has a new girlfriend in every movie. If you're defeating supervillains on a regular basis, I intend to be around for more than one. More of a Lois Lane, I suppose." I've been lying on the couch with my head resting in Owen's lap for most of the movie, and I roll onto my back to look up at him.

Owen has his eyebrows up in question. The man doesn't know who Lois Lane is. I can't bring myself to do any more than shake my head in disbelief.

A pensive look crosses his face. "You know, Charlotte," he starts, and then pauses to brush the hair from my forehead, "I'm really glad you're here."

I smile up at him. "Me too, Owen."

Yet the unsettling thought crosses my mind that he could be confusing his feelings for me with simply having a new confidante. What if the stabbing had happened in front of someone else? Would he now have this intimacy with that person instead?

My face must have dropped, because he squints down at me. "What's wrong?"

I take a moment to decide whether I should tell him. I don't want to convince him that he doesn't actually like me, but at the same time, I don't want to run around thinking this amazing man is falling for me if he's not.

"It's just…" I mumble. "I just worry that for you it could be more about having someone to share this…someone to talk to about what's really been burdening you all these years. Rather than something about me specifically." I focus on my feet, which rest on the arm of the couch.

"Look at me, Charlotte." I do, and his eyes are serious. "It's you," he says. "It's definitely you. It's been you since the day we met."

This is sweet, and it's nice to hear, but I still worry he only *thinks* it's me.

He can tell I'm not completely appeased. "Last weekend when you met my sister…did you notice that she was a little cold to you at first?"

I look up at him, and his eyes are soft now. "I guess so, a little." I had assumed it was just protective-older-sibling skepticism.

"She and I had been arguing," he says. "I know she told you that she'd dropped everything to come out to dinner with me when I called and told her I met a girl. That was true, but not complete. What I really said was 'Isabelle, I met the girl I'm going to show my gift to.'"

My eyes widen.

"She was worried—nothing to do with you." He pauses. "Well, she didn't really love that you work at Genesis, but it was more that she was worried about me, that I could get myself hurt. She argued that I couldn't possibly know after one date that I wanted to share everything with you, and that there was no reason to rush it even if I did. I ended up coming around and agreeing to wait to tell you, but I have to admit that was more out of fear that it would scare you off than anything else. I know it scared you, and I still feel bad about that, but Tuesday night was actually a huge relief, weird as it sounds. Saved me a lot of stress over how to bring it up." The corners of his eyes crinkle as a smile crosses his lips.

My stomach flips around. I have nothing so grand to tell him as this, but I did of course feel very strongly about him from the start too. Really from before the start. I bite my lip.

"Owen, I knew from that first day we talked in the subject reception room that there was something…different about you." My cheeks flush. "I think what I told Maddie when I got home that night was that I'd met the perfect man. And the next day, it wasn't a coincidence that we ran into each other near the elevators. I waited there for you, and I'm not sure what I'd have done if I'd somehow missed you."

Owen smiles his full smile, and leans over to kiss me. It's gentle and sweet. As much as I've been savoring the passionately sexual part of our relationship so far, this is wonderful too, and it comforts me that it's really not just the sex. It does cross my mind, though, that he's in his thirties—he must have dated girls he's liked before. Before I can stop myself, I'm asking him another question.

"Have you never wanted to tell another girlfriend about what you can do?"

"I've never even entertained the idea of showing my healing to any women I've dated. And as soon as I'm sure I can't be honest with someone, that's it. I was twenty-two when I first realized how big of a deal breaker it would be for me. My college girlfriend talked about moving in together when we graduated, but all I could think about was how I couldn't possibly hide what I am from someone in my own home, every single day. That wouldn't be fair to either of us. I was hopeful for a while that I'd find someone I could be comfortable with, but after a few short relationships with girls I found no fault with but still had no desire to tell, I started to lose faith. I hadn't been on more than one date with anyone in a couple years, but I guess because I'd been isolated with this for so long, I was okay being alone."

His eyes are bearing down on me. I nod.

"Why did you want to tell me?"

He blinks a few times. "You're smart and beautiful and witty, all the things any man wants in a woman, but then there's…like a natural strength I've never encountered before. Like you somehow missed the memo on how to act like a girl — to play the part — and just *are* the woman you are. I'm not sure that makes any sense."

I'm pretty much floored. He's seeing something different in me that doesn't fit into the prescribed mold. And maybe doesn't have to.

"I hope I didn't offend you," he says.

"No, not at all. It's just…As an engineer who grew up tossing a football with the boys, I've never thought of myself as particularly womanly." I still have my head in his lap and look up at him, though I'm not sure what I expect him to say.

"Charlotte, being womanly doesn't mean you can't be strong or run fast or be awesome at science." He leans down and kisses me gently again.

Owen Becker, feminist thinker.

The storm has blown over, and as we dress for a walk in the afternoon, I'm glad I so thoroughly packed a bag. I pull out an orange and white summer dress — short, but with flats it doesn't look indecent. I put on my bra from yesterday, throw the dress over my head, and step into a pair of tan canvas flats that I'd jammed into the bag at the last second. I am not a person who goes commando, but when I realize I've only packed dark-colored thongs and that the material of the dress is thin enough to see the contrast, I decide to try another first and go without.

By the time we get back to Owen's apartment, it's almost four. We've chosen a fairly time-intensive meal — fresh pappardelle from the Italian Market with a homemade short rib Bolognese. The short ribs will need to cook at low heat for a couple of hours to get tender enough to shred, so we start on the sauce as soon as we get back. I pull a fancy Japanese Santoku knife from the block and get to work on a couple of onions, reducing them to small and regular squares in seconds.

"You know, Charlotte," he says from the sink, where he's lightly flouring the meat to sear in the pan, "it's pretty sexy that you're so good with a knife."

I *am* good with a knife. I smile and look over at Owen, who has some chopped bacon heating in a Dutch oven. He's changed into a faded blue T-shirt to avoid splattering his white polo with grease, and it's a tiny bit too small, so I can see his upper back muscles under the thin fabric.

"Well, Owen, I think it's pretty sexy that you wanted to stay in and do this rather than go out to dinner. Also, that T-shirt is hot as hell on you."

His posture lifts at my compliment. I realize that despite the fact that I've thought something complimentary about him about every six seconds since the moment we met, I really haven't said many of them out loud. I'm encouraged.

"And I should tell you, that stubble makes me want to remove your clothes with my teeth."

Owen rubs his forehead with both hands and then turns to me. "If you keep talking like that, we'll never eat."

I smile at him again and hold his gaze for a few extra seconds before refocusing on the cutting board at the island. With my back to him, I smash a clove of garlic under the flat part of the knife, and a wave of confidence runs through me.

"Don't let me distract you," I say, planting my feet a little more than shoulder width apart and hinging at the hips to lean forward slowly. My dress pulls up over my butt, and I know that if Owen is looking, he's seeing a lot more than my cheeks.

His breath hisses slowly out.

"Oops." I stand up straight again and pull the fabric back down to cover me. "I guess I didn't realize this was so short." I practically feel Owen's excitement build electricity through the air, and my insides vibrate.

I can turn on this incredible being. Me. He wants me.

"I don't hear any sizzling," I say. Yes, I can turn him on, and I can make him wait for it. "I'm going to have all the vegetables ready in about two minutes. So you better get cracking."

I hear a loud sizzle as the first piece of meat hits the pan. We bought a bunch of short ribs for the sauce, and it's going to take him more than one batch to brown them all. It will take a while, probably ten or fifteen minutes, and I smile to myself knowing that all he'll be thinking about in that time is what he's going to do to me later.

After we've been cooking for about forty minutes, the beef broth and red wine finally get to a simmer. Owen tosses the seared short ribs back into the pot, covers it, and turns the heat to low. It will be at least an hour before we have any more work to do on dinner. I'm still at the island, picking up a few stray pieces of onion and herbs that managed to dance off the cutting board, when I spot a little piece of garlic on the other side of the countertop.

"Can't leave this a mess," I say as I lean slowly forward, arching my back a bit and pushing my butt out behind me as I reach for the stray garlic. It's hot out, but Owen's air conditioning works well, the cool refreshing against my skin when the thin fabric again pulls up over my backside and exposes me. This time I'm not teasing, and when I'm leaning forward enough that my chest touches the granite, I put my elbows down and let my weight rest there.

He sighs quickly—more of a huff—and I wonder what he'll do. I desperately want to turn and look at him, but my body tingles with the excitement of not knowing exactly where he is or what he's doing, and I manage to keep my eyes forward. I hear a couple of soft footsteps behind me. He doesn't touch me, but I sense the warmth of his body.

He makes me wait like this for a moment, and I'm about to turn my head to look when all of a sudden something plunges into me. I'm taken completely by surprise and jerk forward as waves of heat spring suddenly into my lower abdomen. Fingers. It's two fingers he has put inside me, deep inside me, and it's the only physical contact we have.

I close my eyes and focus on the sensation as he moves his fingers slowly in and out of me in complete silence. It's like no other part of me exists beyond the single place he's touching me, and the fire builds quickly. I wonder if I'm going to come like this; I never have before without some kind of touch around my clit, but something about standing here in the kitchen, my legs spread but both of us still clothed, seems forbidden, and the pleasure is multiplying rapidly. My legs start to twitch, and my insides tighten around Owen's fingers.

Just when I think I cannot take a moment longer, they slip out of me. For a brief moment, there is no contact between us before Owen grips my hips with both hands and gently picks me up, turns me around, and sits me on the edge of the island. My dress is still bunched up over my hips, and Owen stares at my bare flesh as he quickly unbuttons his shorts. He pushes the waistband of his boxer briefs down to free his straining erection, and before I've even gotten a good look at it, it's inside me.

Owen's first push into me is so hard that I'm sure I'd have tipped backward if he hadn't grabbed my hips with both hands. His rhythm is already fast, like fingering me has him so worked up already that he doesn't have to build up to it. His hands move my hips back and forth in perfect time with his thrusts. Facing him like this, with his impossibly strong arms pulling me over and over onto his length, he's so deep inside me that it almost hurts. My legs are up in a V in front of me, my knees bent over his arms, and with each pounding drive, his hips bang into that area where my inner thighs meet my butt—that same spot that kills after a spin class. I know I'm going to be bruised, but the pleasure is so intense that I can't be bothered to care.

One of his hands moves to my lower back, and the other between my thighs. My legs are wide apart and I'm leaning back slightly, all of my parts exposed, and Owen drags his thumb lightly across my clit along with a particularly hard thrust. I was already so close that this unexpected touch, this one simple extra movement, pushes me—flings me rather—into the abyss. Everything goes dark, and silent, and there is only the sensation of my orgasm, the sharp, hot pleasure running through every nerve in my body.

We somehow manage to finish preparing dinner without any other breaks. I make sure to scrub the island with soap and water before we sit down to eat. Owen opens a bottle of malbec from another one of his favorite wineries in Argentina as I serve each of us a heaping portion of pappardelle from the Le Creuset on the stove.

"You'd like it there," he says after explaining how his uncle in Buenos Aires introduced him to this particular wine. "Maybe sometime you'll let me take you down and show you off." He's smiling, and

I can't tell if he's just making conversation or really inviting me to Argentina with him. His tone sounds like he means it, but I'm still cautious about making too many assumptions.

"You can show me off anytime, anywhere." I plant a soft kiss on his lips as he hands me a glass of wine.

When I sit on the barstool at the island, I feel a sharp twinge of pain. Those butt bones that Owen assaulted during our kitchen romp might be bruised worse than I thought. I wince and stand back up—it really hurts to put weight on it.

He touches my arm to turn me toward him. "Charlotte, are you okay?" The two little vertical lines running from the bridge of his nose up onto his forehead have deepened.

"I'm okay," I say, then pause, unsure of how to explain that he hurt me without upsetting him. "It's not a big deal, but I think I bruised my butt a little while we were waiting for the short ribs to cook."

His face falls. Shit. I guess it's important that he knows that he's capable of hurting me with his extraordinary strength, but the last thing I want is to be handled carefully. His urgency before, his need to have me fast and hard and right then, was what really turned me on the most.

"You mean *I* bruised you," he says softly. He looks down at his untouched meal. "I hurt you."

"Owen." I take his hand in mine and squeeze it, and he looks back up at me. "It's a couple little bruises, really not a big deal. I *loved* what you did to me." I kiss him, opening my mouth and meeting his tongue with mine. He barely kisses back.

I pull away. His eyes are pained, the normal sparkle in his ice-blue gaze nearly extinguished.

"Can you sit?" he asks.

I tentatively lower my butt onto the stool again, and it's bad. White-hot pain screeches through my backside. I stay there for a moment, trying to steel myself against it, until Owen's hands wrap around my hips and lift me off the stool. A few pulses of residual discomfort meander through me, but a couple seconds after he puts me on my feet, it's largely gone. His hands still grip my hips, but he's hanging his head.

"Owen, really, it's okay," I say. "It will heal. Honestly, I wouldn't change anything. Some people get hickies, some get rug burn, I get a butt bruise. It was worth it."

He begins to speak without lifting his head. "I've had a little worry in the pit of my stomach from the second you found out about me, about what I am. Like being close to me could get you hurt if anybody with bad intentions ever found out." This is clearly about more than a couple of bruises. "I didn't think I'd hurt you myself."

"Hey, hey, hey." I take his face in both of my hands. "For one thing, *hurt* is a bit of a strong word. I've had worse bruises from a bike seat." That's a stretch, but I really don't want him dwelling on this. "You don't need to worry about me. Nobody is going to hurt me, and that includes you. You're just a little stronger than you realize, and we'll figure it out."

He nods, but the strain in his forehead tells me he's still wary. "You have to promise to tell me if I ever hurt you again. During, not after, so I can stop."

I don't think all the strength I have could've made me tell him to stop last time, but this is clearly very important to him.

"I promise."

He takes my arm in one hand and somehow balances both plates in the other. Strong hands. He pulls me into the living room and sets the dishes down in the middle of the floor before tossing a few cushions from the couch on either side of them. He walks back to the island for our wine.

Lying down on his stomach in front of one of the plates, Owen motions for me to do the same. He's willing to eat on the floor in his living room just so that I don't have to sit on my bruised butt. I can't help smiling when I lie down on the cushions across from him. We're facing each other with our bodies out behind us, both propped up on our elbows.

Eating like this takes a little getting used to. Luckily we didn't make anything that needs to be cut; just the fork is difficult enough to maneuver, but I'm glad to have the distraction of our awkward positions with Owen's uneasiness still heavy over us.

The pasta is divine, though it's the quietest meal we've had. Maybe I haven't successfully talked him off the ledge about his ability to hurt me. I'm tempted to bring it up again and try to reassure him, but I can't decide if talking about it is more likely to help or hurt.

He holds up his end up the conversation, which has wandered back to superheroes as I explain the difference between the Avengers and the X-Men, but there's something distant in his tone. After the entire weekend of complete straightforwardness—about his feelings toward me, his ability, his family—Owen is suddenly reserved, and the contrast is stark. A particularly long silence toward the end of the meal fans the ember of unease in my gut to the point where it feels like it's burning me from within.

"I really should head home soon," I say, trying to keep the hurt out of my voice. "I can't go to work tomorrow in the same clothes."

I do need to go home, but part of me wants him to ask me to stay anyway, to reassure me that my growing nervousness is just paranoia and that nothing has changed. But he doesn't even look up from his plate. He just nods, averting his eyes.

"I'll walk you home," he says quietly. "You shouldn't be walking alone in South Philly at this hour."

My instinct is to tell him that I'm perfectly capable of getting home without his protection, that he should only walk me if he actually wants to. But I want to spend the twenty minutes with him regardless, and the idea of just leaving him now with uncertainty pooling inside me makes me want to throw up.

He gets up and picks both of our plates up off the floor.

"I'll help you clean up before we go," I say, hoping a few minutes next to him at the sink will somehow help me get a better read on what he's thinking.

But he manages to make it to the sink without even looking at me and places the plates gently inside.

"I'll do it when I get back," he says, finally glancing up at me. There is pain in his eyes and not a trace of the magnetic force that usually pulls me into him. "You should get some rest for the workweek."

We walk in near silence through Center City toward my apartment. I make a few attempts at starting a conversation, asking Owen if he's been to a restaurant we pass and then about his work schedule for the week. He answers my questions in short sentences and doesn't make any effort to continue our dialogue. Each dropped trail of conversation adds a ring to the sequoia of hurt and disappointment growing inside me.

By the time we reach my building, anger competes with pain and desperation for my attention.

We stand on the stoop of my place, Owen still holding my duffel bag. When I reach out to take it from him, he shakes his head.

"I'll carry it up the stairs for you," he says with a frustrating lack of inflection in his voice.

We walk up in silence, and once we get to my apartment door, anger edges out the hurt for a brief moment.

"Did I do something wrong?" I snap. He remains facing the door for a second, and I see his jaw clench before he turns to me.

"No, Charlotte, of course not," he whispers, and that way he says my name shatters something within me. Desperation wins out.

"Do you want to come inside?" I cringe as my wavering voice sounds like a plea.

He closes his eyes.

"I shouldn't," he breathes so softly I can barely hear him.

"Why?" My stomach caves in on itself in anticipation of an answer I don't want to hear.

His eyes still closed, he bites his lip.

"I don't—" He opens his eyes but stares above my head. "I don't think I can trust myself with you."

He's slipping away from me, and a drip of cold sweat runs down the crease of my back. I take his face in both hands and angle it down toward me, giving him no place else to look.

"I do," I say, forcing strength into my tone. "I trust you."

"But Charlotte—"

"Come in," I demand. Somehow I know in my gut that if I can't get him through this door, he'll be gone for good.

"I don't think I sh—"

I pull his face toward me and cover his mouth with mine, stifling the rejection before he can finish saying it. He stands frozen for a moment, not kissing me back, but I keep moving my lips over his, begging him with my mouth and unsure of what I'll do if he doesn't respond. But after a terrifying few moments, he does.

His tongue moves against mine, and suddenly he has one hand on the back of my head and the other at the small of my back, pulling me so hard into his body that every inch of me is touching him. The rush of relief as he begins to give in is so overwhelming that tears spring to my eyes, and I press my eyelids closed, trying to trap the watery tears within.

Owen's face softens in my hands, and before I can process the emotions sprinting to the front of my mind, he sweeps me off the ground and into his arms. I let my hand drop from his face and fumble through my purse for my keys, still immersed in the desperately intense kiss. When he finally releases my mouth to take a breath, I bury my face between his neck and shoulder and inhale his scent. It's some combination of clean laundry and maybe verbena, I'm not sure. Whatever it is is completely intoxicating.

I manage to unlock the door without Owen putting me down, still scared that he'll float away from me if I give up contact with his body. When he swings the door open, I notice the lights are already on. I've been so wrapped up in the passion and panic that it didn't even occur to me that Maddie might be home.

"Charlieeeeeeeeeee!" I hear from her room. "Charlie, you dirty, dirty girl!"

Owen puts me down quickly, right as she appears in the doorway to her bedroom. I stand awkwardly next to him, and Maddie's jaw basically hits the floor.

"Sorry, I...Hi, Owen," she says with an embarrassed smile, looking back and forth between us.

"Maddie, it's nice to see you again." Snapped out of the emotionally charged moment between us, he turns to me with one eyebrow raised. "Charlie, huh?"

My cheeks flush. "Yeah, it's an old nickname. Only a few people call me that."

"Just the important ones, right?" I'm not really sure what to say to this, but Owen keeps talking anyway. "Would it be okay if I use your bathroom?" he asks Maddie.

"Of course." She motions toward our bathroom door, and I realize she doesn't know he's been here before. As soon as he closes the door, she turns to me.

Oh my God! she mouths, her eyes open as wide as they'll go.

I allow a stupid grin to spread across my face, able to push the heaviness of the last hour or two to the back of my mind for a moment.

"Sorry," I whisper, "I should have texted you. He was just going to drop me off, but I…I didn't want him to leave."

"Who would!" she says excitedly. "Okay, though, Charlie, tomorrow night, let's order in, all right? I'll tell Mark to entertain himself elsewhere because you have to tell me everything. Every single thing."

Just then, Owen emerges from the bathroom, and Maddie smiles at him. It seems the awkwardness has dissipated.

"Well, I'm off to bed," she says. "Owen, lovely to see you. And I'm hoping you'll let me have her to myself tomorrow night?"

"Of course," he says warmly, and maybe a little too quickly. "Have a good night."

"Night, Mads," I say, and she can't resist giving me one more excited grin before shutting her bedroom door.

Owen sits on the edge of my bed as soon as we retreat to my room. There's tension in his posture, the way his shoulders are pulled down, and my dormant panic stirs. Before it can overtake me, knowing only that I need to be touching him, I push Owen onto his back and climb on top, sealing my mouth over his. He starts to harden beneath me, and a tiny weight lifts at the thought that at least his body still wants mine.

I kiss him harder, deeper, desperate to be even closer to him. When his hands wander up my thighs and under my dress, I break our kiss and sit up to disrobe us both as quickly as I can, eager to keep the momentum going and not backslide into the despair of our walk over. I take a moment to enjoy the sight of his naked physique, this Michelangelo's *David* beneath me, noticing for the first time that he has a sprinkling of freckles on his light skin.

"God, you're gorgeous," I whisper, and I lean forward, lifting my hips off of him so I can brush one nipple over his face. He swiftly opens his mouth and catches it between his lips, sucking gently, and the now familiar zing of pleasure shoots straight to my groin. I let out a little gasp and allow the sensation to dissolve the worry in my gut.

Planting my hands on his chest for balance, I slide my hips slowly back and forth, rubbing my wetness along the length of him. He groans and lifts his head to watch. My pleasure builds quickly as I grind my clit up and down his thick, veined cock. Owen starts flexing his hips gently upward in time with the rhythm I'm keeping, and I realize I'm not going to last much longer if I keep rubbing myself along him like this. So I lean forward to kiss him deeply, lifting my hips up to break contact, and while his tongue searches my mouth, I reach behind me for his erection and slowly lower myself onto it.

Owen sighs when he enters me, and he's about halfway inside when he pops his hips upward to meet mine, burying himself completely in me. I feel a slight twinge of pain as his hips touch my bruises, but it's not bad—certainly not bad enough to want to stop. I must have made a face, though, because he snaps out of his daze and lowers his hips slowly back to the bed.

"Did I hurt you?" he asks with breathy concern in his voice.

"Not bad," I whisper, and I continue moving my hips up and down on him. "I don't want to stop."

"You promised." His gaze alternates between my face and where our bodies are joined.

"I did, and I'm okay. If it's too much, I promise I'll tell you. Just… don't stop."

He nods slowly, conflict knitted into his expression, and grips my hips with both hands. He lifts my body so that only the tip of him is still inside, and without saying anything else, starts thrusting hard and fast from beneath me, stopping just short of his hips banging into me each time. The feeling of being weightless above Owen, on top yet completely at his mercy, is like nothing I've ever experienced. I watch him, a sheen of sweat starting to appear across his forehead and chest, and I'm helpless against the pleasure he is rapidly pounding into me, the tangle of worry inside me no match for the onslaught of sensation. I can see the muscles of his arms and shoulders, tense and defined under his skin, as he holds me motionless and thrusts faster and faster into me, his exquisitely defined abs contracting each time. When I look down his abdomen to where he's entering me, the visual is so alarmingly graphic, so shockingly explicit, that the sense that I'm seeing something I shouldn't, that even looking should be forbidden, catapults me unexpectedly over the edge, and I'm coming, suspended there above him. He must have been waiting for me—either that or the sight of me lost on top of him triggers his own finish—because after two more quick thrusts, he stills with his hips flexed, deep inside me as he comes.

After a few moments, when his eyes return to focus, Owen lowers his hips and mine, and I fall forward, still joined, letting my weight rest on his chest as I bury my face in his neck.

"That, Owen," I say haltingly, my breathing still ragged, "most certainly did not hurt."

He says nothing, lifting me off him and rolling both of us onto our sides so he can spoon me tightly from behind. I think I feel apprehension creeping into his taught muscles for a fleeting moment, but I push that thought away and allow the comfort of sleep to wash over me.

July 30th

When my alarm goes off at 5:45 the next morning, I wake quickly. I'm usually a two-or-three snooze kind of girl, but the leftover excitement from the weekend has me ready to go even though I haven't gotten much sleep. But the moment I realize Owen is no longer in bed with me, my stomach plummets, all the fear from last night rushing back in one breath-sucking wave.

I reach over to his side of the bed and it's already cold. Nausea and anger rise together in my throat. I know that I practically begged him to stay, that I kissed him until his body responded and he couldn't bear to leave, but he at least should have woken me before he left. I reach for my phone on my bedside table, my hands shaking.

He's gone.

And there's not even a text from him.

I throw the covers to the foot of the bed and pull my resistant body into a sitting position. I'm still naked, and I notice my clothes from yesterday have been neatly folded and stacked on my desk. On top of them is a piece of paper. I vault to my feet and grab it, flicking on the overhead light.

CHARLOTTE, I AM SORRY. I AM SORRY FOR BRUISING YOU. I AM SORRY FOR LEAVING WITHOUT SAYING GOOD-BYE. MOST OF ALL, I AM SORRY THAT I CAN'T BE WITH YOU WITHOUT PUTTING YOU IN DANGER. I SHOULD NOT HAVE COME UP LAST NIGHT. I WILL THINK OF YOU ALWAYS. ~OWEN

I stagger to the bed and collapse, my emotions spinning out of control as a shuddering sob comes over me. I stifle the wail that wants out and force my face into the pillow, soaking it immediately with the steady flow of tears. Rejection burns into me, mixing with embarrassment. How *pathetic* I was last night, using brute force to convince him to come to bed with me one last time. And how could he — why would he — fuck me like that if he knew it was over?

An image of Owen beneath me, his lean muscles strung taut with pleasure pops unwanted into my mind, and the sobs come faster, harder. Gasping for breath, I try not to think of all the lovely moments from the weekend, but that just makes it worse. Owen telling me he knew on our first date that I was the one he'd share his secret with. The playful way he teased me when he caught me watching him dress. His mussed hair as his head moved between my legs. The gleam in his eye when he showed me how much weight he could curl in the gym.

I can't bear it, my fingers fisting the comforter until my knuckles ache. He's throwing it all away because he bruised my butt? No. It has to be more than that. He's throwing it all away because he thinks his ability is dangerous, that someone could hurt me to get to him. He picks paranoia over me.

Anger trumps the tangled mass of emotions competing in my brain, and I spring off the bed, my eyes drying as I pull on my workout clothes.

My bag is packed and I'm out the door within minutes, practically sprinting toward the gym. I focus only on my body, pushing just to the point of pain on the treadmill and hearing nothing but the pounding of my feet on the ever-rotating belt. An hour passes, and I'm no closer to understanding how I could possibly get over Owen. But my body is physically exhausted, and I hope my sore muscles will divert some small amount of energy to my aching heart.

Hannah arrives at the Garrison just after me. I hold the elevator door open for her so she can catch up.

"Good weekend?" I ask, forcing my voice steady. Perhaps hearing about somebody else's normal weekend will help me forget, just for a moment, the searing pain of loss and shame.

"It was nice enough. Weekends are never the problem," she replies with a tired smile. Hannah isn't a morning person and she tends to keep to herself for the first couple of hours each week. She sighs. "How about you?"

She turns toward me, getting a good look at my face for the first time this morning. I haven't thought of anything to say yet, but she squints at me before I have time to come up with an innocuous response.

"Charlotte, are you okay?" she asks.

I take a deep breath, debating what to even say to carry the conversation on to something else without actually lying. But again, Hannah barely gives me any time to think.

"Guy problems," she says without even the intonation of a question. "What happened?"

The elevator doors open on our floor, but Hannah doesn't move.

Could I possibly be that obvious? I haven't even known her a month and apparently she can read my mind. No wonder I felt like Owen knew what I was thinking all weekend; I evidently have it scrolling across my forehead in plain English.

The elevator doors start closing, and Hannah shoots her arm out to block the sensor, motioning for me to follow her out into the hall. She seems to take my brief silence as confirmation. "Sooo," she says as we get to the row of hooks where our lab coats are hanging. "What's his name?"

I fiddle with my lab coat, digging around in the pockets in an effort to buy myself another few seconds. I do trust Hannah enough to confide in her, but I'm still not a hundred percent comfortable that my dating a subject is kosher at Genesis — or having dated a subject, I should say. And I'm not sure I can talk about Owen without the waterworks starting anyway. But I don't think I should lie, and it would be weird if I refused to answer.

"His name is Owen." My cheeks burn at the mere mention of his name. I don't want to cry, so I paint the picture as optimistically as I can. "It's only been a few dates, but he kind of freaked out yesterday, and now I'm not sure what's going on. I think I…I let myself get in a little too deep too fast. I really like him, though."

As I say the words, it feels like I'm lying. For one, I know that Owen thinks we can't be together. That we're over. My throat tightens around the thought. But what really makes the bottom drop out of my abdomen is that here, standing in the hallway talking to a friend at work, I realize for the first time that I am absolutely, without a shadow of a doubt, completely in love with Owen Becker.

"Hmm." Hannah says. "What do you mean by 'freaked out'?"

What I really mean is that he's convinced he'll hurt me with his superhuman strength brought about by his inexplicable ability to heal from any injury at any time. Moreover, that he's convinced I'm somehow in danger simply by associating with him because of his gift—his affliction. But I can't say that, that would make me sound crazy, and for a split second I wonder if I actually *am* crazy. And then images from the weekend—of Owen cutting his arm, running on his hands, lifting me like I'm a feather—flood my mind, and I wince at the pain of what I've lost.

Again I find myself looking for a way to describe the situation as vaguely as possible.

"Well, we spent the weekend together, and it was going really well. But then he seemed freaked that he's somehow bad for me. He's a little older."

Hannah peers at me. "*Is* he bad for you?"

I decide to steer the conversation toward one small issue in the mess rather than the big one I can't talk about.

"No, he's great. So great. It's just—" I take a breath and lower my voice, even though nobody else is in the lab yet. "It's just a little complicated. I'm not working on the study, but technically he's a subject at Genesis."

A beat later, Hannah's eyes get wide.

"Wait, you're dating Owen Becker?" She gasps, and a disbelieving smile spreads across her face. "Good for you, Charlotte. Good for you. I'm impressed. You met him here in the lab?"

She seems to be shifting to water-cooler, girl-talk mode, so I'm relieved. I can talk about when Owen and I met without nearing dangerous territory, and hopefully without crying.

"Yeah," I begin. "His appointment time for giving samples got mixed up, and I was taking subjects when he came in." With an embarrassed smile, I tell her the truth that I thought he was gorgeous and didn't want to tell him to leave, and how he was a little flirty with me too. "But then when Strickland noticed Owen was here, he swooped in and snatched his file out of my hand like I had stolen something. Do you know what the study is about? It sure seemed like he was trying to keep it under wraps, but maybe that's just because I'm so new?"

I wasn't sure I'd be able to ask Hannah directly about Strickland and Owen—or even that I still wanted to after this morning—but in telling her about the day we met, the question doesn't as seem out of place. And I've just confirmed that, regardless of whether Owen and I are together or not, I desperately want to know what Strickland is up to. Because if Owen is in danger, I have to stop it.

"I'm honestly not sure what the secrecy is about," she says and seems genuine. "There are a few studies like that, but I've always assumed it has to do with privacy issues or something. This place has so much classified information and confidential research going on. Even after five years, there are tons of doors I'm not even allowed to go through, so I don't usually question too much if I'm not allowed to see or work on a particular study."

Hannah is right; there *is* a ton of work being done here that must be kept secret for any number of reasons. Maybe I *am* just paranoid to think something is different about the way Owen's case is handled. I know his family had to sign a load of legal documents when they agreed to the settlement, so maybe confidentiality was just a part of that.

My line of thinking is cut short with Hannah's next question. "Anyway, how did you end up going out, then? Sounds like Strickland was cramping your style. Weasely bastard."

My insides ache as I recount my interaction with Owen in the elevator bank and tell her a little bit about our first date. It was perfect—*he* was perfect, affliction and all. And now he's gone. Hannah must be able to see on my face how much it's killing me to talk about him.

"Okay, so his freaking out," she says, reaching out to touch my arm. "It's possible that he's a total asshole and just saying he's bad for you as an excuse. From what you've said about him, it doesn't really sound like that's his game, but it could be. Door number two is that he really thinks he's doing you a favor, which means he has some sort of self-esteem thing going on or something."

I nod, even though I know with every fiber of my being that he's not just making up an excuse.

"I know it hasn't been that long, but I'm just sure it was real. Absolutely sure."

Hannah watches me for a minute, appraising me. "Okay, then you are not to give up on him. Don't let him decide what's good for you."

She hardly knows the tiniest fraction of the real story yet has somehow come up with exactly what I need to hear. If I want to take some potentially nonexistent risk to be with Owen, who is he to tell me not to? I can't just give up.

"You're right," I say. "If he doesn't want me, that's one thing, but he doesn't get to tell me what I want." Saying that out loud makes me feel fractionally better about the whole thing. It's still like my innards are being twisted around each other and burned with a hot iron, but a portion of that pain hardens into anger.

A smile inches across Hannah's face.

"Plus, Charlotte," she says, eyeing me, "I don't know what your game is like with guys, but I have to think a specimen like Owen Becker doesn't come along every day. That man looks like he stepped out of a *GQ* cover shoot."

My laugh sounds more like a choked cough.

"Strickland will be here soon, so we should get to work. But I'm taking you to lunch today. I was an RA too, so I know how much they pay you, and I know you won't turn down a free lunch."

"Thanks, Hannah."

I head to my lab station. All I have today is a mountain of tests to run — complete busywork — and I don't know how I'll survive with nothing to think about but how to convince Owen not to throw away what we have. But I like this new side of Hannah and believe more and more that she's the one person here at Genesis I can really trust.

The day goes by in slow motion. The lump in my throat doesn't budge, continually restricting my airway and making me worry I could asphyxiate at any moment. Though I've resolved by mid-afternoon to send Owen a text — after much deliberation with Hannah over whether it would be best to text or call or just show up — I now have the stress of figuring out exactly what to say. After a particularly excruciating set of pH tests, I take my phone and head to the bathroom.

Nobody is in the ladies room, so I slump down in the chair next to the mirror. My hands are shaking just enough to make typing on the touchscreen difficult.

You don't get to decide what's good for me.

Too vague. Erase.

You shouldn't have left without saying goodbye, and we are not done.

Threatening? Try again.

My butt bones are fine but my heart hurts more than I can explain.

I'm not a sap. Delete.

The only way you've hurt me is by leaving. You are not bad for me unless you are gone.

It's not perfect, but my legs are bouncing with nerves, and I can't sit here any longer trying to think of something better.

I hit send.

I wet my hands at the sink and try splashing a little water on my face to distract from the deafening silence of waiting for that little ding from my phone.

I don't have to wait long. I'm drying my hands when the message pops up:

Charlotte, you break my heart.
But I'd never forgive myself if you were hurt. I'm sorry.

The breath is sucked from my lungs, and I find myself staggering back to the chair and collapsing, the weight of rejection again settling heavily over me. Staring at his text message, my vision blurs as tears fill my eyes. Pressure builds in my chest, and I want to scream. Scream at myself for getting in so deep so fast, scream at Owen for making this decision on his own, scream at Genesis for causing his affliction, and then for introducing me to him and giving us less than ten days together. I find myself typing.

You're hurting me now.

Immediately after my thumb hits send, a rush of embarrassment piles into my torso with the hurt of loss, trying to crowd out my vital organs.

He doesn't want me. He really doesn't.

And I'm just being pathetic. As Hannah's words echo in my head, I kick myself for dismissing the possibility that he's just using this as an excuse to get rid of me.

Asshole.

I'm the last one left in the lab when I text Maddie to ask if I should pick up dinner for our night in.

When I hang my lab coat on its hook, I hear the incoming message ding.

yes pls and hurry your ass up

I know she expects a night of dishing about fun new relationship details, and a weight develops in my gut at the thought of having to explain what's happened with Owen. I could use her support, but I'm already exhausted knowing more tears are in store for me this evening.

Just as I grab my purse from my lab station, I hear a door.

It's Strickland coming out of his office. I haven't seen him all day, and since I could tell through the clouded glass of his office door that the lights have been off, I just assumed he took the day off and either forgot or didn't care enough to tell me.

He's definitely flustered. "Charlotte, hi. I'm surprised you're still here."

"Just trying to get a little ahead for the week."

Unless he slipped into his office at lunch or when I grabbed a snack in the afternoon, which would be quite a coincidence, he's been in his private lab since before I even got in this morning. His hair looks a little greasy, and he hasn't shaved. Was he in there overnight? I try to keep my face impassive, curiosity about what he's up to elbowing murky despondence into the corner of my mind.

He nods, opens his mouth like he's going to speak, and then closes it again.

Even with the pain and anger I harbor toward Owen right now, I'm overtaken with the instinct to protect him. I bite down on the inside of my lip, as something tells me whatever Strickland is up to has Owen at the center of it.

"So," I say, trying to sound as casual as I can. "Were you engrossed in one of the high-security studies? I haven't seen you all day." That's a normal thing to say, right? Maybe something a little jocular will put him at ease, enough to offer more information. "Here I am, thinking I'm a hero for staying until seven, and you haven't even come up for air."

Strickland laughs weirdly, almost like he's read from my expression that he's supposed to but didn't actually hear what I said. "Yeah, I, uh…guess I got a little caught up and…didn't realize what time it was."

It's not actually weird for a nerd to get carried away and lose touch with time for some period. It used to happen to me in the engineering lab at school once in a while—I'd look up at the clock expecting 8:00 p.m., and it would be the middle of the night. But Strickland is acting like I've caught him doing something he shouldn't be.

It's Owen's study. It has to be.

I remember my dad telling me after a high school lacrosse game that I had a talent for striking when the opponent was on her back foot, for getting a defender flustered enough that she'd lose balance for just a fraction of a second—just long enough to edge past her and put the ball in the goal. I look at Strickland, and that instinct courses through me. He at least thinks I have him on his back foot. Whether I do or not, I don't know, but I don't think it matters.

"You must have made a lot of progress," I say brightly. "Were you working on that guy Owen's samples? Must take forever to get through all those tests!" I do my best to look like I'm just making conversation, not asking him about the man who can heal from anything. The man I love. The man who left me this morning.

Strickland's cheeks flush.

"I, uh…" he mumbles, and I can see the wheels turning behind his eyes. "Y-Yeah, I was."

"Interesting." I dig around in my purse like I'm looking for something, feigning disinterest. "Get any closer to your significant discovery?" I pull my phone out and hold it up like I was more focused on finding it than our conversation.

"Uh, Charlotte, I can't…I have…I have to go." His face grows another shade redder as he walks toward the door.

I touch his forearm when he walks by me, and he stops. "Todd, are you okay? You look like you're not feeling well." I put on my best concerned face.

He stares at me vacantly for a few seconds and then seems to snap out of it. "I'm fine, thanks for asking. I will see you tomorrow. Have a good night." He lets the door slam behind him.

I spend the half-hour walk home schizophrenically jumping between wild speculation about what Strickland is up to, general misery over losing Owen, and debating just calling Owen to tell him about the strange interaction.

Eventually I decide not to call, since I've learned nothing conclusive other than that Strickland was spending time on his study, which shouldn't be a surprise. A call would also seem desperate, and if he doesn't want me, I'm certainly not going to beg. It's really just Strickland's odd behavior that has me thrown for a loop. But, nearing my building, I try to put it out of my mind; I'll need all my facilities to get through a night of dissecting my epically failed romance without telling Maddie the whole story.

As I dig my keys out of my purse on the stoop, it occurs to me that at this point I don't owe Owen anything. I could just tell her the full truth. She'd think I'm crazy, but I could do it. But I know I won't. Frustration claws at my senses when I realize I'm hopelessly loyal to a man who doesn't want me.

"Mads, I'm home!" I shout as I step through the door into our living room. "Just me this time. And two turkey hoagies with sharp provolone!" As I hear it come out of my mouth, I know she isn't going to buy my false excitement.

Maddie comes bolting out of her room in her oldest sweatpants, one of Mark's undershirts, and the huge glasses she reserves for family time only. She doesn't have any siblings and has considered me a sister since we met in Miss Lyon's second grade class. After such an intense weekend, an unbelievably hurtful morning, and a weird end to my work day, it's a relief to see my best friend, and before I can even hope to stop them, the tears start coming.

She stops dead in her tracks, examining me for a moment before running over and pulling me into a bear hug.

"I'll kill him," she says. "You tell me what that fucker did to you."

It's moderately cathartic, really, talking through the situation with Maddie. I include a few more details than I did with Hannah — going as far as telling her that it's something to do with the Genesis study that has him paranoid. She seems to assume I mean that he's sick, that he's protecting me from the pain of losing him to cancer or some other terrible disease, so I feel two little pangs of guilt—one for letting her believe something that isn't true, and another for the miniscule betrayal of even letting on that there's something serious about Owen's physical condition. I grind my teeth against the compulsion to protect this man I love, the man who has pushed me away.

After a good hour or so of relationship dissection, Maddie steers us toward lighter topics, and by the time I shuffle to my room around midnight, we've been through a bottle of Riesling, the better part of a bottle of cheap prosecco, a bag of popcorn, and a pint of cookies and cream. And the focus necessary to meticulously critique every performance on last week's *So You Think You Can Dance* did seem to take my mind at least temporarily off my ruined heart.

I'm drained enough that when I lie down in bed, the darkness of pain only has time to creep around the outer edges of my consciousness before it's all lost to sleep.

July 31st

My alarm jerks me out of a dead sleep, and it takes me a minute to realize that the splitting headache assaulting the back half of my brain is just one symptom of the hangover I've managed to inflict on myself on a Tuesday morning. I reach for the water bottle on my bedside table and gulp down its contents in an effort to battle dehydration, but the influx of fluid makes my stomach wobble.

I take a long shower, walk slowly to work, and make it to my station when the lab is about half full. Every few minutes, I have to push Owen's unreasonably handsome face from my mind, a task made no easier by the pounding in my head or intermittent waves of nausea. Plus, it's another day of simple tests — six racks of blood loom at me from the refrigerator, and the wall clock hanging over the supply cabinet just rubs in how excruciatingly slowly the day is going to go.

About an hour into it, I'm distracted by a text alert. Kyle.

How about that lunch you mentioned? 12:15?

Conflicting emotions tangle with the now fading tendrils of my headache. First to my mind is — of course — Owen and how quickly he dismissed any jealousy over Kyle over the weekend; my chest aches at the memory, at the stark contrast between the loving trust he displayed for me then and the abrupt way he dropped me. Then it's doubt — maybe the reason he showed no jealousy over Kyle was that he was never that interested in me to begin with. This thought burns, and then it's funny, smart, handsome Kyle in my head — along with Maddie's voice because I know exactly what she'd say: *Go for it! Get with that cute guy from work and get this jerk off your mind.* And then it's irritation at myself because I'd like to, but only in the hopes that seeing me with another guy would make Owen want to come back to me. Pathetic.

Pathetic or not, though, I don't have lunch plans. And if nothing else, I should try to make friends, or at least keep the ones I've managed to make already. So I text back.

Sounds good. Meet you then in the lobby?

The rest of the morning crawls by, even with a long coffee break with Hannah. By the time lunch rolls around, I debate canceling and moping with a sandwich at my desk instead, but it is an absolutely gorgeous day, and I can't come up with a good excuse.

Kyle greets me with a hug in the lobby of the Garrison — a little less warm than usual, I think, but then we are at work. And he does think I have a boyfriend.

We talk about work — complain, really, about the busywork of being an RA — while we walk three blocks to a deli nearby and then settle ourselves in the courtyard outside.

I'm almost done with my sandwich when there's a lull in the conversation.

"So," Kyle starts, his voice a bit softer than it's been, "what's the deal with this boyfriend of yours? Owen, I think you said?" He's focused on balling up the paper his hoagie came wrapped in, carefully avoiding eye contact.

I swallow my bite of sandwich, suddenly tasteless.

"I'm not sure he's my boyfriend anymore," I say, unable to keep the waver out of my voice. I fold up the last of my lunch, which has completely lost its appeal.

His eyes snap up to me. "I'm sorry. I didn't mean to pry, just curious. Never mind. Maybe we should get back?" He stands up and tosses his trash into a nearby bin, and I follow.

After a brief, slightly uncomfortable silence, we get back to talking about work.

"How's it going with your boss?" Kyle asks. "Is he really as difficult as everybody says?"

I have no trouble talking about the tough parts of working with Strickland for a few minutes, and then I ask Kyle about his boss, who seems eminently reasonable in comparison.

We're almost back to the Garrison when he asks me one more question.

"That guy Owen, he's a subject, isn't he?"

"Yeah," I say slowly. "Why?"

Kyle turns to me. "Do you know what his study is about?"

I shake my head, my mouth suddenly dry.

"I'm sorry," he says quickly, touching my arm. "I thought I saw him coming in last week, and I was just curious. I shouldn't have brought it up." Before I can think of something to say, he keeps going. "Look, whatever happened, you don't deserve to be sad. Let me buy you a drink one night this weekend."

He has a gleam in his eye now, but something strikes me as just a bit disingenuous about his tone. But then I hear Maddie in my head again. Telling me to quit being paranoid and just say yes.

"Yeah, Kyle, I'd like that."

He grins as we show the security guards our badges and make our way back to the lab. Then he hugs me again as the elevator doors open for my floor, a little tighter this time. I should be happy, I think, but as I get settled back at my station, my skin feels just slightly prickly under my clothes.

August 2nd

When my alarm sounds Thursday morning, the crushing weight of reality presses down on my chest before I've even had time to take a breath.

Three days since I've spoken with Owen. Three days since he left this bed and didn't come back. Three long and excruciatingly painful days. I walk around in a haze, robotically going through the motions of life, only able to distract myself occasionally and temporarily from the dense fog of unhappiness closing in around me.

It's another start to a strange day at work. With my misery-induced punctuality—I cannot fall back to sleep for the life of me—I arrive at work a few minutes early and find Strickland milling around my lab station.

"Charlotte, good morning!" he says, a little too enthusiastically. He's never chipper in the morning, or ever for that matter.

"Hi, Todd. Good morning." I nod toward him.

He takes a breath like he's gathering himself. "Well, Charlotte, I'm glad I caught you. First off, sorry I've been fairly unavailable this week. I hope I haven't slowed you down if you've had questions for me."

I did actually have a few, but I'm not sure where he's going with this, so I don't want to complain. "It's no problem. Hannah has been a big help."

"Ah, very good. I have something else I need to talk to you about as well. Let's step into my office."

I drop my purse on my station and follow him, sipping my iced coffee as we walk. He closes the door and motions for me to sit.

"Well, Charlotte, I think you've been doing a good job, and I'm going to be a little preoccupied on some confidential work for the next few days. I'd like you to delay the tests you'd planned to do today and tomorrow and take over as lead researcher on the Anemorin study. I think you're ready."

This is…quite unexpected. One part of me is happy—even if it's only temporary, playing lead researcher on a major study like this is a huge step, one that most RAs don't make until their second or third year at Genesis. The rest of me—the majority, really—is suspicious. Is Strickland irresponsibly passing work off on me so he can spend time on something shady? I have to think the head of research at Genesis would not approve of an RA who started less than a month ago as lead on Anemorin. I'm also nervous. I do think I'm doing a good job, but I have no reason to think I'm equipped to run lead on a big study, and it's going to be extra hard with Strickland locked in his private lab, inaccessible again. Regardless of the reason or my nerves, though, this is a big step, and I need to do a good job.

"Todd, that's…I'm surprised but very excited to take on the challenge."

"Good!" Strickland claps me on the back in a way that I think was meant to be encouraging but instead comes off as awkward. "Let me show you where I've left off."

He takes me through the study thus far, and after some questions, I at least know what needs to get done today. He tells me I can knock on his office door if there are any emergencies but that he'll come out to check on me periodically, so I should wait on any non-urgent questions. Then he disappears into his office, and after maybe ten minutes, the motion sensor light goes out. He's in his strange private lab.

Hannah is a little late this morning, and I'm immersed in the new study at my station when she walks in nursing an even bigger coffee than usual. I wave her over immediately.

"Hannah," I say. "How weird is this? Strickland asked me to take over lead on Anemorin this morning. Said he needed to work on a confidential study instead."

"Lead? That's…Well, good for you, but that's…unusual. How is it going?"

"I guess it's okay so far. I mean, I'm glad to have the opportunity, but it seems a little sketchy, doesn't it?" This is the first time I've voiced a real suspicion about Strickland to her.

She frowns. "Maybe. I really have no idea why that would be, but there must be some explanation. No offense to you, of course, but RAs just don't get lead after less than a month."

"I know." I decide to push it a little further. "Hannah, tell me this. Have you ever seen anyone go in or out of Strickland's private lab in his office?"

She looks genuinely confused. "Private lab?"

"The door behind his desk, where he works on his confidential studies, right?" I search her face, but she really doesn't seem to know what I'm talking about.

"Why do you think that's a lab? I thought all the senior guys in our pod were supposed to do their confidential research in the high-security lab past the bathrooms on the left, the one with the retina scanner."

Well, that's pretty strange. Hannah has been working with Strickland for five years and he's never mentioned that lab?

"Strickland saw me staring at that door in his office one day and told me it was a high-security lab that I wasn't allowed to go near. What did you think that door was?"

Hannah presses her lips together. "I guess I never really thought anything of it. Maybe a supply closet or something."

"He's in there now," I say. "He told me to knock on his office door if I have an urgent question on the study, but the light in there went off shortly after he went in. So either he's behind that door or he's asleep."

"Wow. I've never particularly liked the guy, no one really does, but I didn't ever think he might be up to something devious."

I bite my lip and decide to forge ahead and tell her about Monday night, when I was the last one in the lab and saw Strickland stumble out of his office. How he looked disheveled and flustered as if he thought the lab would be empty.

"Wait. Strickland was at work Monday? I didn't see him once. I even went into his office in the afternoon to leave some results on his desk. It didn't look like he'd been there." Hannah is pacing a little now.

"Yeah, I hadn't seen him either. Which, unless he really snuck by us, means he was in that room before any of us got in that morning. From the looks of him, he could have been in there a couple days."

"This is fucked up," she says. "There is no way whatever he's doing in there is above board. I'd at least have known about the lab."

"It doesn't have an ID reader on it either."

She stops pacing and looks over at me. "I have a friend in the maintenance department. My husband's second cousin. They must have floor plans, right?" Before I can even respond, she picks up her cell phone and makes a call.

"Rick, hi," she says. "Any chance I could ask you a huge favor? I'm trying to get my hands on a floor plan for my lab floor." She pauses, listening. "You are just too nice, Rick…Yes, a photocopy would be great…Thanks again."

Five minutes haven't gone by when Rick walks into the lab holding a legal-sized piece of paper. Hannah introduces me and thanks him profusely, and he's on his way.

Looking over the plan, I locate the elevators and our big shared lab pretty quickly. There are six private offices off our main lab, and before I can pick out which one Strickland's should be, Hannah slams her finger down onto the paper.

It's Strickland's office, and it looks just like the other five. A small square on the paper that's the office itself, and then a door on the back wall attaching it to another slightly larger room. There's a little square divot cut out of the room, bearing tiny photocopied letters that read *HALF BATH*. And over the remaining part of the rectangle, there is no mistaking it:

STORAGE

"Maybe this is outdated," I say. "Who knows how often they update these things. Maybe it's five years old and he's gotten approval since then to put in a lab?"

Hannah drums her fingers on the lab bench, thinking. "Well, it would've had to be before I started here, because I'd have noticed the workers coming in and out to build it. If you even move a desk in this place, the Garrison union has to do it, and to build even a small lab would be a few days' work for those guys." She pauses for a second, then picks up her cell phone.

"Sorry to bug you again. I just forgot to ask you, when is this floor plan from? I know things get moved around pretty frequently in this place." After another pause, she shakes her head at me. "Thanks again, Rick. You're the best."

She turns to me. "Updated monthly. He said the financial floors have a lot of moving around, so policy is that the whole building is updated on the first business day of each month."

"So…either Strickland lied to me about having a lab back there and is, what, napping all day in his supply closet? Or he's surreptitiously running a secret lab that Genesis doesn't know about and, for some inexplicable reason, decided to tell me about it."

"Neither of those makes any sense."

"I know."

As if summoned, Strickland appears from his office and walks up to my station. I flip over the floor plan as inconspicuously as I can.

"Everything going okay so far, Charlotte?"

"Yes. Thanks, Todd. Hannah was just talking me through how to interpret some of the pH results." I hope he doesn't ask any questions about that, because I haven't even gotten to the pH results. Hannah must be thinking the same thing, because she talks right away.

"Quite impressive, Charlotte covering lead on a big study like this so early on." She smiles at him, but I can hear a little irritation in her voice. Hannah takes her work quite seriously, so maybe she's personally offended that it appears Strickland is both working on something he shouldn't be and acting carelessly with what he should.

Yet he smiles too. "Quite the prodigy we have here," he says through clenched teeth.

"So, Todd, how is the work in your high-security lab going?" I ask innocently, doing my best to sound earnest. While I'm sure it's no mistake that Strickland hasn't told Hannah about the lab in his office, he never told me explicitly to keep it to myself. "Making good progress?"

His expression doesn't change, but his cheeks redden a shade as he looks back and forth between Hannah and me. "Yes, I, uh… well, I've kept you ladies long enough." Another forced smile, and he walks awkwardly out of the lab.

"What the fuck kind of weirdness was that?" Hannah whisper-shouts to me as soon as the door closes behind Strickland. "We have to tell Levin."

We *cannot* tell Levin. Aaron Levin runs all of research at Genesis, and the first thing he'll do is launch an investigation into anything and everything in Strickland's secret lab—including something that could expose Owen.

"Wait," I say, "let's think this through." I can't think of a way to explain to her, though, why we can't just turn Strickland in without basically begging her to ask me what Owen would have to hide. And something twists deep in my gut at the thought of Owen's secret coming out. His paranoia—real or put on—was contagious.

"Maybe we need more evidence."

Hannah rolls her eyes at me. "Charlotte, did you *see* the man's face just now? At least we know he's not going into acting after he gets fired from here."

"I'm just thinking…if there's some other explanation, like he's having some personal issues or something, and we turn him in? If he doesn't get fired, he'll make both of our lives living hell."

I'm grasping at straws here, but she puts her chin in her hand and looks pensively up at the ceiling.

"You mean like his wife kicked him out and he's living in his storage closet? And he made up some confidential lab to tell you about so he could pass his work off on you and sleep or cry or do drugs or whatever back there without any higher-ups finding out?"

"Look, I'm not saying that's likely, just that there's no hurry and we might as well give it a little time. I think he's working on something shady in there, but if there's even a chance we're wrong, we're both risking our reputations at Genesis." I'm winging it but actually starting to convince myself as well.

Hannah looks up at the ceiling again and, after a few moments, nods slowly. "I think you're right," she says. "Last thing we want as the only girls in this pod is for everyone to think we're hysterical. And given that display from Strickland, I wouldn't be surprised if he gives us something better to work with anyway."

I feel a little rush of relief at having guarded Owen's secret, even if I'm only buying time.

"Yeah, maybe we can get him flustered later and he'll give up what he's working on. For now, though, he'll know something's off if neither of us get any work done all day."

She still has her morning coffee in her hand and hasn't even been over to her lab station. "Ugh, you're right about that." She shakes her head as she walks across the lab to her bench.

It's actually a good thing I'm totally out of my depth working on the Anemorin study. It takes virtually all of my concentration just to make sure I don't totally screw it up, so I have minimal brain space to obsess over Owen, Strickland, and Hannah's potential over-involvement.

Late morning, I've hit a roadblock in my work, and Hannah isn't sure how to help. I knock on Strickland's office door, then realize I can hear him talking on the phone. It's a little bit muffled, but I can just make out the words.

"Thanks, Owen, for being willing to come in on such short notice," he says and then pauses before yelling for me to come in.

I open the door and poke my head through. He still has the phone held to his ear.

"Twelve thirty. Great. See you in a half hour." Strickland hangs up and looks up at me, a glint of irritation in his eye.

I draw a blank for a moment, the question I meant to ask gone as my mind fills only with the realization that Strickland has just scheduled an appointment with Owen — my Owen — for thirty minutes from now. My chest contracts when I picture him — in crisp gray slacks and a white button down — stepping off the elevator. Into the elevator bank where he first kissed me, drawing me in and pinning me against the door, taking me like I'd never been taken.

Strickland's voice pulls me back to the present.

"Yes?" he says impatiently.

I open my mouth to speak, but nothing comes out.

"Charlotte, what do you need?"

I rack my brain for a moment before remembering why I'm here. "The alkaline phosphatase levels. What algorithm do I use to analyze the data in conjunction with the GGT results?"

Strickland nods, motioning for me to come around the desk. His irritation is gone — or at least he does a good job of hiding it — while he explains the procedure, jotting formulas onto a piece of paper on his desk. After a few minutes of explanation, he looks up at me.

"Was there anything else?"

I stand silently for a moment, trying to come up with some way to ask about Owen, but nothing comes and I shake my head.

"Close the door on your way out."

Back at my station, my head barely contains a pressurized cloud of confusion. Scenarios dance through my mind, each one more upsetting than the last.

Owen was just in two weeks ago for samples, so Strickland shouldn't need more so soon. Perhaps he forgot one, but this seems unlikely. Could Strickland have actually isolated whatever it is that gave Owen his ability? Maybe he's planning to bring him into some sort of shady business deal. My stomach plummets and my throat constricts at the possibility that they've been working together all along. It would explain the paranoia—maybe Owen knows there really is something to be worried about because he's already involved.

I can't focus my eyes on the lab results in front of me and have just about twenty-five minutes to decide what, if anything, I'm going to do when Owen gets to the office. Part of me wants to corner him in the elevator bank and force him to see me—to *see* me—like he did that first day. And to tell him that whatever Strickland is up to doesn't matter because he and I can just leave and go somewhere far away and never look back. Even letting that thought into my mind, an image of Owen holding my hand as we board a plane with a one-way ticket, makes me feel like a pathetic idiot, and my jaw clenches.

If nothing else, I have to find out why Strickland has called him in. Because if Owen's not already mixed up in something, there's a chance his paranoia is not for nothing and he could be in danger.

I spin my wheels, coming up with no brilliant plan. I try to make the numbers and formulas in my lab notebook make sense again, but when 12:25 rolls around, I've done virtually nothing, and the tension rises through my chest as we tick closer to Owen's arrival.

I pull out my phone.

Are you coming to Genesis?

I don't know what I'm hoping to accomplish, but I hit send before I can overthink it. My knee bounces under my station as I wait for a response.

I've already stood up and headed for the bathroom, unable to contain the nervous energy, when he responds.

**Yes—Strickland called begging me to come back in.
Said he'd contaminated a sample and needed
another vial of blood. Getting to reception now.
I am dying to see you but know it's not fair to ask.**

There's a tiny smear of relief in some far corner of my mind at his response, but panic fogs my eyes and outstrips any other competing emotion. Owen could be lying about why he's meeting Strickland—and about wanting to see me—yet somehow any suspicions about his own involvement in some nefarious plot evaporate and are immediately replaced with a sense of dread so strong that my knees try to give out and send me stumbling through the bathroom door.

I know in my soul that Strickland didn't contaminate a sample. That Owen is in danger at this very moment. That I should have put our relationship—or lack thereof—aside and called him when my suspicions about Strickland went from vague conspiracy theory to almost definitely holding water.

I take a deep breath and lean up against the bathroom wall. The cold tile against my cheek jumpstarts my senses, and I know that I have to do something.

Hands shaking, I pull up Owen's number on my phone and hit call as quickly as I can. I don't know what I'm trying to stop, or how I'm going to stop it, but my sense of looming dread is so strong that I can taste it closing in around me.

Ring.

I hurry out into the hallway and head toward subject reception.

Ring.

The thought occurs to me that even if Strickland wants to hurt Owen for some reason, he won't be able to, or at least not in any lasting way, but I'm only comforted for a brief second.

Ring.

Genesis produced whatever it was that caused Owen to be the way he is, and I have no idea what Strickland has been up to—he could be concocting something that will counteract Owen's abilities for all I know.

Ring.

Voice mail.

I throw the door to subject reception open, but the room is empty. He's already with Strickland.

I swing around the desk and open the door to the hallway of the exam rooms as quietly as I can. I still have no idea what I'm planning to do and have fabricated no excuse for being back here, so I don't want Strickland to see me.

Three of the exam room doors are open, and the lights are off in each. The fourth is closed. Maybe I should just swing the door open and spew some bullshit excuse about looking for a supply we're out of in the lab. That's not believable at all, but I'm creeping toward the door anyway when I notice the rooms aren't anywhere close to soundproof. I can hear muffled male voices, and by the time I'm right outside the door, I can pretty much make out their words.

"I apologize again for asking you to come in on such short notice," Strickland is saying. "I'm usually not clumsy, but I somehow managed to knock the stand with your samples out of the refrigerator, and with the rest of the chemicals already mixed and ready to go, I'd have lost a lot of work if I couldn't replace them by the end of the day."

This doesn't make sense—I don't know of any tests where the other chemicals involved go bad within hours.

"It's no problem," I hear Owen say, my gut fluttering unexpectedly at the mere sound of his voice.

My heart is pounding out of my chest. Could I be crazy? Maybe Strickland really did ruin some samples and is just trying to replace them. Clearly whatever research he's doing with them is suspect, but it's possible he did just ask Owen here for more blood.

There's a moment of near silence—just some ruffling around—and then Owen speaks.

"Uh, Todd." His voice is uneasy. "What's that for?"

"Oh, ha, don't worry. I just need to open a new pack of needles, and I can't find the scissors in here. One of the research assistants must have misplaced them. Just going to—"

All of a sudden, there's a crash, and I hear Owen cry out. I instinctively lunge for the doorknob, but it's locked. I jiggle it and push as hard as I can, but it doesn't budge. I'm about to bang on the door, my breath fast and shallow, but I stop myself. If Strickland wanted the door locked, he's probably not going to open it for me even if I make a ruckus. And there was enough noise going on in the room when I grabbed the doorknob that he might not have noticed.

"Oh my God, Owen," Strickland shrieks. "I am so sorry! Are you okay? I can't believe I just…Here let me see…Hold pressure." He's not winning any Oscars.

"It's—I got it. Don't touch me," Owen says with an edge of anger that I've never heard before.

"Owen, I'm a doctor. Let me take a look."

"I'm fine." There's another little crash. "I said, do not touch me. You fucking meant to do that."

"Owen, let me see it." Strickland's tone is cold.

There's a brief moment of silence, then some shuffling, and another muffled cry from Owen.

"You fucking bastard," he shouts, and I hear the doorknob jiggling from the inside.

"Owen, calm down. That door locks from in here, and I have the key. You can't cover both of those gashes at the same time." A pause. "Holy shit, it already stopped bleeding!"

"You can't get away with this, Todd. I'll call the police." Owen's voice is even, but I've never heard such fire in it.

"And tell them what? Actually, Owen, I *am* going to get away with it. I know what you are, and if you tell anybody about this, anybody at all, I might…forget my subject confidentiality rules long enough to call a few papers." Strickland sounds crazed.

"And who would believe you?"

There are a few moments of uncomfortable silence.

"You can pull it down and break it if you want, but the feed is connected wirelessly to a computer elsewhere, so you can't destroy the footage."

"So you'd show the world footage of yourself slashing me—twice—with a scalpel just to, what, prove a point? What point is it that you're trying to prove, exactly?"

I'd be worried if I were Strickland—trapped in a tiny room with someone who is super pissed and essentially invincible.

"Owen, I'm not trying to prove a point." Strickland's voice is measured now. Also frightening. "I'm just asking you to be reasonable. There is no reason to involve the police, or anybody else for that matter. The camera is just to give you a little incentive to agree with me on that point. As for the police, I could have this blood cleaned up by the time anyone got here, and if I'm not mistaken, you have no evidence left on your arm. Is that correct?"

Owen's voice is soft now, simmering but maybe partially defeated. "Why are you doing this?"

"I have no interest in hurting you. But it took me twelve years — *twelve years* — to figure out what your father's team was working on. And another three to figure out why you survived the accident. I had to be sure."

"Sure of what?"

"That the original serum worked. That what I have resynthesized will work too." Strickland sounds excited, validated.

"Why did I survive the accident?" Owen asks quietly.

"I've read the file a thousand times. The blast was so strong it killed eight men instantly. There is no way a six-year-old boy should have survived. Somehow, the serum ended up in your bloodstream, and it was enough to save you from what should have been fatal injuries. I spent three years trying to isolate it in your blood, and now I have it."

That doesn't sound anything like Owen's recollection of the explosion; someone must have covered up the details of the accident. But maybe what Strickland has isolated really is what gives Owen his ability. Or maybe it's what killed the seven men who were only moderately injured but then died within hours. In that event, it might just as likely kill whomever he tries it on as enhance their healing.

"What are you going to do with it now that you have it?" Owen isn't going to bring up the inaccuracy in what Strickland just said, and I'm glad.

Strickland snorts. "Retire," he says. "Okay, I really can't thank you or your fantastic blood enough for making me a billionaire." I can hear a little shuffling around again. "But as you might guess, I have work to do ahead of some very important business next week. I think we're all cleaned up here."

I hear the door unlock from the inside, so I dive into the exam room across the hall and tuck myself out of sight. Through the little crack between the door and the frame, I see Strickland step into the hallway. Owen follows him, his face obscured, but I've never seen his posture so limp. Strickland stops, then turns toward him and extends his hand. Owen doesn't take it.

"Look, Owen, I'm sorry if my unconventional methods today upset you. But I know you've worked hard to keep that secret for all these years, and I see absolutely no reason to break that streak for you. All I ask is that you keep my secret too. At least until next week. Do we have an understanding?"

Owen hesitantly shakes his hand.

"Wonderful!" Strickland says. "Well, as always it's been a pleasure. I trust you know your way out." He nods, then disappears through the door back to the lab.

Owen has made it back to reception by the time the door clicks into place behind Strickland. He hears me bolting up behind him and turns, startled. I'm not sure he's even had time to register who it is before I throw my arms around him with all my might. He closes me into a tight hug, and I'm completely overwhelmed—by the feel of his body against mine, by his scent, by relief that he's okay, by simply touching him again after three unbelievably miserable days.

He sighs deeply into my hair. "Charlotte, I…" The unfathomable abyss between us since Monday morning drains away, the distance reduced to nothing as he pulls me so hard against him that it's almost painful.

"I'm sorry," I say into his chest. "I should have called you before… and then I got your text and tried to get you, but you…you were already in with him. I…heard everything."

I pull out of our embrace and hold him about a foot away from me by the shoulders. It's the first good look I've gotten at his face. Dark circles ring his eyes; he hasn't shaved since I've seen him, and he's a shade paler than normal. He has years on the Owen I spent the weekend in bed with. My heart aches for him, for this lovely soul haunted by an incredible ability that he never asked for.

He still has one sleeve rolled up, a few tiny drops of blood marring the crisp white fabric.

"Owen," I breathe. I gently unroll his sleeve, buttoning his cuff at the bottom. "Are you okay?"

He's watching my hands, his eyelids heavy as he looks down. "I don't know…It's…He knows."

I look up at his face, and there is real pain behind his eyes. Before I can say anything, he starts talking again.

"Charlotte, these last few days…on my own again…I can barely function." His eyes bear down on me, a little deeper set than last I saw him. "But…"

But. But he can't be with me. But I'm better off without him. But he doesn't want to hurt me.

He already has. And maybe I was right that it was never about me specifically as much as Owen just having someone to talk to. As good as it feels to be near him, as much as my skin tingles just at the thought of pressing my lips to his, I think of his note and the texts, how quickly he left me, and my cheeks flush again. I'm not ready to forgive him regardless, but I can't hear his excuses again.

"It's fine, Owen," I say, though I'm sure my tone says the opposite. My knees shake beneath me, and I lock them in the hopes of staying upright. "You don't have to explain. But you can't fix this on your own."

"This mess I'm in…I can't—"

"You don't get to decide what I do," I snap.

His gaze flashes to mine.

"I heard everything, Owen. This isn't just about you and me anymore, and you know it."

His eyes widen, and then he looks down at the floor. I've never seen Owen quite like this before—unsure, exhausted, broken. It wears at me, but Strickland's words echo in my head: *Very important business next week.* I don't have the time to let my muddled feelings about Owen get in the way. Or his fears about hurting me.

"We don't know who Strickland is dealing with," I say. "It's just a risk that we're going to have to take."

"You didn't ask for this."

I force a breath into my contracting lungs.

"Neither did you." My voice trembles over the words.

He stares into me, the blue of his eyes intensifying with every passing moment. A pang of unexpected desire runs through me. And then the door back to the lab catches my eye.

"Look, we need to talk some more and figure out what we're going to do. But it can't be here."

After a long second, he nods. "I'm going to work from home the rest of the day."

"I'll come by after work?"

He nods again, then steps toward me. I feel the heat of his body a moment before he touches me, pulling me into another hug. I melt into him, my arms wrapping around his back against my better judgment. His chest expands with a long inhale, pressing against mine, and I find myself leaning into him for a few seconds before I gather some willpower, take him by the shoulders, and push away.

He blinks a few times. "Sorry. I shouldn't have—"

"It's fine. I'll see you in a few hours." Before I have any more time to get pulled in, and before he has time to say anything else, I turn on my heel and hurry back to the lab.

The rest of the afternoon crawls by. I manage somehow—miraculously—to stay relatively focused on my work, but a lingering worry mills around my brain, and by the time six o'clock rolls around, the knot in my stomach is so gigantic that I'm not sure I'll be able to stand up straight. Strickland hasn't come in or out of his office all afternoon.

It's the thought that Owen might be in real danger that gives me the strength to actually get up and gather my things to leave.

I change into my flats in the elevator and hurry to his building. The security guy at the front desk greets me warmly and waves me over to the elevators; he must remember me from the weekend. The thought makes my heart twist—how quickly all the intimacy and fun of the weekend was displaced by such anguish.

Owen answers the door less than a second after I've knocked.

He's in his underwear—just a gray pair of tight boxer briefs—and he's dripping sweat.

The knot in my stomach all but disappears as any coherent thought fades from my mind. A drop of sweat rolls first over his collarbone, then his left pec and down over his abs, settling into the waistband of his underwear. I indulge myself for a few seconds, just admiring his expertly built physique, and then I look up at his face. Which, even still a little pale, is just as perfectly formed as the rest of him. His eyes pull at me. He's not mine, I think, and the knot comes back in full force.

"Charlotte," he says, that gravel creeping into his voice. I fight against the impulse to break at the way he says my name. He gestures for me to walk by him into the apartment. "Sorry, I meant to clean up, but I lost track of time."

I tear my eyes from his body and step into his place. The island is covered in work — binders packed with papers, loose sheets, and a notebook. There are a few dishes in the sink and Owen's work clothes are draped haphazardly over the backs of two of his barstools.

He sees me looking around.

"Sorry," he says again, picking up some of the papers on the island and stacking them neatly. "I've been a mess this week and am a little off after what happened today. I was going to work, but I couldn't concentrate, so I ended up just practicing some exercises all afternoon." He seems a little embarrassed.

"Owen," I say, putting my hand on his arm to stop him from frantically cleaning up. "It's fine."

He freezes at my touch, his eyes closing. After a few beats, he nods.

"Let me at least put a shirt on," he says, unmoving.

I stand there for a second, wondering what would happen if I pulled him to me by the hips and ran my hands over the thin material covering his package. Would he push me away, or would he let his body respond? Would I feel him hardening into my hand? But then an image of Strickland wielding a syringe pops into my head, and I remember why I'm here. I take a step back.

"Go ahead," I say, and he disappears into the bedroom.

My breath still shallow, I notice that he's moved all the furniture to the edges of his living room. There's a little crack in the ceiling above the center of the carpet. With the misery of the last few days and the drama with Strickland today, I've barely contemplated Owen's ever-increasing strength. But I find my heart rate quickening now at the thought of it.

He reappears, looking no less sexy in a thin white undershirt and pair of mesh athletic shorts. He sees me eyeing the crack in the ceiling.

"That, uh…I hit my head. But I think I can fill it with spackle and just paint over it."

I nod. My instinct is to ask him if he's okay, but of course he's okay. So then I want to ask him what he's been up to, what he possibly could have been doing to hit his head on what I'd guess is a fourteen-foot ceiling, but I stop myself. Strickland. Strickland is why I'm here.

"So," I start, forcing my thoughts to the real topic at hand. "Strickland's been acting strange all week."

I launch into a quick explanation of his erratic behavior over the last few days—staying in his lab all day Monday and maybe even the night before, how Hannah and I determined that he turned his storage room into a makeshift unsanctioned lab, the inappropriate passing off of work way past my level to give himself more time.

Owen nods through all of it. "So he's been staying in there day in and day out trying to recreate the serum my father's team made. And now he thinks he's going to sell it to God-knows-who for ten digits."

"That's what I think. What I don't understand, though, is the discrepancy between your memory of how the accident went and what Strickland seems to have read from whatever official report got filed."

He squints. "They must have wanted to cover up the fact that the serum killed all those men. Who knows why—they could have just filed it as an explosion involving toxic chemicals, but maybe that would have brought more questions. If I'm right that the serum killed my father and the others, and Strickland has managed to recreate it exactly, then I have to think whoever he tests it on is going to die." His eyes darken.

I nod. "We have to find some way to stop him. Even if he tests it on himself, Genesis will find whatever is in that back room, and he must have something back there that would give you up."

Owen nods slowly and then looks at me, his gaze soft and pained. "Charlotte, you can't put yourself in any kind of danger just so that I can keep a secret. It's not worth it, and I'd never forgive myself if you ended up getting hurt just because I don't want anyone to know what I am. It's bad enough that you're involved in the first place."

My throat constricts. I step forward and find my hands on his shoulders. His muscles are tense and warm under the fabric.

"We'll figure this out. First and foremost, we have to find out what serum Strickland has actually made, and we have to stop him from selling it. Then we'll worry about how far we go to keep your secret. I'm not going to get hurt, and we have a little time. Strickland said he's selling it next week, right? So I think the first step is for me to just figure out how to get into his little lab when he's not there, and then we can decide what to do. Maybe I can just destroy it."

Owen shakes his head and doesn't look up at me. "That's too dangerous. What if he catches you? If he thinks you're the only thing between him and a billion dollars, there's no telling what he'll do."

He's right about one thing—we really have no idea what Strickland would do if he caught me meddling. But at least he doesn't know how much I know.

"Look, Owen, we have to do something, and I have to be involved, because you can't get into the lab on your own. We're not just talking about the two of us. Maybe it's some eccentric billionaire who wants to pay Strickland for the serum so he can go heli-skiing without worry or some shit, or maybe it's a foreign government or terrorist group. And…what if he really did get it right?"

Owen looks up at me, his eyes wide. He hadn't thought that far. He's clearly a person who has a lot of control over his life—he has to, to have kept his secret this long—and he appears to be at a loss in this situation, which seems to get more and more out of control with every passing moment. He needs me, and even with everything so uncertain between us, I let myself enjoy the thought, just for a moment.

I squeeze his shoulders. "Okay," I say, "this is what we're going to do. At nine or ten, we go back to the lab. I'll pretend to have left my keys at work if anybody sees us. Your visitor pass from today should still work to get you in, and we'll figure out how to get into his office together. Until we see what he has in there, there's probably not a ton of planning we can do."

A little color returns to his face. "Charlotte…Charlie, you do impress me."

He leans toward me infinitesimally just as I take my hands off his shoulders, feeling a chill along my palms as I break contact with his body.

He blinks, and I glance at the oversized clock on the kitchen wall. 6:45. It's going to be a long two and a half hours.

"Charlotte—I'm really sorry I got you into this mess."

The intensity of his blue eyes clouds over. Before I can come up with something to say in response, he continues.

"At least let me buy you dinner."

After an uncomfortably quiet and fairly long walk to a tapas place called Bar Ferdinand, dinner is increasingly relaxed despite the tension hanging like a waterlogged tarp over our table. The pitcher of sangria may be acting to calm our nerves, though I'm barely tipsy by the time we finish it. We do talk briefly about the evening's task, but other than some very minor details, there's not much we can think of to plan until we—hopefully—see what's in that little lab.

We order several rounds of tapas, and by the time the last few dishes come, we've settled back into the rhythm of engaged conversation I'd so enjoyed over the weekend. My anger toward him for the way he left, though still clinging to life deep in my gut, has dissipated enormously. When our dessert arrives, I find Owen eyeing me over the table like he's trying to work something out in his head, and a little ember of hope lights in me.

After what feels like a good minute locked in eye contact, our almond ice cream melting on the table between us, I can't take it any longer.

"What?" I ask him.

He looks down at the table, then picks up his spoon like he was surprised to see our dessert waiting for us.

"It's just…" he starts, struggling to find the words. "This is just… nice. It's nice to see you."

I wait for more, wait for him to say something else, but just then our waiter arrives to fill our water glasses, and the moment floats away.

Owen looks at his watch.

"The check when you have a chance, *por favor?*" he says to the waiter and then turns to me, a veil of sadness already shading that energy I saw just a second ago. "It's nine fifteen. We should…" He sighs. "We should get out of here."

It's the first time I've been in a cab with Owen since our first date, consciously at least, and the memory of that short, sexually charged ride sits right at the front of my mind, taunting me, from the second he slides into the backseat after me. When his knee brushes against mine, a shiver of electricity shoots up my thigh and heats my core. I force my thoughts back to what we are about to do.

"Owen," I say. "What do we say if Strickland, or anybody else, sees us together? What are we doing out at this hour?"

When he turns to look at me, his leg shifts on the seat, and the entire length of his thigh ends up right against mine. My skin tingles.

"Well," he says, "you're going back because you forgot your keys. I think the only believable explanation for why I'm with you is that we were on a date, and I'm just making sure you get home okay."

A date. Like the one we were on when we couldn't keep our hands off each other on the cab ride home.

But he's right. I nod.

I'm not one hundred percent sure that this *wasn't* a date and almost say as much, but for once I manage to stop myself. We have too much to worry about to mix our failed relationship back into everything. With his leg against mine, though, the thought of exactly what's underneath his jeans proves too much, and my eyes close, the world around me evaporating as I'm transported back to that first time with him, completely enveloped by the imaginary sensation.

I don't know how much time has passed when the trance is broken by the cab jerking to a stop. I look out the window to see the entrance to the Garrison looming not ten yards away. The fire that was building is smothered as my mind refocuses on what we're here to do, and the floaty sensation in my middle is immediately replaced by that familiar knot.

Owen pays the cabbie and steps onto the sidewalk, holding his hand out to me. I take it instinctually, and he pulls me from the cab. With no resolution to us, no clarification of what we are, I think I should drop his hand, but I can't seem to make my fingers loosen their grip. Glancing upward at the intimidating tower of steel and glass, I give myself permission to fight that battle later and decide it's okay to lean on the one source of comfort I have at the moment.

He pulls me tight against his side as we walk the few steps to the entrance. We step through the door.

The night security guard glances at my badge and Owen's visitor pass and lets us by. Owen's pass says it's good until midnight, but Strickland could have had it deactivated, so I hold my breath as he waves it over the scanner. The knot in my gut loosens just slightly when the glass panels at the security gate glide noiselessly out of his way.

By the time we're halfway up to the forty-seventh floor, the little space between our palms is getting damp. I can't tell if it's my sweat or his. Probably both.

Owen squeezes my hand and heads for the men's room when we get off the elevator. He'll wait there for a text from me as I check the lab and see if Strickland, or anyone else, is still hanging around.

My heart races as I step into the empty lab. Strickland's office is dark.

I knock loudly three times and hold my breath. If he answers, I'll ask him if he's seen my keys. It's a bit of a stretch, but I can say I think I dropped them somewhere in the lab and thought maybe I hadn't put them down yet when he called me into his office this morning.

No answer.

I knock again and wait.

Nothing.

I press my ear to the glass and still hear nothing. I listen for what seems like a full minute, and then I wave my badge in front of the reader on Strickland's door. I hear a click as it unlocks. This is not a surprise — it's Genesis policy that RAs are given mirror badge access as their bosses, minus anything prohibited by security clearance. For those researchers who work on confidential studies, there are locking file cabinets for miscellaneous material, but work on high-security studies is supposed to be contained to the restricted-access labs.

I push the door open slowly, causing the motion sensor light to click on. Looking around, nothing catches my eye as out of the ordinary. As usual, Strickland's office is tidy and organized, with most surfaces clear of clutter. There are two neat stacks on top of his desk — one of papers that look like Anemorin results, the other unopened mail. The stack of mail is actually a little big; maybe it's been a while since he's kept up with the day-to-day.

"Todd?" I say as loudly as I can without yelling. I try to conjure a panicky tone — if I was actually worried enough about finding my keys to be looking for my boss at this hour, I'd have to be pretty frazzled. It's really not that much of a stretch.

I don't hear anything. "Todd?" I call again, and this time I walk over and put my ear to the door behind his desk. Silence. I wait, my ear pressed to the wood, and count to fifty in my head. Still nothing. Either he's not in there, or he's doing his absolute best to stay silent until I leave. I really hope it's the former as I try the doorknob. It's locked, and listening once more, I still can't hear anything.

I text Owen:

No sign of him, meet you at the lab door

Leaving Strickland's office, I drop a pen from the mug on his desk onto the floor between the door and the frame to keep it from locking. Owen is just a couple of steps away when I get to the hallway, and I hold the door open and motion for him to come in.

"The door to the little lab is locked," I say, "but I don't think he's in there."

Owen nods as we walk toward the door to Strickland's office. "You still think he has no idea anyone would try to get in, right?"

"Right. I can't see why he would. I don't think he'd even suspect anybody knows about it other than me and maybe Hannah now, but I can't imagine he'd expect her to go snooping."

"Maybe there's a key in here somewhere, then."

This seems like a long shot to me—I'm pretty sure that we'll have to use Owen's strength to break the door, or maybe take the doorknob off entirely if we're lucky. If Strickland installed the lock himself, we can at least hope he's not much of a locksmith. But we might as well look.

"Wait a second." I make a detour to my lab station. I drop my keys onto the desk, obscure them with a page of lab results, then pull two pairs of purple latex gloves from the box on my bench and grab some alcohol wipes from my bottom drawer. I don't know if Strickland would know how to dust for fingerprints or what to do with them if he did, but there's no reason to take the chance.

When I get back to the office, I carefully wipe down the doorknob and the pen I used to prop the door open—the only two things I touched, I think.

I hand Owen a pair of gloves, and he pulls them on. He starts opening drawers while I run my fingers carefully over each shelf in

Strickland's two bookcases. I don't find anything, so I start picking up and looking under each item on his desk. Nothing taped to the bottom of his stapler, nothing underneath his mug of pens. I can't think of anywhere else to look, and Owen has just finished searching the drawers to no avail.

I'm about to walk around the desk to get a better look at the doorknob when his eyes light up. He's running his hands along the underside of the desk. A close-lipped smile sneaks across his face as he pulls something free.

It's a small gold key, stuck to a piece of Scotch tape. It looks like any house key. Owen carefully peels the tape off and sticks it gently to the edge of the desk.

"Ready?" he asks, holding up the key.

I nod, and he slips the key into the lock on the doorknob. I have a moment of panic that it might be a key to something else, that my heart could be pounding out of my chest for a false alarm, but then Owen closes his eyes and turns the knob. He pushes the door slightly—maybe only a few centimeters—but it's enough to see that there are no lights on behind the door. He looks back at me. I nod again, and he swings the door open all the way.

The light from Strickland's office pours through the door, and we can see that directly in front of us is a desk with several computer screens on it. Owen steps inside, and I follow him hesitantly. I feel around on the wall by the door and find a light switch. I flick it on.

The room is not large—maybe twelve by fifteen, and to our right is the little half bath, making the lab part itself a fat L shape. To our left is a lab bench. It looks like the ones in my high school chemistry lab, only older and more beat-up. There are lots of cords and cables on the floor running in various directions and a power strip hanging out of a wall outlet next to us, jammed with extension cords. One of these runs to the back left corner of the room, where three dorm-size refrigerators are stacked. The back right corner has two metal shelving units packed with old equipment. There's a file cabinet on the back wall with papers basically bursting out of it.

The lab looks nothing like the other spaces I've seen Strickland operate in. His office is tidy, and his station in our main lab is generally spotless, but this space is messy and cluttered. The trashcan in the back corner by the bookshelves is overflowing with papers, used lab stuff like pH strips and broken test tubes, and food wrappers of all kinds. Next to the desk with the computer screens—four of them, actually—is a stack of bedding. A couple of poorly folded blankets, two pillows, and a blue rolled camping mattress. I glance in the bathroom, and in a mug by the sink, there's a toothbrush and toothpaste, a stick of deodorant and a razor. Seeing Strickland's personal items unexpectedly and completely grosses me out.

Owen has made his way over to the mini fridges. He opens the top one, and I can see from where I'm standing that there's a lot of Red Bull in it—maybe a dozen cans—and some other miscellaneous food items like a half a block of cheap cheddar and a few yogurts. Inside the second are samples—lots of samples. Most notably, there's a rack with a bunch of vials of blood, all labeled with the same tag: *Subject X.* The third fridge houses just one item, a similar rack containing only sealed test tubes of a clear fluid. I quickly count—there are five rows of six. Thirty vials.

"His serum?" Owen asks me.

"I think so."

A hard look crosses his face. "Let's destroy it."

"I think we should, but let's see what else we can figure out first. Plus, we should be careful. If it's the same thing your dad's group was making, it must be pretty dangerous."

"Good point," Owen says. "I have to be the only one to touch it. Actually when we're ready to do it, you should leave."

I don't like that idea. When it comes down to it, we have no way to be sure how coming into contact with the serum could affect him. For all we know, it could be just as dangerous to him. I bite my lip.

"We'll cross that bridge when we come to it," I offer.

Owen nods and closes the fridge.

The desk seems a reasonable next step. Unlike the one in Strickland's office, this desk is a mess. There are loose papers all over the place, some with unlabeled lab results on them, some with scribbled formulas and notes. Three open Red Bull cans sit on top of a book called *Regenerative Blood Therapy: A Stem Cell Study.* There's a spiral bound notebook with a chewed pen resting on top of it.

"Maybe this is his lab notebook," I say, picking it up. On the cover, written in black marker, it says *STRICKLAND: July 19th* with a blank spot for another date, and then the number fourteen. I look around and notice a row of similar notebooks on the top shelf of one of the metal bookcases—thirteen of them. Their edges are a little tattered, like they've been heavily used for a long time. "I think those are his old notebooks, and this is his current one." I open to the first page to find a series of equations and some chemical diagrams. Without context, it looks pretty foreign to me. I flip through the entries—all written in the last two weeks—until I find the most recent one. It's dated today. Written in all caps, it says:

SUBJECT X HEALS. PROOF OF CONCEPT. TWO DEEP CUTS WITH A SCALPEL TO THE FOREARM HEALED IN LESS THAN THREE MINUTES. THE STRUCTURE HAS BEEN CONFIRMED AS...

What follows is two and a half pages of very neat chemical diagramming. I recognize elements here and there—a couple of protein chains—but the vast majority of the structures are completely incomprehensible to me. I hold the notebook out to Owen so he can see, and as I put my other hand down on the desk, I inadvertently bump the mouse.

The four screens flash to life.

The screen on the left looks like a normal Windows screen. There's an Excel spreadsheet up on it. The other three, however, startle me. Badly.

The next screen is a video feed—of us. Looking at the angle of the shot, I realize the camera must be back and to the left of us. I whip around, and sure enough, tucked into the corner between the wall and the ceiling is a tiny security camera. The third screen is almost completely dark, but I'm just able to make out the exam table and counter of one of the exam rooms—the one he swiped Owen in today, I'm sure. And the last is a shot of our lab, from just outside Strickland's door.

My stomach basically implodes.

When I'm finally able to tear my eyes from the three surveillance screens, I can barely breathe. I turn to look at Owen, and he's still studying the screens with cold intensity. I struggle even to remember why we're here and what we're trying to do—the realization that we may well already be caught has catapulted me so far off track that I just stand there, paralyzed, completely unable to form a plan about what to do next.

Owen turns slowly toward me, his eyes fixated on the screens for a moment even after his head starts to turn. His look is one of pensive worry, not the complete and utter panic that I'm sure is written on my face. He must be able to read that I'm freaking out because he puts his hands on my shoulders and pulls me toward him until I'm just an inch or two away. His gaze locks on mine, and I think he's seeing right into my soul.

"Charlotte," he begins, and even in the midst of this emergency, something dances a little inside me at the way he softly handles my name. "We knew there was a good chance we'd get caught in here. And we don't even know that we are yet. Our goal here is still the same whether Strickland is watching us or not. At least we know he can't call security or the police on us. He'd get in more trouble than we would."

He squeezes my shoulders slightly and goes on. "You keep looking through his research while I try to at least disable the camera and figure out where, if anywhere, the footage is being sent. If he shows up, we're going to get you out of here. I'll hold him back and break the door down if it comes to it, and then I'll deal with him."

I open my mouth to protest this last part, but Owen puts a finger up to my lips before I can get a word out. The bit of heat from the pad of his pointer feels good against my mouth, and I momentarily lose my train of thought. I find my gaze has instinctively shifted to Owen's slightly parted lips, and for a brief moment, all I can think of is how that mouth should be against mine, warm and wet, soft but commanding. Maybe the best way to take care of the surveillance issue is sweeping everything from the desk in one dramatic movement, letting it crash to the floor like in the movies, and then fucking fast and hard on the newly clear surface.

I have to close my eyes for a minute to extricate this thought from my brain. When I think I may have had some moderate success and slowly reopen my eyes, Owen is still staring intently at me, but a trace of a knowing smile has crept across that gorgeous mouth.

He releases my shoulders, then pulls the swivel chair out from the desk, sinking into it quietly and redirecting his attention to the computer in front of him.

"Why don't you see if you can figure out whether what's in that fridge is all of the serum he's produced?" he suggests over his shoulder. "Maybe he recorded amounts in his notebook."

I'm grateful for the direction—that's exactly what I should be doing, but my usual practicality has not yet returned. I like this side of Owen, the one that takes charge in stressful situations and comforts me even though he has more on the line than I do. Though I guess there is some risk of bodily harm to both of us should Strickland show up, what's really at stake for Owen is his secret—his privacy—and the way he's lived nearly his entire life. I could lose the job I've had for less than a month, which seems embarrassingly trivial in comparison. And he's the one keeping it together.

This thought snaps me back to reality, and I smooth my hands over my ponytail as I walk to the large bookcase in the corner and remove notebooks ten through thirteen. I pull a rickety aluminum stool out from under the bench, plop down and begin to work backward through the most recent one.

Despite the absolutely cluttered and chaotic appearance of the lab, Strickland has actually taken meticulously detailed notes. He's recorded every interaction with or about Owen that he's had, always referring to him only as Subject X. He has even noted the interactions he's had with me regarding Owen—referring to the day he ran into us in the exam room hallway as a "close call" and noting that there seemed to be some kind of "flirtation or friendliness" between Owen and me that he "will be sure to follow up on."

I grab a pad of Post-it Notes from Strickland's desk, making a mental note to replace it with a fresh one, and flip rapidly through the pages. It's fairly clear to me which entries are from days of actual lab work and which are just observations or general notes, and I start marking the lab days with the sticky notes.

I have about fifteen tabs with scribbled notes on them sticking out of the notebook when I begin to really piece together the timeline of events. I recognize some of the diagramming, at least in the context of Strickland's work, and I can see a pattern emerge as the dates start to come together.

"Owen," I say, my nose buried in the pages, "I think I figured out when he isolated the formula. There's an entry here from the end of June where he's diagrammed the same structure that's in the one from today."

The version from June isn't as neat—there are lots of parts scribbled out and other components squeezed into the margins. Today's entry seems to be what Strickland must think is the final version.

"So," I continue, "from what I can tell, he spent most of the last month trying to synthesize that formula. I am fairly certain that's the serum in the fridge."

Owen has gotten up from his post at the desk and now hovers behind me, his hand on my shoulder as he leans over me to follow along in the notebook. I can feel the heat from his body, and my mind clears just for a second when his stomach brushes my upper back.

"The only thing is," I say, pointing down at the page in front of me, "it looks like he should have made thirty-six vials in this inaugural batch."

When I look up at Owen, he's staring at the little fridge across the room before his eyes snap to mine.

"There are only thirty vials in the fridge," he says slowly.

"There are only thirty," I repeat numbly. "We're missing six."

Neither Owen nor I can come up with any way to account for the missing serum, and after a few minutes of fretting unproductively, we decide to just ignore it for now and focus on the surveillance issue.

He seems to have successfully erased the footage from outside Strickland's office of us coming in. He's managed to loop in some video from right before we got there instead, and when he plays back the transition for me, I can't even pick out exactly when it is.

"What I can't tell," Owen says as he begins to cut out the footage of us poking around the lab, "is whether or not the raw video is being recorded anywhere else. But if I'm editing the only copy, he'd have to be watching in real time to see us."

"So, the faster you cut us out of that tape, the less likely he is to know we were here, right?"

"I think so," he says, leaning toward the screen and clicking away.

I busy myself searching for the missing six vials of serum. My instinct tells me they're not in the lab—that he's taken them elsewhere for safekeeping—but staring over Owen's shoulder at the screen is just making me antsy, and there is no reason not to at least look. I do a pretty thorough once-over, moving equipment around, pulling books from the shelves, and taking every item out of each little fridge, making sure to place everything back exactly where I found it. I've all but exhausted the potential hiding places when I run my hands along the underside of the lab bench and come across something cold and hard—Strickland has hidden what feels like a metal box under there. My breath catches in my throat.

A glance in Owen's direction tells me that he's not done with the video yet. He's still completely immersed in his task, and as the surveillance issue is certainly the most time-sensitive problem we're dealing with, I decide not to disturb him.

I slip quietly off the stool and shimmy underneath the lab bench. Leaning back, I can get a good look up at the object attached to the underside of the table, a small metal lock box, maybe eight inches long, six inches wide, and four inches deep. It takes me a moment to notice that Strickland has actually secured two clamps underneath the bench to hold the box in place. It's removable.

I put one hand against the box, steadying it carefully while I try to release the clamps with the other. The first clasp snaps open easily, but the other is a little sticky, and my heart pounds against my ribcage as I try to jiggle it free. If the serum is anywhere near as dangerous as we fear, the last thing we need is a shattered vial. After a few nerve-racking moments, the clamp pops open and the weight of the box falls into my hand. Nothing sounds broken or feels wet, so I slide out from under the table and stand up, placing the box on the lab bench.

I stand paralyzed for a moment while I work up the courage to open it, pleading silently that what's inside is the missing serum and that I'll be able to announce this victory to Owen right as he finishes erasing the evidence that we were here. This could be perfect—we destroy all the serum and Strickland doesn't know we were here, so we buy ourselves some serious time to come up with a way to stop him from making more. This optimistic thought gives me the extra push I need, so I pop open the latch on the box.

That is certainly *not* serum.

For a second, I'm not sure if I'm going to laugh or vomit. A giggle escapes my throat before I can stop it.

"What's funny?" Owen asks.

"It's nothing…Well, just tell me when you're done with the footage."

"Almost done. Two minutes," he says, turning his attention back to the computer.

Thank God. Hopefully I can stay sane for two more minutes.

It's really not funny. It's ridiculous. In the span of a few weeks, I've gone from being a bright-eyed young scientist, whose biggest problems were boring lab tests and a cranky boss, to this. To breaking into said boss's secret lab. To dating, or not dating, I don't really know, a man — a very sexy man — who can heal from what should be a fatal wound in minutes, an absolute medical impossibility. To trying to stop my boss from selling some janky serum that does God-knows-what to God-knows-who. And now, to staring down into what I'm almost positive is a small but potentially powerful bomb.

As the gravity of the situation starts to sink in, a heavy blanket of dread settles over me and the brief moment of levity over the absolute absurdity of it all is gone as quickly as it came.

Peering down into the box, I study its contents as carefully as I can without touching anything. Against the left side is an old-school flip phone. It's sitting on top of a rectangular black case, which, on further inspection, appears to be a battery — Strickland must have wired up some special long-life battery to replace the phone's original one. The right-side panel of the phone has been removed, and there are three tiny wires connecting its innards to a plastic microchip on the right side of the box. The microchip is fastened to a device with two clear cylindrical chambers connected by a little tube with a valve in it. One of the chambers holds a cloudy liquid, and the other has a bluish tinge to it. I don't know much about bombs, anything really, but instinct tells me exactly what this is — a homemade remote-controlled explosive device. A signal from that cell phone activates the chip, which then causes the valve to open, the fluids to mix, and a little bit of heat from a current in the exposed wire running through the connector tube sets it off.

I don't know what the substances are, so I don't know how powerful an explosion this thing could reasonably produce, but I do know that Strickland is a very accomplished chemist. If anyone could make a bomb small enough to fit in this little box but strong enough to blow up the entire lab, or the entire floor for that matter, it's Strickland.

I'm thinking through how quickly we could get out of the building when Owen's voice interrupts my thought.

"That should do it," he says triumphantly. "Let's just hope he hasn't been watching these feeds for the last half hour. I believe the evidence is gone as long as he didn't see it real-time."

A corner of that thick layer of dread lifts at this news. If he was planning to blow up the lab with any intrusion, he probably would have already done it. Hopefully we at least have time to get the box remounted under the desk, grab the serum, and get out.

"Owen," I start, and I can tell by the way his eyes shoot to mine that he can read the panic in my voice. "We need to get out of—"

"Is that…" He's eyeing the little box now.

"A bomb. I think so. I'm going to put it back where I found it. You get the serum, and let's go."

Owen stands there dumbfounded for a second but then snaps to attention, nods, and strides quickly to the little refrigerator. With his back toward me as he opens the fridge door, he asks, "Do you think all he has to do is call that cell and it…goes off?"

"I'm not sure. It could be that or a text, maybe a text of a specific word or something," I ramble as I slide back underneath the lab bench.

Focused on carefully clamping the box back in place, I don't even hear the door.

"Actually Charlotte, you're right. Just a text of one word and this whole place goes. *Blow*. Fitting, isn't it?"

I'm so startled by Strickland's voice that I crack my head on the leg of the bench trying to get out from underneath it. I'm stumbling to my feet when he grabs me.

"Now, Owen," he says, and I feel a tiny prick on my neck—a needle. "You're not going to take another step closer. Unless you want your dear little girlfriend to become my first test subject. I know you're stronger and faster than I am and have no reason to fear bodily harm, and that's great and all, but I can have this needle deep into her jugular before you even touch me."

Owen slowly sets the rack of test tubes on the bench between us and puts his hands up in front of him.

"Todd, you don't want to do that," he says, a barely noticeable quiver in his voice. "Charlotte has nothing to do with this. It's between you and me. I put her up to getting me in here. Let her go and the two of us will work this out."

Strickland shifts, and I can't keep from wincing when the needle pokes slightly farther into my neck. Owen's eyes widen as he stands staring at me, frozen in place. He can't use his energy worrying about me right now, so I nod slightly, mouthing the words *I'm okay* in an effort to calm him and help him focus on the task at hand—on getting us both out of this mess. This rigged-to-blow mess with a literal mad scientist ready to inject what may well be a lethal serum into my neck.

"While it does not surprise me, Owen, that you're able to convince impressionable young women to do whatever you damn well please," Strickland says, an edge of disgust in his voice, "it seems to me that Charlotte involved herself pretty deeply the second she decided to break into my office." He tightens his grip around me.

Owen looks back and forth between Strickland and me and opens his mouth to speak, but I cut him off.

"Todd, if that serum really does what you think it does, shouldn't you be testing it on yourself, not me? If you use it on me, you'll be stuck in a room with two people who can overpower you and can't be harmed. If you use it on yourself, nobody can stop you from doing what you want." I know this is a risk, but it's clear to me that Strickland never thought through what he'd do in this situation. If he had, he'd be holding a gun to my head, not threatening to stick me with a needle. I can tell by the way he huffs that he's actually thinking about what I said.

"You think it won't work. You would only say that if you didn't think it was going to work." There's a nervous anger in his voice, an instability that makes me think he could go in any direction. Including trying to grab the serum, run, and then trigger the cell phone bomb.

"Honestly, I have no idea if it's going to work or not," I say, trying to sound as earnest as possible. "But if you've promised this thing to someone for ten digits, I can only assume you'll be in some pretty deep trouble if it doesn't. Either way, it doesn't benefit you to have me involved, or Owen for that matter." Owen's eyes flicker to Strickland for a moment when I pause and then back to me. The almost imperceptible nod of encouragement he gives me is exactly what I need to press on. "Listen, Todd, you are a good researcher and a good man. I think you may have just gotten a little bit over your skis on this. If you're in some kind of trouble already, the last thing you need is to end up in jail for hurting one of your employees."

I'm not positive this makes sense, but I need to keep him thinking, and I know if he lowers the needle even for a fraction of a second, Owen will be able to get between us.

"I can't let you leave here knowing what you know." The needle digs farther into my skin.

"You're no murderer, Todd. We both know that," I say, feigning confidence. I don't think he'd kill me, but when it comes down to it, I have no idea what he'd do for a billion dollars. "And I can never tell anyone about this anyway. To do that, I'd have to admit that I broke into an area of Genesis that I wasn't cleared to be in. I need this job."

Owen takes a step closer to us.

"Todd," he says quietly but evenly, "just let go of her, and we'll leave."

Strickland takes a couple of somewhat labored breaths behind me, and the few moments of silence pass like hours.

It seems he's bought my argument, though, because after an absolutely excruciating silence, he lowers the needle from my neck and takes a small step back. Owen is between us before I can even register what's happening. He pushes me behind him, blocking me with his body and leaving one hand on my hip. The front of my body is right up against the back of his. I've never been protected like this—never needed to be protected like this—and having my chest pressed against Owen's back both reassures me and makes me want to tear his shirt off with my teeth. Strickland's voice interrupts that inappropriate thought.

"So, Owen," he says, his voice wavering a bit, "why are you here?" He's placed himself between us and the door and is holding the syringe out in front of him, vaguely aimed at us like he can't decide if it's a magic wand or a weapon.

I feel Owen's chest expand as he takes a deep breath.

"Todd, you of all people know I've been living with this secret for most of my life. Do you think that's been easy for me? Today you told me you know why I'm this way. I'm here looking for answers." Owen's voice sounds strong and confident—he's selling it well.

"You're trying to steal my serum," Strickland rasps.

I tremble against Owen's back.

"I wouldn't wish this on anybody," Owen snaps. I know he's trying to convince Strickland that he's here just for information and not the actual formula, but this statement sounds sincere. For Owen, it's not a fun party trick or an amazing miracle of biology; it's the shameful secret that has isolated him for most of his life. What's kept him from playing sports, from having close friends, from dating.

Strickland squints at him.

"I live a quiet life," Owen continues, his voice steady now. "I make decent money, and I've learned to manage my ability in a way that lets me live fairly normally. You think I'd put that at risk by getting into bed with the kind of people who would buy this sort of thing? Not that I'd know how to find them anyway."

Strickland looks down at the floor and then back up at Owen. "What am I supposed to do then?" He runs his hands through his greasy hair and slumps back against the desk behind him. "I can't have people out there knowing what I've done." He fiddles with the syringe in his hand and looks up at Owen with confusion and, I think, pain in his eyes.

I find myself actually feeling sorry for him—his rapid transition from needle-wielding tough guy to lost scientist only emphasizes how absolutely in over his head he must be.

"Todd, how about you take what you need to take, and the three of us walk out of here together," I venture. He seems like he's breaking down and really just unsure of what to do. "And then you trigger the bomb. It will look like a freak accident in a storage closet, the evidence will be gone, and you know the two of us will never say anything again. Owen's not about to expose the secret he's kept all these years, and I wouldn't put my own career in jeopardy over it."

He seems to actually listen and nods a little. In this unsure state, he's like a completely different person, small and vulnerable.

"But I can't destroy the lab unless I know it works. If I bring them serum that doesn't do what I told them, they'll kill me." His voice is quiet as he inspects the floor. "We could…" he starts, his eyes on me.

"No," Owen says. "You don't touch her. I swear to you, Strickland, you come one step closer with that and you won't need to worry about your buyers coming after you."

I press my body tighter against Owen's back, squeezing his shoulder.

Strickland's eyes are vacant, bouncing around the room with no obvious destination. After a few seconds, he opens his mouth to speak, freezes for a second, and then closes it. His pupils are dilated, and he raises the tiny syringe, his thumb on the plunger.

I try to yell out to stop him, but before I can force a sound from my paralyzed vocal chords, Strickland jams the needle into his thigh, right through his wrinkled khakis, and pushes the plunger all the way down. The clear liquid vanishes into his leg.

He looks up at us, eyes ablaze with nervous excitement. Owen and I both stand frozen, and nobody says anything for what feels like several minutes.

I find myself actually hoping the serum works — I'm pretty sure it's either that or Owen and I watch Strickland die right here and now.

My curiosity gets the better of me, and I step out from behind Owen to get a better look. Strickland looks back and forth between the two of us.

"So," he says, focusing on Owen, "what happens now?"

"Todd…I was six…I really don't know. I didn't notice any change until weeks after the explosion."

I'm glad he doesn't bring up what happened to the other researchers. If it's going to happen to Strickland, it's too late to do anything about it now.

"How did you find out?" Strickland asks, the unfriendly tension in the room all but gone, a buzz of agitation in its wake.

Owen begins to tell the story about skinning his knee, but within a few sentences, the color drains from Strickland's face.

"Todd, are you okay?" Owen asks, interrupting himself.

"Yeah…I think…I maybe just need to sit down," he replies and crumples into his desk chair.

Owen looks at me, hopeful for some kind of direction, but I'm just as lost as he is.

"I'm not sure there's anything we can do," I whisper to him.

I wish there was—I really do—but we can only watch in stunned silence as Strickland's face gets paler and paler. Some beads of sweat appear around his hairline, and he wipes at them clumsily with the back of his hand. He leans over to put his elbows on his knees, his head resting in his hands, and his breathing has become labored and audible.

We both automatically lunge to catch him when he topples forward out of his chair. We lay him as carefully as we can on the floor, and when I ask him what we can do, it's clear he can't hear me.

"Why is this happening so fast? I thought it would take hours given what happened to my dad," Owen says to me over Strickland's now-seizing body.

"Maybe if a trace of serum from a shard of glass was enough to cause what happened to your father, a syringe full is enough to do it in minutes?" It's the only explanation I can come up with, but the fact of the matter is I have no idea. "Should we call someone? Should we call nine-one-one?"

"I—I'm not sure how they could help him." Owen puts two fingers under Strickland's jaw. "They won't know what to do, and… and I can't find a pulse. He's not breathing."

Some instinct kicks in within me, and I'm suddenly filled with adrenaline—pulled out of my stunned helplessness. In moments, I'm straddling Strickland and performing the best CPR I know how. I've practiced it many times in classes, but this is the first time I've done it in real life. After a few chest compressions, a rib breaks. I remember learning in my CPR course that this is normal—necessary even—but it still startles me, and the snapping sound turns my stomach. After three breaths into Strickland's lungs, I'm nearly thrown off him when he sputters back to life with a coughing fit.

I scramble off and kneel at his side.

"Todd, can you hear me?" I shout into his ear.

He looks up, his eyes focusing on mine for just a moment, and his hand latches onto my forearm with a surprisingly strong grip.

"I'm…I'm sorry. Destroy it. Destroy it all," he whispers before devolving into another coughing fit. I can't tell when exactly the coughing stops and the seizure starts, but soon he's convulsing on the floor. I grab a blanket from the pile of bedding next to us and stuff a corner of it into his mouth in a vain attempt to keep him from biting off his tongue.

When the shaking slows, Owen checks for his pulse again, shaking his head at me, and tears spring to my eyes. I frantically climb on top of Strickland again and start chest compressions, but I know it's futile. I can't help myself from keeping at it for a few painful seconds before rolling off him — off the body — and into Owen's arms, sobbing uncontrollably. Owen hugs me tight to him and whispers into my hair.

"It's okay, Charlotte. We're going to be okay."

When I finally get my tears under control, Owen picks me up and sets me on my feet like I weigh nothing. Then he takes my face in both hands. My vision is still blurry, but the sight of his concerned eyes, even through the haze of salty water, transports me out of this nightmare scenario, just for a moment.

"Charlotte, we have to get out of here," he says, looking right into my eyes, urging me slowly back toward reality.

I nod in agreement and turn to look at the rest of the room. It's the first time I've really looked around since Strickland arrived, and seeing the rack of test tubes containing the lethal serum somehow plucks me out of the last of my emotional daze. I know exactly what we have to do.

"His phone," I say. "We have to take his phone."

Owen freezes. "You want to set off Strickland's bomb."

"We don't have any other choice. This — all of this — has to go." Strickland's strangled last words echo through my head: *Destroy it. Destroy it all.*

"But…" He's clearly trying to think of another option.

"Even if we managed to get the serum out of here and destroyed without hurting anyone — and that's a big if — there's too much in here that could give you away. The notebooks, the computer, who knows what else. It all has to go."

"You should go to the director of research, tell him what happened."

I take him by the shoulders.

"Owen. I am not going to risk that any information about you, about what you can do, falls into the wrong hands. It will look like an accident. Help me find his phone."

He squeezes his eyes shut. "You don't have to do this. He almost killed you tonight."

"He didn't." I kneel down and run my hands over Strickland's pockets looking for the phone. "I'm fine, but I won't be if something happens to you. It's the only way."

He nods slowly, finally accepting that I'm not going to change my mind, and when he sees me struggling to roll Strickland over to check his back pockets, he bends down and quickly flips the body. There's a rectangular shape showing through his right back pocket.

Owen seems to be on board now, and he grabs the serum, placing it on the lab bench directly over the metal box's hiding place. I like his idea and stack Strickland's notebooks next to the serum. When I turn around, he's pulling out the cables from the back of the CPU tower under the desk. Once it's all unhooked, he pulls the computer out and lays it down on the floor directly under the bomb.

"Let me just make sure the number is in here." I open the contacts folder on Strickland's phone. There aren't very many entries, maybe thirty or so. I recognize a few names from Genesis—a couple of the other senior researchers and a few people from our lab. Scrolling down, a name catches my eye.

"Project X," I say. "That has to be it."

"Well," Owen says, grabbing my hand and leading me toward the door, "let's hope so because we're certainly not going to test it."

Stepping out of Strickland's office and back into the lab is surreal. It looks exactly as we left it, like we've completely shut the door on the ridiculous turn of events we just endured. Like waking up from a bizarre nightmare to find yourself safe in bed.

When I reach my lab bench to pick up my purse and uncover my keys, I realize I still have Strickland's phone in my hand, and the brief moment of post-nightmare calm is ripped away from me instantaneously. Owen must be watching my face, because right at this moment, he lightly grabs my arm and pulls me into a tight hug.

"You can still change your mind," he says, and I pull away to look at him. "You don't have to—"

I plant my lips right on his. The nightmare is pushed, just for a moment, to a remote corner of my mind as Owen's tongue finds its way into my mouth. I allow the indulgence for a few seconds longer than I should, and my body starts to respond. His hand is moving down my lower back when he begins to harden against my stomach, and I know I have to pull away. In my state of emotional fatigue, I know I'll be powerless to stop if I let this go on even a second more.

I push Owen away by his shoulders. He looks confused, maybe even hurt, just for a moment, then shakes his head slightly as if to physically snap himself out of it.

"Sorry, I…" He stares at my lips, and my heart takes a little leap at the thought that I have the power to make this man forget where he is and what he's doing with just a kiss.

"I know." I grab his hand and pull him toward the door. "We need to get out of here."

We're still holding hands when we get to the elevator, palpable sexual tension between us, like all the fear and nervous energy, all the emotion of the last hour has been converted straight to lust.

"Charlotte, can I see the phone?" he asks, breaking my escalating thoughts.

I hand it to him, and he begins tapping on the screen.

"What are you—" I start, and then think better of it. I'm sure there's a camera in this elevator, and it could have sound. "Never mind."

Owen must be on the same page, because he nods and drops the phone into his pocket.

I am hyper-aware of my surroundings as we walk through the lobby; I try to act as normal as possible, but even though neither of the night security guards even looks up, I feel like everybody is watching us. The privacy of Owen's apartment really cannot come soon enough.

I look around when we get outside, and nobody is within earshot. Fear briefly flashes through me that he somehow deleted Strickland's contacts, thinking he was protecting me.

But before I can even ask him what he was doing on the phone, he says, "I turned off the GPS," and grips my hand. "In case there's enough left of the lab for them to figure out how the explosion happened, it's better if they can't find the phone. Even so, we should wipe it down and get rid of it as soon as we send the text."

"You're right. And we might as well send it from a public place, just in case there's still some way to locate where the signal came from."

I've never really tried to get away with something before — at least nothing that would warrant more than a slap on the wrist from my high school advisor. I am way out of my depth here. But there's no way I'm risking Owen being exposed or someone else picking up where Strickland left off, so we're sending that text one way or another. We'd just really better think it through first.

"We should wait a few hours to do it," I say as we practically speed walk in the direction of his place. "They'll have us swiping in around nine thirty, and presumably on the elevator camera as well." I pull my own phone from my purse to check the time and can't believe it's only eleven. It feels like we were in the Garrison for a week. "We'll have to come up with some believable explanation for being in the lab for an hour and a half, and the more time between us leaving and you-know-what, the better."

Owen bites his lip and looks at me. "Has to be before anybody else is likely to come into work tomorrow morning. We can't risk someone else getting hurt if that device is strong enough to damage more than just Strickland's area. When do you think is the earliest someone could be in?"

I think for a second. "Nobody in my lab is in before eight. I'm not sure about the other labs, but I doubt anybody comes in before six. Maybe before five?"

We're coming up on a group of twenty-somethings talking and laughing. I can't imagine anybody piecing together what we're talking about, but paranoia gets the better of me.

"Let's figure the rest out upstairs," I say before Owen has a chance to respond, and he nods in agreement.

We spend the next hour or so going over our story: why we were at Genesis, what we spent ninety minutes in the Garrison doing, what I'll tell the higher-ups about Strickland's erratic behavior, and what I will and will not share with Hannah. Owen makes us a turkey sandwich to split, and by the time we're done eating, I'm fairly comfortable that we've come up with a pretty believable story given the unbelievable circumstances.

I look at the clock in the kitchen and it's about 12:30 a.m.

"We should probably try to sleep a little," I say, though I'm not sure that's possible. My body is spent, and I'm completely drained emotionally, but I'm not sure the residual worry in my belly is going to allow me any real rest.

Owen doesn't stand up. "Do you want me to sleep on the couch?" he says, uncertainty in his tone.

I close my eyes. I don't want to go to sleep without some idea of what's going on between him and me, but I'm not sure I have the strength for another difficult conversation tonight.

"No, Owen, I don't."

I open my eyes to find him looking down at his fidgeting hands in his lap.

"I've already dragged you into such a mess."

"We're both in this mess, and you didn't cause it. Your ability may have, but you didn't cause that either." In a way he is right—being with someone as different as Owen is not without risk. But I'm already in too deep, and his unbelievable ability has only drawn me to him further. This man, this beautiful, sweet man, is a masterpiece of scientific art, a walking breakthrough in medical science. "I'm not afraid of being with you. But if you don't want me, you're just going to have to tell me, because I'm not accepting you pushing me away for my own good any longer."

His eyes snap up to mine, a worry in them that I haven't seen before.

"Is that what you thought?"

I take a breath, the beginnings of relief sprouting within me at his reaction.

"I had the best weekend of my life with you, and then I woke up and you were gone," I say. "I didn't know what to think. Of course it crossed my mind."

"God, Charlotte, no." He reaches over the island and pulls my hands into his, his grip warm and strong. "It was the best weekend of my life too. I've never wanted anything as much as I want to be with you."

My heart thumps against my ribs as the last of my anger toward him drifts away, my forgiveness complete.

"Then why?"

His eyes burn into me. "I'm not normal, and I never will be. It will always be something, whether it's Strickland or my own strength or something else, and you don't deserve that."

A giggle pops out of me, unexpected.

His brow creases. "What?"

"Owen, I *know* you're not normal," I say, exercising a bit of restraint not to call him Captain Obvious. "And I knew you were different before I knew what you could do. But what makes you think I want normal? And why should you decide what I want? You at least owe me enough respect to let me make my own decisions."

He rubs the backs of my hands with his thumbs, the touch sending a tingle up my forearms. It's a few seconds before he speaks again.

"Knowing everything you know about me, you'd really still want to be with me?" His tone is unsteady. "I'm not good at this."

I inch toward him. "Yes." I pull one hand free and cup his jaw, his stubble tickling my skin. "God, yes." I kiss him lightly on the lips, careful not to linger too long.

"You're the smartest, most capable person I know. If it's really what you want, then I guess I have no choice but to let you decide for yourself. There's never been any question that I want you."

I pass my finger over his lower lip, and his mouth opens slightly as his eyes close. He presses his eyelids together and shakes his head slowly.

"What?" I ask.

When his eyes reopen a moment later, there's a clarity in them, his confidence returned.

"It's just," he says, standing and closing the small gap between us, "a relief. I was ruined without you these last few days. Knowing you exist and not having you—it's devastating. But I realize now that I don't necessarily know what's best for you…and that I at least owe you the respect of letting you decide what you want. It's like a huge weight has been lifted."

My lower eyelids moisten, just slightly, and I stand up, pressing my body closer to his. His arms wrap around me, and I collapse into him, burying my face in his chest.

"Come on." He lifts me off the floor in one smooth movement. "Let's get a few hours of rest."

Owen carries me to the bedroom, setting me gently on the bed before warmly undressing me. He picks an old, soft tee from his top drawer and lifts my arms, pulling the shirt down over my head. His own clothes end up in a pile at the end of the bed when he strips down to his underwear, but I don't even get a good look at him before he has both of us under the covers. He spoons me tightly and kisses the side of my neck.

"Good night, my Charlotte."

August 3rd

The alarm wrenches me violently out of a dead sleep at 4:00 a.m. My stomach drops immediately when the unavoidable reality of today comes rushing to the front of my mind. Owen is sitting up in bed next to me, and he leans down to kiss me lightly on the lips.

"Coffee?" He brushes a piece of hair from my forehead.

My spirits lift just slightly at his touch. I nod.

Owen hops out of bed and walks toward the door. I can't help but stare after him, the ideal male triangle. Broad, square shoulders, an exquisitely muscled back, slim hips with an ass that makes me want to pull him back to bed and never leave.

When he returns a minute later with two steaming mugs of coffee, my eyes are immediately drawn to the impressive package between his legs. He still has a trace of morning wood, just slightly visible through the thin fabric of his boxer briefs.

"Charlotte, if you keep looking at me like that, we'll never get out of this bedroom."

On any other day, I'd take that as an invitation to show him exactly what I'm thinking about doing to him, but we have a rough task ahead of us. Owen hands me the coffee as I force my eyes from his crotch and pull myself out of bed.

I dig around in my gym bag and pull on yesterday's leggings and running tank while he dresses too.

"Clean socks?" Owen asks from behind me, handing me a pair of short sport socks. He looks as hot as ever in a paper-thin gray

Stanford tee, and I smile to myself at the small intimacy of having something of his against my skin—even if it's just socks.

Within a few minutes, my coffee is finished, my teeth are brushed, and my running shoes are tied. I carefully tuck Strickland's phone into the little pocket in my waistband. When the cool glass back of the iPhone touches my stomach, a shiver runs through me at the thought of what we are about to do.

I wouldn't call myself a rule follower—sometimes I bend the rules or choose to disregard particularly mundane ones—but this will be by far the riskiest thing I've ever done. I didn't build the bomb or operate a rogue lab in my supply closet, but I did break into my boss's office, I didn't alert anyone when he died, and now I'm about to knowingly activate a device that will blow up some undetermined amount of Genesis labs.

Owen must notice I'm ruminating, because he comes up from behind me, wraps his arms around me, and buries his face between my shoulder and neck.

"You know you can still—" he starts, but I can't let him finish.

"I'm not going to change my mind." I turn my head toward his. "Strickland cut you with a scalpel just to prove he was right about you. Who knows what someone else could do if they thought they could get at what you have."

"Do you want me to take the phone at least?" He rubs his hands slowly down my upper arms. "You shouldn't even be in the middle of this."

I turn around to face him and wrap my arms around his waist.

"Neither should you." I stand on my toes so I can kiss him. "We're in it together."

I kiss him again, this time letting my lips part slightly when he responds. He traces my lips slowly with his tongue, and blood starts flowing toward my core. I allow the heat to pool for a few seconds before I pull away.

"Let's get this done," I say, my eyes still focused on Owen's mouth for a moment. "It'll be over fast."

We're holding hands when we cross the street into the center of Rittenhouse Square. It's still dark, but the beginnings of pre-dawn light creep into the purple morning sky. It's quiet but not deserted—walking to the gazebo in the middle of the park, we're passed by a competitive-looking runner in a Philadelphia Marathon tank, and two people are taking dogs for their morning bathroom breaks in the grass.

My hand is shaking when I pull out the phone. I really have no idea what to expect—we're a good five blocks from the Garrison, and I don't even know if we should hear something from this distance or not. I also have no concept of how powerful Strickland's little device is meant to be—I'm sure from its size that it can't level the Garrison or anything, but I don't know if it will take out just his little lab, my entire pod, or even the whole floor. And who knows if it will even work. Knowing Strickland, it should, but I hope for at least some small confirmation so we can move on to the second step of our plan—to wipe down the phone and drop it into the Schuylkill River.

Owen still has a firm grip on my left hand, which he squeezes reassuringly. The warmth of his body brushing my side is a comfort, but it still takes all the energy I can muster just to move my thumb across the surface of the iPhone. As I select *Project X* from Strickland's address book, I notice Owen's breath has become just slightly audible—he's nervous too.

My hands are still shaky, so it takes me three tries to type out the one-word text message. As soon as I type the W, I read the word one last time on the screen to make sure it's right.

BLOW

I don't allow myself any time to think.

I just hit send.

I listen so hard for some sign of an explosion that the little chime on Strickland's phone indicating the text has gone through nearly causes me to jump out of my skin.

I've barely gotten my breathing back under control when I hear the boom.

It's not deafening—if I heard it on any other day, I'd suspect a SEPTA bus had backfired or that perhaps it was a gunshot muffled by a few buildings. But the timing is too perfect, and in the quiet of the pre-dawn summer morning, I know in my gut that it worked. Strickland's bizarre cell phone bomb worked.

I'm almost numb, a strange sort of bleak quiet settling over my mind. I don't even notice that I'm emotional until a tear drips onto my cheek. Owen wraps me in a tight hug, and the tears come faster as I bury my face in his chest.

"It's okay," he whispers into my hair. "It's over."

I sob quietly into his pecs for a few seconds, not even sure what exactly has triggered my reaction. It's a lot of conflicting emotion—relief that it seems to have worked, sadness over Strickland, happiness that we've done what we can to protect Owen's secret, worry that our involvement could somehow be found out.

I pick my face up from the fabric of Owen's tear-soaked shirt so I can see his face. We can't go over to the Garrison for fear of being spotted so soon after the explosion, so I'm about to ask him how we can be sure that's it's over, how we can be absolutely positive that the boom was not some coincidentally timed but unrelated event—but just then I hear the first siren.

A police car zips up Eighteenth Street along the eastern edge of the park with its lights on and sirens blaring. Within maybe fifteen seconds, we can hear a chorus of other sirens, seemingly from every direction. Two firetrucks come barreling up Eighteenth after the police car. We stand dumbfounded for a few minutes, watching service vehicles rush through the streets from the middle of the square. I don't see any ambulances, which makes me feel a tiny bit better even though I can't ignore the possibility that one has taken another route to the Garrison.

As much as I want to know what the damage is, I'm suddenly and completely overwhelmed by the urge to run—to get myself away from the blare of sirens and the speeding cop cars and the heavy sense of dread.

"Let's go," I say to Owen, and he nods quickly like he was having the same feeling.

I take off toward the northwest corner of the park. Sprinting, really, as I find my legs carrying me faster than I thought possible. I barely stop to check for cars when we cross the street to head up Walnut to the river, and my lungs contract as they struggle to pull enough oxygen from the humid summer air to power my fleeing legs.

Owen is right by my side, easily matching my pace. Within three blocks, I'm so winded that I can't even think about talking, but Owen seems as content as I am to run in silence.

We reach the Walnut Street bridge and run down the stairs to the path along the river, the sirens receding in the distance and the dread surrendering to the sheer physical pain of moving much faster than my body is meant to. We tear north along the path, passing several serious-looking runners even before we reach the art museum, and my quads burn with the aggressive pace. I don't slow down.

A drop of sweat drips from my brow onto my cheek, and my tank sticks to my lower back as my body fights to cool itself against the rising summer temperature. I glance at Owen; the tear splotch I left on his shirt has been replaced with sweat, his chiseled upper body even more obvious now beneath his thin, wet shirt. I focus on the regular rhythm of his graceful stride and take comfort in having him right next to me while I force my body to fly across the pavement.

I pump my legs into the pain, ignoring the growing heaviness of my feet, which seem to gain weight with every step. It's getting hard to breathe, and I have to concentrate to keep my breathing even and deep against the instinct to pant and hyperventilate.

Between the searing pain building in my legs and the struggle to get enough air into my lungs to continue this assault on my body, I have little space left in my brain to consider what has happened with Strickland and the uncertainty of the day ahead. All of the emotion and worry is pushed into some dusty corner of my mind as every active part of my being unites in an effort to keep moving.

We pass Boathouse Row, our pace never wavering. Several bridges later, a sound finally startles me out of my weird running trance. It's a shrill noise, out of place in the beautiful scenery of the river, and it's coming from my person.

Strickland's cell phone is ringing.

I have so much momentum built up that I almost trip as I abruptly attempt to stop. My hands shake as I remove the phone from the pocket of my leggings. My stomach flips over on itself when I see the number flashing on the screen—I don't recognize the whole thing, but the first six digits tell me it's coming from Genesis.

"Should I?" I ask Owen, who has also come to a stop beside me. His clothing and hair are now completely saturated.

"I don't know…Might not be a great—"

But I find my finger gliding across the screen anyway.

Regret immediately courses through me.

The call connects quickly, and I hold it up to my ear without saying anything. As soon as I hear the computer-generated voice on the other end, I glance around to make sure nobody is within earshot, then put the call on speaker so Owen can hear.

"Hello. This is the Genesis Life Systems emergency preparedness system with a message for Genesis employees from the forty-seventh floor of Garrison Headquarters. Please listen carefully to the following recorded message."

I look over at Owen and he's staring intently at the phone, his brow furrowed.

"Good morning. This is Aaron Levin, director of research at Genesis. This morning at approximately four thirty a.m., there was an explosion in Lab Pod F. The cause of the explosion is still unknown, but there was extensive damage to the floor. Several offices and storage areas have been completely destroyed, and we have yet to determine if any of the main lab space of Pod F will be salvageable. Though Pods E, G, and H do not currently seem to be affected beyond minor smoke damage, we are still investigating the cause of the explosion, and no employees are permitted to enter the forty-seventh floor until we have safety clearance from maintenance and engineering. We appreciate your patience and will be in contact as soon as we have more information to share. Thank you."

The call disconnects. Without a word, Owen pulls an alcohol wipe from his pocket and tears open the tiny package. He takes the phone from my paralyzed hand, turning it off before rubbing it down carefully with the little wipe. Then he looks around, nods in my direction, and pitches it soundlessly into the river.

I've been so completely focused on the message from Genesis that I haven't even noticed I'm still completely winded and my legs are shaking. Looking around, I see that we're just a few hundred yards from East Falls—we must be close to five miles from where we started.

"Charlie, breathe," Owen says, picking my hands up and placing them on top of my head. "Big breaths. There's a water fountain right up there. Do you need a drink?"

I nod, but when I go to take a step in the direction he's pointing, my leg gives out under me. He sees my stumble and catches me by the torso, lifting me easily back onto my feet. He squats with his back to me.

"Climb," he orders. "We'll draw less attention if I give you a piggyback than if I just carry you."

"I think I can—"

"Charlotte, climb," he says a little more sternly, so I put my arms over his shoulders, unable to muster the energy to argue. He stands fluidly, hooking his forearms under my thighs and holding me tight against him.

"Since I have to be careful not to draw attention to myself when I run," Owen says while he walks briskly toward the water fountain, "I've gotten pretty good at pacing. We were doing somewhere between a six-minute mile and six and a quarter. You need water."

"That can't—no way," I pant, my breathing still labored. A six-minute mile is way too fast. That's over two minutes faster than my normal treadmill pace.

Owen shifts my weight to his right arm and holds his left up so I can see his watch, an older but classic stainless Rolex. It's not even five o'clock—he must be right. I knew I was moving a lot faster than my normal speed, but I didn't think it was even physically possible for me to run five miles in thirty minutes.

"A little adrenaline can go a long way," he says, replacing his arm under my leg.

Even though my body is overheated, it feels good to be pressed against his back like this. Between the humidity and the frantic pace of our run, we're both completely soaked with sweat, and I run my hands over his chest, tracing the firm muscles through the wet fabric. My breathing slows to a nearly normal rate as my mind wanders toward what I might do to Owen if we weren't in a public place. While my body is absolutely exhausted, overwhelmed by physical, mental, and emotional fatigue, some tiny fire inside me remains lit, and something about being up against his body with my legs splayed apart seems to be stoking that fire, fanning it gently.

"Charlotte, if you keep touching me like that—" he lowers me to the ground right next to the water fountain "—you're going to make me embarrass myself."

I raise an eyebrow at him, unsure of his meaning, and then lean down to take a drink of water.

"These shorts are thin," he says, and I smile to myself while I suck down gulp after gulp of not-quite-cool water from the fountain.

I must have had a liter by the time I come up for air, and my legs are still jelly. I'm a little lightheaded.

"Here is what we're going to do." He has a sexy authority in his voice. "You're pale, and you need to eat something. You're going to get on my back, and we'll run to my apartment. You rolled your ankle if anybody looks at us funny. We'll eat and take a shower, and you can get some rest. Sound good?"

I manage a nod, and he immediately ducks in front of me, reaching back to grab my legs before I even muster the energy to throw my arms over his toned shoulders. Then we're off and running toward the city at what must be a ridiculous speed. I wrap my arms tight across Owen's upper chest to keep from tipping backward off him. We round a soft bend in the path, and a thin older man is visible maybe a hundred yards away, running toward us. Owen slows considerably, down to an easy jog, and as we come closer to the runner, he starts breathing pretty heavily. The runner gives us a funny look but just keeps moving, and the moment we pass him, Owen is back to Kenyan marathon speed.

My chest is pressed against his upper back, and I lean my head forward to put my mouth right to his ear.

"I spend a lot of time thinking about riding you," I whisper, my lips brushing against his earlobe. "But this isn't exactly what I pictured."

"Charlotte," Owen says, "what did I just tell you about these shorts?"

I decide not to play with him anymore—he has a point about the shorts—but I do let my thoughts wander, enjoying the feel of his muscled back against my breasts and his strong collarbones under my fingers. It's keeping my mind off Genesis.

We make exceptional time getting back, slowing to pass four or five more runners along the way, and then to a fast walk once we're back in the city. When we're within a few blocks of Owen's place, I give myself permission to toy with him once more to avoid obsessing over the explosion.

"If only I were a little more flexible," I murmur into his ear, spreading my legs as far apart as they'll go. "I think I'd be able to come like this."

A long breath hisses out of Owen, and he picks up the pace, just past the point of what would be reasonable for a normal human.

"Slow," I purr. "We didn't go through all of this just to have someone spot you sprinting at a superhuman pace through Rittenhouse Square."

He does slow, a guttural groan rumbling through him and vibrating into my body.

"Make that sound again," I whisper, pressing myself harder against his back. "That felt good."

He does, a little louder this time, sending little currents of heat through my midsection, and then we're a block from his building.

"You can put me down, Owen," I say as we cover the last few yards to his building. "I can walk."

He complies, setting me down gently on the sidewalk. He picks up my hand to steady me, but my legs are no longer like jelly. A little tired, maybe, but that's it. I don't have much time to think about this, though, because Owen has started tracing small circles on my palm with his thumb. He leans down and puts his lips to my ear, his breath hot on my skin.

"Feel that?" he asks, changing the pattern on my palm. I think he's drawing figure eights now. "When we get upstairs, I'm going to draw that same pattern on you." He pauses, and I can tell he's smiling even though I'm looking ahead. "With my tongue."

I take a deep breath and can actually feel the fabric of my thong soaking through between my legs. And from the way his shorts are hanging, I can see that he's stiffened underneath them. We're about half a block from the door to the Huntington now, and I'm barely able to keep myself from breaking into a sprint. Just a few more seconds, I tell myself, another minute tops. At last, we enter his building, and as we wait for the elevator doors to open, he leans down to put his mouth to my ear one more time.

"Poor Arthur is about to see something he shouldn't."

Arthur is the kindly, older night security guard. The one that watches the surveillance feeds from the elevators.

Just then the ding of the elevator door comes, and Owen follows me in. I press twenty-eight, and the doors aren't even fully closed by the time I'm pinned against the wall, Owen's mouth hot and wet over mine. One of his hands finds its way to my hair, and he cradles the back of my head, protecting me from the hard marble of the elevator wall, then presses his tongue into my mouth like he has to have me, right here and now. He nudges my thighs apart with his knee, and his kiss hasn't let up at all when his hand slides under my leggings and between my legs. My thighs part farther, giving him as much access as possible. He pushes my thong to the side, and my body wills his fingers to touch me, wills him to penetrate me.

But he doesn't, and all of a sudden his mouth is no longer on mine. I look up at the digital display above the buttons, and we're only passing floor nine now. This is happening really fast. I'm thinking that we don't have much longer, though, maybe thirty seconds or so, when Owen suddenly and silently drops to his knees.

I know I should stop him, should close my legs and pull him back up to standing, but I can't seem to force any sort of sound from my mouth. I hear an abrupt rip and look down to see my workout pants split from the front straight down through the crotch, Owen's knuckles white where he still grasps the fabric. My shock is short-lived as his tongue touches me right then, eliciting a gasp that forces the air from my lungs. The pleasure is so sharp, so sudden and powerful that my knees start to give out, but Owen catches me before I fall, supporting me easily by my butt. He's tracing slow figure eights over my clit, just like he promised, and electric waves radiate outward through my abdomen. We pass twenty-two. Almost there.

"Owen," I breath, barely audible, though it's as loud as I can speak. "Owen, we're almost… We're almost—"

"I know," he says, and the low vibration of his voice sends a new pang of pleasure, so sharp it almost hurts, rippling through me. "Don't come yet," he orders. "I want to be inside you when you—"

"Then you better stop," I pant, so close to the edge that even one more word might tip me over.

Just then Owen stands, lifting me by my butt and setting me on his hipbones as the elevator door opens. I wrap my legs around his waist as he steps out of the elevator, his erection pressing against me through the taut fabric of his shorts.

There are four apartments on this floor, and Owen's is maybe twenty yards down the hall on the right. We've only taken a few steps in that direction when I lean my head forward and take his left earlobe into my mouth, sucking gently.

A shudder runs through his body, and suddenly my back is against the wall in the corridor and his mouth seals over mine, his kiss desperate and uncontrolled. I run one of my hands through his hair, pulling his head closer and sucking his tongue. One of his hands leaves my behind, and then my weight shifts in his other hand as he reaches below me and into his shorts.

I pull my mouth from his.

"Owen, what are—"

He plunges into me, filling me so completely that I can hardly bear it. My insides quiver and tense around him, and his cock thickens and pulses in response. He thrusts fast and hard, the base of his penis rubbing against my clit with each stroke. A soft groan escapes my lips at the delicious friction inside and out. Then a hand clasps over my mouth.

"Shhh," he whispers into my ear as he keeps pounding into me. "Come quietly for me this time. Next time you can scream."

My body gives in. Rhythmic waves of pleasure course through every part of me, radiating outward from my most sensitive parts. I dig my fingers into his shoulder as my back arches off the wall, resisting the scream that wants out. He stills with one last thrust, and I'm pinned even harder against the wall as he empties himself into me.

Owen's hand slides from my mouth, and I watch a tiny drop of sweat trickle from his hairline. He blinks a few times.

"Fuck," he whispers, and runs his hand through his hair before placing it back under my butt, lifting me from the wall, and hurrying the few steps to his apartment, still inside me.

Once we get inside and the door is latched behind us, he sets me on one of the barstools and gently pulls himself out of me.

"Charlotte…that was…I'm sorry, I just—"

"Made me come," I say, looking him dead in the eye. "That's one." I let a half-smile cross my face. "Let's aim for three."

Needing little encouragement, we fall into bed together and manage to make it to two.

Cocooned in Owen's embrace afterward, I must drift off for some time, but I'm eventually awakened by the strangest sensation.

The slow and regular rhythm of his breathing indicates he's dozed off too. But something has just moved inside me, the tiniest of slippery movements.

Another little slip causes my insides to contract, and suddenly I know exactly what's happening. I feel Owen's chest expand as he pulls in a deep breath—the movement has woken him too. We must have fallen asleep still linked together in the most intimate spot. And now he's getting hard again inside me.

"Charlotte," he murmurs, his voiced laced with sleep, "I was dreaming about you."

This thought—that he was stiffening in his sleep thinking of me—and the bizarre sensation of his member expanding within me, pushing the sensitive tissue apart, forces my fatigued body to arouse once again. I arch my back slightly, pushing my hips back into him. He grumbles that same sexy rasp of a groan in response, and his cock continues to grow.

I'm still sensitive from my last orgasm, and as he starts to gently rock his hips into mine, I'm not sure I can take it, the sharp sensation verging on pain.

"Owen," I whisper, "I'm not sure I can…again…" I trail off as I can't help my body from matching his slow movements.

He sighs, pausing briefly to kiss the thin skin behind my ear, which is unexpectedly sensitive to his touch, tingling warmly. "You asked me to make you come three times." His words are slow and deliberate, still carrying the weight of sleep. He's fully hard now, pushing in and out of me with a metronomic cadence. "And I intend to do everything in my power to give you exactly what you want."

This gives me the control I need to focus on his movements, on the place inside me that the head of his penis is slowly and methodically kneading into submission. My body yields to him, swelling and quivering around his thick and now rock-hard member.

"That's it," he continues, kissing my neck. "You can do this."

He's right, and the simmering energy of orgasm has already started to collect in my core, swirling and churning like a coming storm.

Owen makes me eggs and toast while I'm in the shower.

I sit down at the island in his white bathrobe and barely manage to thank him before I'm shoveling food in so fast that I hardly have time to breathe in between bites. I'm not sure I've been this ravenous in my life.

He sits next to me, digging into his own monster-sized plate and watching me, smiling quietly to himself. He's already poured a mug of coffee and set it by my plate. I put my fork down for a moment and take a few sips. When I lower the mug, Owen is biting his lip.

"You okay?" he asks.

It's the first calm we've had together—awake at least, and not physically engaged—since the weekend. Which could be a lifetime ago.

"I am, actually," I say. "I think we did it, Owen. I think it's over." There's a little piece of hair sticking up on his head, and I fight the urge to fix it, because I know where even the simplest touch can lead between us.

"I think so too." He takes a big bite and washes it down with coffee. "I'm also quite sure I've given my last blood sample to that place."

"Let's go with no samples of any kind, to anybody," I say. "And Genesis Life Systems Policy number thirty-eight be damned. It's just you and me now, no excuses."

Owen sets his fork down and goes quiet. His eyes fix on a crumb on the counter in front of him. I reach out to pick it up with my napkin, and when I look back up, he's staring at me, still silent.

"What?" I run my fingers through my damp hair, all of a sudden a little self-conscious. I don't even have my usual tinted moisturizer on.

"It's…I want you to have this." He lays a key on the granite between our plates.

My heart races. Is he giving me a key to his apartment? After two weeks?

"Is this…" I start, but he picks up when I pause.

"A key to my place, yes." He sounds a little timid. "I have a few meetings this morning that I have to get to, but I thought you might want to stay here and relax. You should be able to come and go, though, so I don't want you getting locked out if you decide to run out for something."

My spirits fall just a touch. He's being thoughtful and practical, but he's not offering me the key to keep.

"That's great, Owen, thank you. I am pretty pooped." I try not to sound disappointed. "I can get it back to you tonight when you get home."

He looks at his plate. "I…don't want it back." He takes a deep breath and looks up at me, a bit of renewed intensity in his eyes. "I want you to have it. Charlotte, I love you."

This is fast—I know Maddie would tell me it's too fast—but I can't help a huge smile from spreading across my face. He's sure about me. And I've never been as sure of anything in my life as I am that I want Owen, that I need him, that I love him.

I lean forward on the stool and kiss him lightly on the lips.

"I love you too, Owen." I kiss him again, a little longer this time. "Of course I love you."

"So it's not too much?" he asks when my lips leave his. "I haven't scared you away?"

I put my hand on his bare knee and look him right in the eye.

"You, Owen Becker, are never too much for me. You couldn't scare me off if you tried."

Epilogue

The ring of my cell phone rips me from a deep sleep. Owen is next to me in bed, sitting up with a binder of papers in his lap; I don't know when he came home from his meetings. He hands the phone to me from his bedside table, and my heart jumps when I see the number on the screen. The same one that rang on Strickland's this morning just before Owen tossed it into the Schuykill River.

I answer, then put the call on speaker as soon as it's clear that it's another recorded message from Genesis. Owen's hand finds its way to my shoulder, its warmth and weight reassuring when the director of research again begins to speak.

"This is Aaron Levin with an update regarding the explosion at Genesis. The investigation is ongoing, and the cause of the accident is still unclear, though we have received safety clearance that the floor is stable. However, the forty-seventh floor will remain closed to researchers until further notice as the necessary repairs are quite extensive. We ask all employees from lab pods E through H to report to the Rittenhouse Conference room on floor sixty-two at one thirty p.m. for a meeting to brief you on the situation. We will answer any questions we can at that time. Thank you again for your patience and understanding."

Part of me is relieved. Though Levin's first message made it clear that little, if anything, is left of Strickland's lab, it does feel odd to not know when to return to work or what I'll be doing when I do. So hopefully I'll at least get a little clarity on that at this meeting.

Owen's hand slides down my back as I scoot my butt toward the headboard to sit next to him. I look at him, just noticing now that he's stripped down to an undershirt and boxer briefs. His work clothes are draped over the armchair in the corner.

He leans over to kiss me, and his lips are soft against my own. My skin starts to warm, but he doesn't linger too long.

"Let's get you home," he says, his face just inches from mine. It takes some effort to listen to his actual words rather than just watch his gorgeous mouth move. "You can't very well go to work dressed like that."

I too am in one of Owen's undershirts and nothing else. My phone is still in my hand, and I check the time—just after noon. Though what I really want to do is rid both of us of our white tees and stay in bed all afternoon, he's right. I nod.

"Come on," he says, hopping out of bed and extending his hand to me. "I'll drive you."

There's about an hour to the meeting when we get in the elevator and head down to the lobby of the Hutchinson.

"Owen, your car is ready for you, as requested," says the doorman.

Owen thanks him and then leads us through a door in the back of the lobby. After a short corridor, we emerge into the brightly lit entrance to a parking garage. There's a young man, maybe about my age, in a valet outfit, standing at the curb.

"Mr. Becker," he says, handing Owen a set of car keys. "Should be good to go."

"Thanks, Matt, and, really, it's Owen." He claps the young man on the back. He takes the keys and turns to me. "Shall we?"

There's only one car parked at the curb, and it's a gunmetal gray Porsche 911. It's spotless and beautiful and absolutely gleaming. He opens the door for me, and I duck inside, noticing immediately that the inside of the car is just as absolutely immaculate as the outside. The leather is an exquisite saddle brown with deep gray accents and trim.

"I guess it's my one real indulgence," he says. "Do you like it?"

"It's gorgeous, I love it."

A proud smile crosses his lips as he starts the rumbly engine and puts the car in first gear, driving slowly to the exit of the garage where a metal door raises in front of us. Sunlight streams in, and he pulls a pair of old-school black plastic Ray-Bans from the cup holder and puts them on. Driving stick shift in an immaculate Porsche 911, wearing navy slacks, a gray-and-white-striped dress shirt, and those sunglasses, he has never looked so sexy.

"Honestly, I didn't think you could possibly look any hotter, but you seem to have topped yourself." I put my hand on his knee and trace that runner's muscle with my index finger.

Before he has a chance to respond with any more than a sharp inhalation of breath, I hear an incoming text chime from my purse. I dig out my phone and find a message from Maddie.

> *i heard there was an explosion at genesis—*
> *txt me asap so i can stop worrying*

I tap out a message back to her.

> *it was on my floor, my lab is closed, have a meeting*
> *at 1:30 about it. am back on with owen,*
> *on my way to the apt now for a change of clothes.*
> *will txt you when i know more*

I'm not used to keeping any secrets from Maddie, so it feels weird to leave so much out. She texts me back right away.

> *ok phew, and yay re owen. tell me everything tonight*

"Everything okay?" Owen glances at me quickly and then back at the road.

"Just Maddie checking in. The explosion must be on the local news." I wonder if I should call my parents. I don't think it would have made national news, but I wouldn't put it past my dad to have Genesis on Google Alert. I decide to call them after the meeting, when I'll hopefully have at least a little more information that doesn't involve the full truth of what really happened.

My legs feel surprisingly light when I eventually hop out of Owen's car and onto the curb in front of Genesis, now dressed in a fresh blouse and skirt after a quick pit stop at my apartment. I turn to him before I shut the door, leaning down so I can see him in the low driver's seat of the sports car. He has the wayfarers on and his hand on the stick, and I can't tell if I think it's hot when a man really knows his way around a car, or if it's just that everything this particular man can do is hot. Even after the embarrassing amount of sex in the last twenty-four hours, I can't help imagining what it would be like to slide on top of him and ride him like that, our movements restricted by the tight space of the car.

"I'll see you at your place later, right?"

He tips his head forward so he can peer at me over his sunglasses. "One more meeting, but I should be home early," he says with a wicked grin. "You better get some more rest. I fully intend to wear you out again tonight."

"Do you now?" I call over my shoulder as I walk away. I guess there are some advantages to a boyfriend who can't get tired.

The cool of the air-conditioned lobby hits me like a wall when I pass through the Garrison's rotating door, snapping me back to reality. It's 1:26 p.m., so I head straight for the elevators that service the top floors. The entire elevator bank that leads to the Genesis floors is blocked off with caution tape, and there are maybe fifteen or twenty police officers and firemen milling around the area.

My feet have stopped moving, and I'm just taking in the commotion when I feel a tap on my shoulder. I turn.

"Charlotte, are you okay?" Kyle pulls me into a hug before I have time to react. It lasts a little longer than seems appropriate, especially given what I spent the majority of the morning doing with Owen.

"Thanks, Kyle. I'm fine," I say, detaching myself from his embrace.

"If you need anything, you let me know, okay?"

I nod, and something darker shades his eyes, just for a fraction of a second.

"Do you think," he starts, and bites his lip. Something about the small movement doesn't read as genuine to me. "Do you think it had something to do with that guy, what was his name? Owen?"

I gape at him for a second. "Why would you think that?"

"I don't know," he says in what seems like an attempt to sound casual. "You'd said that Strickland seemed a little weird about him. Never mind." He looks at his watch. "You should get to your meeting."

I want to ask him why he's pressing for information about Owen—for the second time now—but something tells me I shouldn't. So I just nod and head for the elevators.

The conference room is about two-thirds full when I walk through the door. I'm about to sit in an empty row near the back when Hannah appears out of nowhere and pulls me by the elbow to the back corner of the room. Her eyes are wide and her hair is a mess.

"Rick told me the explosion happened near Strickland's office. He said there's basically nothing left of his office or that half of the lab." She's talking faster than I've ever heard. "It has to have something to do with what he was doing in that little back room, doesn't it? It has to!"

It feels strange to again leave out the majority of the truth with someone I trust, but telling Hannah any more than the bare minimum is completely out of the question.

"Wow, really? It must," I fake. "Can I tell you something really scary? I went back to the lab after dinner last night because I forgot my keys, and I ran into Strickland, who was acting about the same amount of weird as he was with us during the day. Do you think he was testing something overnight and it went wrong? It's too scary to think it could have happened while people were in the lab…" I trail off, hoping to sound like I'm just speaking off the top of my head.

"Have you heard from Strickland?" I didn't think Hannah's eyes could get any wider, but they suddenly do. "Do you think he was in there when it happened?" She claps her hand over her mouth.

"I haven't heard from him. I hope he wasn't there." I look at my feet to hide the fact that I'm not even sure what reaction I'm supposed to be faking.

Luckily, Levin has just taken the podium, and the hum of voices fades out as he waits for people to take their seats. Hannah pulls me into the back row and sits next to me, her right knee bouncing shakily.

"Thank you all for coming," Levin begins in a somber tone, noticeably different from his usual animated pep. "I regret to inform you that after a terrible accident in the Pod F lab in the early hours of this morning, we've lost one of our most talented researchers, Todd Strickland."

Levin goes on to give a brief summary of Strickland's achievements at Genesis—which are quite numerous and impressive—and then speaks for some time about how much he will be missed. A minute or two in, Hannah picks up my hand and holds it in her lap, and when I turn to look at her, there are a few tears dripping down her cheeks. I find myself surprisingly emotional too, a mix of sadness and a shred of lingering worry, and by the time Levin wraps up his makeshift eulogy, a single tear spills over my bottom lid onto my cheekbone.

"I'm sure you are all wondering what caused the explosion," he continues, "and unfortunately I'm not sure we will ever know for certain. We've had forensic engineers surveying the damage all day, and all we know at this point is that the explosion originated from the supply room behind Todd's office."

Hannah squeezes my hand.

"The damage to Pod F's lab has been quite severe, and we ask the researchers in that group to please be patient with us while we recover what we can of your work and find temporary lab space for you while we renovate. We will contact you by email, but I expect the earliest we'll be able to have you in temporary space is mid-next week, so please at least enjoy the silver lining of a few days off." He manages a bleak smile.

"Our best guess at this point is that Todd was working very early this morning, and some sort of chemical spill and some extremely unfortunate luck resulted in a combination of volatile materials. I remember from our days as RAs together that Todd would occasionally become so engrossed in his work that he'd find himself working nearly round the clock," he adds, a little wistfully. "Unfortunately there is so little left of the supply area or even Todd's office itself, we likely will never know exactly what happened."

He wraps up his speech with a few more nice comments about Strickland, and then a woman from HR takes the podium to inform us about grief-counseling options.

When we're dismissed, Hannah pulls me out of the way of the bewildered-looking crowd exiting the room and back into the corner.

"I don't think we should tell anyone," she whispers. "Because whatever he was doing is over now, and he paid for it with his life." Another tear slips down her cheek. "He was a tough boss, but he was good at his job, and it just seems wrong to tarnish that at this point. Levin said there's nothing left. It's not like they'll be able to recover his work anyway."

I'm a little surprised at Hannah's reaction — I'd prepared myself to deal with talking to Levin and the rest of management about the secret lab — but her unexpected loyalty to Strickland actually makes it much easier.

"You're right." I pull her into a brief hug. "There's no reason to bring it up at this point." I decide to change the subject before she can rethink her decision. "What are you going to do with your extra-long weekend?"

Hannah is about to answer when I hear my name called from across the room. It's Levin, beckoning me to him.

"Call me," I say to Hannah before I walk away. "Let's do something together with one of the days off."

When I get across the room to Levin, I'm struck by how run-down he looks. I've never talked to him one-on-one, so my heart beats a little faster than normal.

"Charlotte, our security records show that you entered the building last night after work hours, just about the same time as one of Todd's subjects, Owen Becker. Is that correct?"

"Yes," I eek out. "I'd forgotten my keys, and I came back to the lab to look for them. Owen is…We're dating, and we'd been out to dinner, so rather than wait outside for me, he came up." I can feel my cheeks flushing. I can't believe the first conversation I have with the head of research is even peripherally about my love life.

"Ah, I see," he says. "We have Strickland swiping in a little bit later. Did you see him?"

"Yes. It took me a little while to find the keys. They had somehow fallen into a drawer in my lab station. Strickland came through just before I found them." I'm hoping our story sounds believable.

Levin perks up at this, but I detect no suspicion in his expression. "Did you notice anything off, did Strickland say anything to you that seemed out of the ordinary? We're just trying to gather as much information as we can that might help us figure out what happened."

A little pang of guilt hits me for lying. "Nothing specific, really, though I will say he seemed a little zoned out and flustered. And I don't know how to put this, but I'm not sure he'd been home to shower in a while. He certainly seemed engrossed in whatever he was working on."

He nods. "Thank you, Charlotte. Terrible loss, but at least it didn't happen during work hours when the lab would have been full of people. I do hope you will come to me if you have any questions once we shuffle everyone around. My door is always open to you."

"Thank you, Mr. Levin," I say awkwardly.

"Aaron," he corrects, and I nod.

"Thank you, Aaron." And with that, I turn on my heel and hurry out of the building as quickly as I can.

I walk straight to Owen's apartment, using my cell phone to call my mother on the way and give her the abridged account of what happened. As expected, she sounds freaked out, and offers to pay for a plane ticket to New Hampshire for me to spend a few days of my unexpected vacation at home. I tell her I'll look into it, and briefly consider inviting Owen for the weekend, but then decide I've had enough big decisions in the last twenty-four hours so table that for later.

When I slip the key into the lock on Owen's door, I feel an unexpected little rush of triumph and pride. After an absolutely ridiculous and stressful few days, I can at least relish the fact that Owen, exquisite, indestructible Owen, wants me. Wants me in his space, in his life.

I stop for a glass of water in the kitchen, still parched from the morning's activities, and then head straight for the bedroom, where I strip down to nothing before climbing into his bed. I pull the crisp, white bedding up to my neck and take a long inhale of his scent, letting my mind wander briefly to how it will feel when he climbs in next to me later. What I really need is some pure distraction, so I take my tablet from where I'd left it on the bedside table and pull up the futuristic YA novel my older brother raved to me about last week. Snuggling deeper into Owen's bed, I lose myself in the fantastical story, noticing after a few chapters that it's only marginally more far-fetched than my own.

"How was your meeting?" Owen asks just as my eyes are opening. He's woken me in the gentlest way — by climbing into bed next to me, removing the tablet from my chest, and allowing the touch of his body up the length of mine to bring me back from sleep. I wasn't planning to nap again, but I suppose the events of last night and this morning did take their toll.

"Mmm." I press my body into his, indulging in the closeness for a moment before I answer. "It was fine," I say, not yet in the mindset to rehash the details. I roll onto my side, which leaves me facing him, not an inch between our faces. "Kiss me," I whisper.

Owen doesn't argue.

When we eventually make it back onto our feet and into our clothes, my stomach is grumbling. Owen rattles off a list of delivery options for me and listens without complaint while I talk myself back and forth between Thai and Indian for a few minutes. Then he pours me some iced tea, and I settle at the island while he calls in an order for massaman curry, pad see ew, and enough Thai appetizers for a family of six.

Once he's off the phone, I launch into a play-by-play of the meeting at Genesis, as detailed as I can manage. I've just finished telling him about Hannah's reaction and am about to summarize Levin's speech when Kyle pops into my head. I'd been so focused on the meeting that I haven't properly analyzed the one vaguely unsettling interaction from the afternoon.

"Do you remember that RA you met? Kyle?" I ask.

Owen is across the island, and he leans toward me, his elbows on the granite.

"Shake Shack guy?" he says, and I nod. "He likes you, but you like me?"

His tone is playful, and I lean toward him too, planting a chaste kiss on his lips.

"No, handsome, I don't like you, I love you," I tease, and that wide grin appears on Owen's face.

"Just making sure," he says.

"Anyway," I continue, combatting the instinct to let the conversation derail further into silliness, "I ran into him on the way into the Garrison. And he asked me about you."

Owen puts his glass down mid-sip.

"Asked about me—how?"

"He said I'd mentioned that Strickland has been weird about you, and asked if I thought that had something to do with the explosion. The thing is, I don't remember ever saying anything like that to him." I tell him about the lunch I had with Kyle the other day, and about how he'd brought up Owen being a subject then too.

"That's odd," Owen says as he traces the rim of the glass with his index finger.

"Do you think I should be worried about him?"

"Well, I have been coming to Genesis for a very long time. I can't imagine Strickland has never said anything to any other researchers about me. Maybe Kyle heard something unrelated and is just speculating from there?"

"Could be," I say, but my suspicions are not fully alleviated. "I'll keep an eye on it, and if he presses it again, we can figure out what to do. Back to the meeting."

I'm halfway through explaining Levin's heartfelt words about Strickland when our food arrives. Noodles and dumplings slow my progress somewhat, and we've cleared our plates by the time I get to my slightly embarrassing conversation with the director of research.

A whooshing sound interrupts my monologue, and it takes me a second to process that it came from the entryway to the apartment. Owen is one step ahead of me, already on his feet and swinging around the island toward the door. It's a few paces before I clear the refrigerator and have a direct view.

Someone has slid something underneath the door.

I'm right behind Owen as he bends to pick it up, and my organs liquefy when I catch a glimpse over his shoulder. It's an eight-by-ten black-and-white photograph with an index card paper-clipped to it. Even with the card obscuring a section of the picture, it's immediately obvious to me that it's a still from a surveillance feed from Strickland's unsanctioned lab—and that both Owen and I are clearly visible. The card has just a few handwritten words on it:

> *Owen Becker:*
> *Your life is in danger. I can help you.*
> *Jack Green*

I've barely read the 215 phone number at the end of the short note when Owen shoves the papers into my hands and lunges for the door, throwing it open and darting into the hall. I sprint after him but know even before we reach the closed elevator doors—the messenger is gone.

Acknowledgments

I owe thanks to many parties in the writing and editing of *Subject X*, including:

Anthony, whose real-life superpower of tolerating the glow of and tapping on my (okay fine, his) laptop from the other side of the bed, late into the night, even with rounds at 5:00 a.m. the next day, made possible the writing of this novel. Thank you for being my partner in everything. I love you.

Katie, the best BFF any girl could ever ask for. Thank you for helping me navigate this world of publishing, and for the endless discussion of every important aspect of life for the last twenty-five years, from second grade social dynamics to motherhood to The Real Housewives of Beverly Hills. You are the best.

Alexandra, proof that one really can win the sister-in-law lottery. Thank you for being the very first set of eyes on *Subject X* and for your helpful feedback, but most of all for supporting me throughout the writing process and making me comfortable enough to share my writing to begin with. Especially since it's not exactly G-rated, and I am married to your brother after all! How you made that into a non-awkward experience, I will never know.

Colleen, who made this story better in a few really big ways and about a million small ones. Thank you for immediately understanding these characters at least as well as I do, and for inexplicably making the editing process fun and exciting rather than stressful and laborious. It is a true pleasure to work with you.

Jennifer, and the rest of the Omnific team. Thank you for your guidance and patience, and for answering all of this first-timer's questions, no matter how silly."

About the Author

Emma Hunter lives with her family in Philadelphia. With a career in finance and a degree in mechanical engineering, she has taken the only logical next step and begun writing novels. Outside of reading and writing, Emma's main hobbies revolve around food—she's been known to spend hours at a clip in the kitchen, will drive many miles out of her way for an exceptional meal, and rarely shows up to a holiday gathering without way too many desserts. *Subject X* is her first novel.